Geoff Tristram has been a professional artist and cartoonist for over twenty-five years, working for a diverse range of clients including Embassy World Snooker, The BBC, Tarmac, Past Times, Winsor & Newton, Trivial Pursuit and the television show, 'They Think It's All Over!', to name but a few.

He has painted celebrities such as Jonathan Ross, Ian Botham, David Vine, Alan Shearer, Ian Hislop and Gary Lineker, not to mention virtually every famous snooker player that ever lifted a cue. You may have even noticed him at the World Championships on TV, interviewing them as he drew their caricatures!

He has also designed many book covers, album sleeves for bands such as UB40, The Maisonettes and City Boy, (remember them?) and postage stamps, notably 'Charles and Diana - The Royal Wedding', 'Lake Placid Winter Olympics' and 'Spain 1982 World Cup Football' editions.

Geoff's younger brother, David, is a well-known and extremely successful comedy playwright, so it was no real surprise when Geoff eventually turned his hand to comedy writing, hence this, his second full-length novel, featuring the accident-prone artist, David Day.

In order to make up for lost time, Geoff has now written three more novels, which follow this dreamy, scatterbrained character as he grows up and eventually gets a real job. Geoff's family wonder if he will do likewise.

Monet Trouble

By Geoff Tristram.

For Larry, who ate all the pies.

First published in 2006 by Geoff Tristram Ltd.

Printed and bound by Antony Rowe Ltd.

Contact the author on gt@geofftristram.co.uk

ISBN 0-9551428-1-4

ISBN 987-0-9551428-1-9

Cover illustration by Geoff Tristram.

With sincere thanks to the incredibly clever Aileen Fraser for editing this book.

If you find any mistakes now, it's her bloody falt.

DIALECTIC DILEMMA.

After several sleepless nights and much deliberation, I have decided not to use dialect in my book as a general rule (though I have broken my own rule occasionally when it suited me!). This is certainly not a slight on those authors who choose to include phonetic spellings and so on. It's just that, personally, I feel it is hard to decipher in written form, and somewhat limits the readership. Therefore, when you are told that a young light-bulb tester from the Black Country spoke with a really broad accent that no one from more than twenty miles away could understand, and you subsequently observe that his dialogue is in perfect English, I'm hoping you'll employ your vivid imagination and hear it the way it was spoken. If you have no concept of the accent anyway, feel free to hear it in any accent you like. A good story is a good story, no matter what language it's in, and this one, though I say it myself, is a cracker!

A POTTED HISTORY

Those who were lucky enough to read of his exploits as an eleven-year-old will know that David Day, the hero of this book, was the kind of lad that things happened to; a perfectly normal little boy, but one who just seemed to act as an unwitting catalyst for all manner of odd incidents.

If you are already familiar with my first novel (which was incredibly good, by the way) you may find this an opportune time to pop to the kitchen and make tea, or phone what's-his-name from next-door-but-two about borrowing the power tool again. For the uninitiated amongst you, a brief potted history may come in useful, and then again, having just re-read it myself, it may not.

David Day at eleven was something of a dreamer. Nothing much had changed by the age of nineteen, except maybe the dreams had become more erotic every now and again. As a child, he had found himself embroiled in a drama that saw, in no particular order, the Jesus-like resurrection of his beloved pet hamster, (which had been unceremoniously laid to rest in a refuse bin and covered in cold baked beans) and its eventual replacement squashed flat by a vintage steam roller, a toy shop owner who was 'killed' four times by burglars, a letter to Scotland Yard, imploring them to apprehend the killers of the woman, who was still very much alive, and a police sergeant coshing his own son into a state of unconsciousness in David's back garden.

Add to this the discovery of a priceless set of Shakespeare manuscripts, (purchased for two pounds) which were then feared eaten and recycled by a Staffordshire bull terrier, and I feel we have the makings of a decent plot.

While all this was going on, David was using his rare quieter moments to cut out three plywood sheep (at the expense of some 234 jigsaw blades) which disappeared into thin air during the opening night's performance of the school Nativity play, as if by magic. Oh, yes - he also managed to donate a fifty-thousand-pound cheque for the new school roof, and all this whilst sporting a less-than-fetching Adolf Hitler hairdo that his barber insisted on setting fire to once a month in order to prevent him from catching cold. (David that is, not the barber.)

This is admittedly a rather viciously edited précis, and you would be better advised to spend the money on a full version, but you must surely agree, now that you are abreast of the basic facts, that this was a young lad worth keeping an eye on. Those borrowing power tools or brewing tea can now rejoin the fold. The newcomers are more or less up to speed.

'A Nasty Bump on the Head' featured David as an eleven-year-old just about to leave junior school. 'Monet Trouble' picks up the tale as he is leaving Grammar School to go to Art College. Unlike its predecessor, this book, though humorous from the off, builds quite slowly, and for a while you may even begin to think, "Hilarious, I'll grant you, but where on earth is it all leading?"

Have faith. In this case, the journey is every bit as pleasurable as the destination, and if I remember rightly, the plot 'proper' doesn't even kick in until around page 150. How relaxed is that?

Now, I realize that it is my duty to grip the reader, but I deliberately wanted this tale to unfold at its own gentle pace. Even Captain Corelli's Mandolin took its time before you were hooked, if you will recall, and look how good that was! (Not that Monet Trouble is remotely like Captain Corelli's Mandolin, I hasten to add. It's a lot funnier for a start!)

Be patient, enjoy the ride, and you will be rewarded with a plot so wondrous that you'll feel truly bereaved when it's all over.

I give you my word! Now would I lie to you?

Geoff Tristram.

Oh what a tangled web we weave,

When first we practise to deceive.

William Shakespeare.

My computer has just informed me that the above quote is a 'fragment', (which apparently is not good) and that I should consider revising it.

This is worrying news. If Shakespeare couldn't get it right, what bloody chance have I got?

Show me the seven-year-old's pullover,
and I will show you the man. *Anon.*

CHAPTER 1

The girl with the pearl earring

Café 'Duomo'. Florence. Autumn 1972.

David reached into his handbag and took out a fuchsia-pink lipstick. It was a hot, sweaty day and he desperately needed to freshen up his appearance.

There were hideous mascara smudges down his cheeks and a blue five o'clock shadow was beginning to show through his foundation. He took a good, long look at himself in the cracked mirror of the café's tiny, malodorous lavatory and wondered how on earth he'd ended up this way.

Less than six months before, he'd been a perfectly normal grammar school boy; now here he was, not only an accomplished forger of Monets and Botticellis, but also a woman.

* * * * *

"That Mohammed's been tossing himself off in the bathroom again!"

Nicole was livid.

"There's liquid everywhere. All over the walls, on the taps, up ze mirror. It's disgusting!"

"That's probably not the best way of putting it," suggested Suzanne. "You probably meant *shaking* himself off. What you just said is really rather rude in England, dear."

"Well, whatever. He must get out of ze bath, and just shake, like a dog. Ze water goes everywhere. Don't these Arab types use towels like us? I sink not."

"That 'Arab type', as you call him, was born in West Bromwich, near Birmingham. He's never been to Saudi in his life, dear, and anyway, I think he said his family were from Pakistan."

"Whatever! He's a bloody pig. He blows his nose like a footballer, if he thinks nobody's looking."

"The reason for that is more likely to be because he's from Tipperton Grammar School, rather than any foreign influence," explained Suzanne, a trifle snootily, considering that she was only from Selly Oak herself, all of about ten miles away.

The upper-sixth formers of Tipperton Grammar - once described rather unkindly by one of the inmates as a borstal for clever kids - were youth-hostelling in Stow on the Wold, that idyllic and genteel Cotswolds village. At least, the male ones were. The females had gone off to a theme park to scare themselves to death in the name of entertainment. The excuse for this debauched, Guinness-fuelled expedition was that it heralded the last of the A Level exams. From then until the end of term they could let off steam, and woe-betide anyone who got in their way. Residents of Stow, meanwhile, were battening down the hatches, raising their drawbridges and preparing vats of boiling oil in preparation for the philistine invasion. The Youth Hostel, on hearing that it was to play host to Tipperton School, had insisted on money up-front as insurance against damage to their property, and the educational establishment that was to share the facilities that weekend - Birmingham's elite Royal Grammar School for Girls, was asking for sizeable discounts.

The superior offspring of Edgbaston's middle classes were more than a little miffed about the state that the Viking marauders from Tipperton had been leaving the bathrooms in. Pigs, they argued, were better bred, and for that matter, with few exceptions, better looking. Nor were these refined young ladies too impressed with the shenanigans that the rougher element got up to at night, once they had returned for lights-out, full to the gills with Guinness and peanuts. Beds were booby-trapped. Eggs were thrown, and lurid suggestions made about the best way to warm up a sleeping bag during a cold night in the Cotswolds. To French girl Nicole, recently relocated to Solihull because of her mother's new P.A. job, the multiple culture shocks were a bit much to bear. First England, which was bad enough, then youth-hostelling, which had none of the comforts she was accustomed to, and now *this* uncouth lot.

"Zey are nothing but Palestines!" she complained to Suzanne, exasperated. "Ze French men are far superior."

David Day walked into the Tipperton dormitory, soggy towel wrapped around even soggier soap under his arm. He was wearing a stripy cheesecloth shirt, baseball boots and bellbottoms, and his long, straight hair was soaking wet and

3

forming into rat's tails. He looked warily around his Spartan bed, and then inside it. So far so good - no booby-traps, no flattened, leathery hedgehog smuggled in from the day's sixteen-mile walk. No doctored sheets, folded back to make entry impossible. No bag of flour suspended from the ceiling. Part of him actually felt disappointed, because no one had found him worthy of playing a trick on that evening. He was sure things would change, after last orders at the King's Arms.

His closest ally at Tipperton was Dennis Wills, who was sitting cross-legged on his bunk reading a paperback. He was a fairly studious type who had visions of joining the army to become a career soldier. They say opposites attract.

"Nice shower, mate?" he asked, nonchalantly. Too nonchalantly for David's liking.

"Why, what did you do?"

"Nothing. You know me."

"Yes, I bloody well do. Where are my best clothes?" David had realized that his duffle bag was missing.

"Oh, in bed, snuggled up."

"Which bed, arsehole?"

"It's in a posh, Birmingham Girl's Grammar-type bed. Can't remember which one off hand, I'm afraid."

"Shit bag!" said David, a grin spreading across his face.

"Oh, I don't know, I thought it was a rather nice bag," said Dennis, without looking up from his book.

"Well, in a strange way, that makes me feel a tad better, I suppose," admitted David, as he headed off towards the girl's dorm.

"Explain?" asked Dennis, puzzled.

"It makes me feel better about sellotaping your walking boots to that light fitting right up there," he grinned, exiting at speed.

* * * * *

David knocked politely on the door of the girl's dormitory, and was invited in. It was almost empty, with the exception of Nicole and Suzanne, who were applying their make-up prior to going out to the local pub for dinner.

"Excuse me," he mumbled to the floor, for he was very shy with the opposite sex. "Have you seen a blue duffle bag? I think someone has played a little prank on me. Apparently, it's in here somewhere."

Most ventriloquists opened their mouths wider. He glanced at Nicole as he spoke, and when their eyes met, the intimacy made him uncomfortable - he felt safer gazing at the floor. She was beautiful, with petite, chiselled features, huge, soulful brown eyes and long brown hair, which was taken up into a loose bun arrangement at the back. It showed off her incredibly long, slender neck and tiny ears, which were set off with a small pair of pearl earrings. When she spoke, it was, for David, like fine icing being piped onto an already delicious cake, though the actual content of her opening gambit was a little bizarre.

"Ah yes!" she said. "One of your friends 'as done a shit in my bed."

She didn't seem too pleased, and who, given the facts, could blame her?

5

"Er, Nic, that's pronounced 'sheet'," said Suzanne, smiling sweetly at David. "She's French, you see." As if that somehow excused her for everything. Which, indeed, in David's eyes it did.

"Zat's what I said, shit," she replied, quizzically. "Zey have turned my shit around to stop me getting in, and also hidden your bloody duffing bag at ze bottom. Very funny!"

Her face suggested that she thought otherwise. "Here!" she gestured, throwing the bag at him. "Tell your friends to grow up."

Had she shoved a red-hot poker into his eye, he would still have found her totally gorgeous. A mild rebuke he could live with.

"Oh, don't blame me for that lot next door," he said. "They mean well, but they're a bit crazy. Just letting off steam you know, after the A Levels."

This explanation did nothing to lighten her mood. He could feel his cheeks reddening. Why did she make him feel slightly less worthy than a dollop of dog mess on a walking boot? He scooped up the bag.

"Putting your make-up on I see," he observed, mentally recoiling in horror at his stupid, inane chat-up line. He desperately needed to redress the balance with something clever, or they'd think him a buffoon. "God gave you one face, and you paint for yourself another! That's from Hamlet. I can't remember the exact words, but it's what he says to Ophelia after he's supposedly gone loony."

It was going from bad to worse.

"Thanks very much," said Suzanne, "very informative." She turned her back on him, thereby suspending the interview at approximately six-fifty p.m. David mumbled a sort of apology and hastily took his leave, making a complete hash of his exit and ending up having to back out of the store room and try again.

"He was quite cute, in a straggly-long-haired, hopeless kind of way," admitted Suzanne, once he'd gone. "It's a shame he had to spoil things by speaking."

"But he's from Tipperton," argued Nicole, "so he will naturally be uncouth. If he is anything like 'is friends, he probably doesn't even get out of ze bath to 'ave a piss."

"Another charming French expression, dear?" asked Suzanne, wincing. "He's not too bad looking though."

"I'd put him somewhere between Quasimodo and Robert Redford," replied Nicole, filing her nails.

"Oh, I don't know. I'd give him one," confessed Suzanne, blushing ever-so slightly.

"You'd fancy anything wiz a pulse," sneered Nicole, strapping on her high heels.

"I'm not even that fussy," admitted Suzanne, wickedly.

* * * * *

David walked back into his dormitory, which was now buzzing with wet-haired young men sitting on the edge of beds, slipping into crumpled clean shirts and trousers. The walk had been a hard one, and they were all feeling aches and pains. A hot shower and five minutes rest on their bunks had prepared them for alcohol. There is nothing to compare

7

with a pint of lager after walking sixteen miles in heavy boots, and the lads were itching to explore Stow.

They had decided to split into manageable groups, after a previous excursion had proved problematic. The landlord had taken a dim view of twenty eighteen and nineteen-year-olds barging into his pub. He smelt trouble, and, in fairness, he was not to know that these were high-spirited but essentially harmless individuals. Landlords were also suspicious about their ages. It is a fact of life that, given any typical group of sixth-formers, some will look far too young, and not be able to grow facial hair, whilst others look like middle-aged men wearing school uniforms for a bet. Luckily, both David and Dennis looked more-or-less how they should have looked for their age, and were usually able to get served without too many problems. They duly set off to find a good cosy local pub that served food, as they were starving after the long walk, and promised to meet up with the others later, at the King's Arms.

After a bit of searching, they came upon such a hostelry, which boasted home-made food, though it wasn't made clear whose home it was made in, or indeed if the home-owner knew how to cook. It could, after all, reasoned Dennis, have been concocted in the home of Sweeney Todd.

Unperturbed by this admittedly remote possibility and seriously ravenous, they ventured through the heavy oak door and scanned the various rooms on offer, finally settling for the empty little snug at the back of the pub, which had a television and cosy armchairs. After a hard day's walking, they needed to stretch out and relax. David had snatched a menu from the bar *en route*, and was perusing it, calling out the various meals on offer to Dennis, who had his feet up on the low pub table and was watching the television.

Just at this moment, a man came into the room and studied them for a few seconds in silence. He sat down.

"Can I help you, lads?" he asked politely. "I'm the landlord."

Dennis replied that he certainly could. He put in a request for two pints of Guinness, and after a brief consultation with David, added that he wished to place an order for a Steak and Ale pie and the Gammon and Pineapple.

"I'm afraid that won't be possible," replied the landlord. "I'm going to have to ask you both to leave."

"Hang on," complained Dennis, with all the righteous indignation of one who had come of age the month before. "I'm eighteen, mate. I've got a copy of my birth certificate with me, and he's a bit older than me."

"I don't care if you're fifty-six," replied the landlord, colouring slightly. "You're in my bloody living room. I go to the lavatory during the commercial break, and I come back to find you pair sitting in my favourite armchair, watching my telly. I see you've even changed channels. Now do me a huge favour, as fully-fledged, responsible adults. Sod off!"

After a battered cod of dubious vintage, eaten *in situ* at the town's chip shop, the two met up with the others at the King's Arms. David excitedly nudged his friend as they queued patiently for drinks at the bar. Suzanne and Nicole were seated in the dining area, ordering wine from a waiter. Nicole had taken delivery of the duck, while her friend had opted for chicken.

"Those are the two girls I told you about," whispered David, his heart fluttering.

Dennis looked over. "They're having a beautiful candlelit dinner, and we had stale cod and cardboard chips. We could have asked them out for something to eat if we'd known."

Nicole haughtily summoned the waiter back to the table. These French women were so assertive, thought David. She was drinking wine and everything!

"Zis duck has got bollocks!" she said, stabbing a tetchy fork into her bird.

"Erm. I think you mean bullets, Nic," corrected Suzanne, "but we call it 'shot'."

"Good job we didn't take 'em out after all, Dave," said Dennis, wincing. "That French one might be gorgeous, but she's a bloody nightmare!"

The two young men stood by the bar drinking, and occasionally glancing over at the girls, who were now having desserts. After brief eye-contact, the diners would turn away and snigger. Nicole summoned the long-suffering waiter once more, with an aristocratic slender finger. As he approached, she checked with her friend.

"If you *can't* eat it, it's inaudible, yes?"

Suzanne replied that the word she was groping for was 'inedible'.

The waiter arrived, looking apprehensive. Nicole let fly.

"Sorry! Zis crap, it's inedible."

"Nic!" protested Suzanne, flushing maroon, and clearly embarrassed by her friend's forthright attitude. "It's pronounced 'crape'. Surely you know that. It's a French word, isn't it?"

"Yes," she sneered. "It's a *crepe*, and it tastes bloody crap! Zat's an English expression, *n'est-ce pas?*"

* * * * *

The Youth Hostel closed its doors at eleven. If its clientèle weren't back by then, they slept somewhere else - house rules. At one minute to eleven, Dennis and David staggered into the front entrance and bid a cheery goodnight to the warden, who seemed less inclined than they were to engage in small talk. The rest of the Tipperton gang had romped home five minutes earlier, and were probably already dismantling beds and setting booby traps. As the pair walked into the dormitory, there was a deathly silence, which told them immediately that something was going on.

"Yeah, yeah! Come on. Get on with it; let's get this over with then," moaned Dennis wearily.

No one spoke. A particularly vicious and anonymous fart caused a ripple of laughter, but other than that, nothing seemed particularly untoward. David examined his bed, and Dennis ditto. No booby traps.

The others were already tucked up in their bunks, and some were staring intensely at their paperbacks. A few, exhausted by the walking, had opted for an early night. David got undressed, eyeing his friend as he did so. A few hours ago, they'd been playing tricks on each other. Now they were united in their suspicion of the others. Dennis sat on the edge of his bed, rubbing his sore feet, while David, clad only in his Y Fronts, took his toothbrush and paste to the shower block next door to complete his bedtime regime. He squeezed the paste onto his brush, and began to

11

vigorously clean his teeth. David was fastidious about dental hygiene, cleaning them up to six times a day. He looked in the mirror, and staring back at him was a rabid werewolf-like creature, with long straggly, greasy hair and a mouthful of foaming froth. What he saw was something of a shock; he didn't realize how much he had let himself go on this walking weekend. He resolved to clean up his act, and shave, first thing in the morning.

What he saw next was also something of a shock. In fact, it was a damn-sight more shocking than the werewolf had been.

In the mirror behind him, approximately fifteen lads had appeared, with treachery gleaming in their eyes. Nobby Jones, who was the biggest and ugliest of the bunch, grabbed him firmly from behind. David struggled furiously, but Nobby was just too strong. The other lads grabbed what parts of him they could, rendering him utterly helpless.

Dennis, that turncoat whom he had trusted, skilfully removed the Y Fronts, leaving the hapless werewolf-boy stark naked and foaming heavily from the mouth. David's writhing body was then roughly manhandled to the door of Dormitory B. Dennis opened the door, whereupon the others threw him into the pitch-black room. Nobby quickly closed the door and turned the key, which he had purloined earlier from the cork notice-board in the office. The fifteen plotters then fled back to the safely of their room, flicked their lights off and scampered into bed.

Meanwhile, inside Dormitory B, startled Birmingham Grammar School girls in their baby-doll nighties were leaping from their beds screaming. Suzanne located the light switch, to reveal, in the middle of the floor, stark naked and foaming heavily from the mouth, stick-thin David, covering his less than impressive manhood with a tartan sock that he had managed to grab hold of as he hit the floor. His face was now a bright Alizarin Crimson, which contrasted beautifully with the pure white froth bubbling out of his mouth. He looked like a giant matchstick that had been dipped in crazy foam. Suzanne and Nicole were too doubled-up with laughter to speak, or even breathe. They found it painful to look at him. Other girls were falling about the place too, and one was screaming hysterically. Just then, the door burst open, and the warden came in with his torch.

"This had better be good, son," he said. "This had better be bloody good!"

David tried his best to look nonchalant and devil-may-care, but missed by at least sixteen miles. He backed out of the room to a soundtrack of wild cheers and wolf whistles, to find a dark corner where he could lie down and die of shame.

CHAPTER 2

David's Michelangelo

It was Monday morning, and David and Dennis both had free periods. They lounged in two moth-eaten dusty armchairs in the sixth form common room, drinking tea from David's flask. This act alone required considerable bravado, because untold horrors lurked down the backs of the common room chairs. Long-dead sandwiches decomposed, as did the rats that had dived in to eat them. What went into these chairs never surfaced again - they were the chairs of doom. If money was ever lost inside them, it stayed lost. No one was ever brave enough to retrieve it.

"Anyway, thanks very flipping much," said David.

"No problem at all," replied Dennis, nibbling on the skeletal remains of an apple, before flinging it across the other end of the room in the vague direction of the wastepaper basket.

"Yes, let's recap shall we?" said David. "You, my so-called best mate in this leper colony, aided by a gang of your hand-picked cretins, manhandle me stark-bollock-naked and foaming at the mouth like a rabid animal, into a girl's dormitory. The girl that I totally adore sees my weedy

14

white body and its appendage, which incidentally had shrunk to half its already feeble size due to shock, thus causing it to closely resemble an acorn in a sparrow's nest. Correct so far?"

"Yes sir," spluttered a red-faced Dennis, who was dangerously close to embarking on one of his renowned giggling fits.

"I get booted out and threatened with expulsion by a livid warden. I'm made to look like a complete nutter in front of the woman I love. Following me, are you?"

"Hmph!"

"The aforementioned girl, who, incidentally, shunned me *totally* on the Sunday, when I went to apologize, and just walked off."

"She didn't *just* walk off, in fairness," argued Dennis, with one of his 'mock-concerned' faces.

"Oh no," agreed David. "No, she stopped, turned and wiggled her little finger at me, suggestively. I wanted to die. I'll probably never pluck up the courage to talk to a girl ever again. This marks my descent into homosexuality; you know that don't you? I'll have to make do with playing the pink piccolo now, thanks to you. I couldn't stand the bloody ignominy of being rejected by another female."

"Perhaps wiggling your little finger is a French greeting of some sort," offered Dennis helpfully, his stupid face about to explode with laughter.

"Yeah! You're right. It's French for 'Hey, you vile frothing stick-insect, haven't you got a ridiculously underdeveloped dick!' That's what it's French for."

"Look on the bright side," grinned his friend. "You'll never have to see her again. Okay, it was a shame, but there are loads more frogs in the sea. It's no good fancying someone who patently finds you absurd, is it? You'll soon be finished here, and hopefully, as long as you haven't totally screwed up your A Levels, heading off to Art College. These Art Colleges are famous for women. They've all got long, Pre-Raphaelite hair and they don't wear bras, and because they're arty, they believe in free love and stuff. You'll thank me for saving you from that French woman. She's a right bitch for a start, and if you had been going out with her, think of all the sexy Art College types you couldn't be going out with."

David wasn't convinced.

"It's all ahead of you, son," continued Dennis, warming to his theme. "Just think of poor old me. I'll be applying for the Army or the Police Force or something equally regimental. Either way, it's a life of discipline and duty. You'll be swanning around in baseball boots with your long hair, drawing gorgeous naked life-models, who'll probably offer themselves to you after your passionate eyes have burnt into them for a few hours. They'll all want to hold your little stick of charcoal, you'll see."

"I don't think art students still draw naked people. That was in Victorian times," said David, unimpressed.

"Was it bollocks!" replied Dennis. "You don't know much do you? They still draw from life, you mark my words. You'll be at it from day one, and then Nicole will be but a distant memory, my son."

At this point in the debate, around ten boisterous sixth-formers burst into the common room, fresh from a riveting German lesson, and the conversation was suspended. Dennis

16

grabbed his duffle bag and sloped off to double maths, whilst David sat looking out of the window, in a reverie, wondering if his friend was right.

* * * * *

The following week, David had arranged a day off from school to go to his foundation course interview in Wolverhampton. He lived in Brierley Bank, Staffordshire, a Black Country town around five miles from Dudley, and he couldn't drive. He'd looked into the train times, and decided that catching a bus to Dudley and changing there for Wolverhampton seemed the best bet. His dad, Len, would drop him off at the bus terminal on the way to work, which he could easily do each day, should David be accepted onto the course.

On the day of his interview, his mother, Ruby, made him some sandwiches and put them in his small red tartan attaché case, next to his portfolio, which he was to take to the college. His dad also had a small attaché case for his flask and sandwiches, and to distinguish between the two, his was green. Father and son walked down to the garage at the back of their small council house and set off for the bus terminal. His mother shouted good luck, and returned to the kitchen, where she duly discovered David's attaché case, still sitting where she'd left it, on the breakfast bar. She ran down to the garage, shouting for them to hold on, but the car had already gone. Luckily, she knew that David had a few pounds in cash on him, so he could get lunch from somewhere in Wolverhampton. She mumbled something to herself about what a dreamer he was, and carried on vacuuming the carpet.

Len arrived at the bus terminal, and David jumped out. He grabbed his portfolio, and absent-mindedly gathered up his dad's attaché case. Len, not noticing what had happened, wished him good luck and David hopped straight onto the virtually empty bus, just as it was about to leave the station.

"That was close!" he said to the driver. "I nearly missed the bus, which would have made me late for an important interview. Not very clever."

He sat down, a little flustered, and dropped the attaché case onto the seat opposite. He put the portfolio in front of his legs, took a few deep breaths to compose himself, and stared out of the window. The bus pulled away, and was chugging along in its usual fume-ridden merry way towards Dudley, when David glanced over to the opposite row of seats, and noticed an attaché case. He knew it wasn't *his*, as *his* was red. Obviously, he concluded, someone had left it behind. He grabbed it and ricocheted up to the driver, a large and jolly West Indian man of some sixty summers.

"Sorry to trouble you," said David politely. "I've just noticed this case on the seat opposite. I thought I'd hand it in."

"Ah, they's always leavin' stuff!" said the driver. "I'll keep it safe. I'll keep it safe. I'll keep it safe."

David concluded from this that the driver intended to keep it safe. He thanked him, sat down, and continued to daydream. He was rudely awoken from his trance-like state by the sound of a car horn peeping furiously, accompanied by the anguished voice of the bus driver.

"What's up with this madman? What's up with this madman? What's up with this madman?" This driver liked to have things in triplicate. His mental filing system insisted on it. David looked behind him, through the back windows of the bus.

"This bloody crazy man," continued the driver, "Swervin' all across the road, peepin' his damn horn, tryin' to get past, get past, get past! Eel get us hall killed!"

"Some people are so bloody impatient!" frowned David, sympathetically.

The lunatic driver was trying desperately to overtake in a crowded high street, and it was proving impossible. Finally, the bus had to pull into a lay-by to collect passengers, and the lunatic exploited the moment. He screeched past the bus and parked diagonally in front of it, American cop-style.

"Good God!" squawked the driver, in fear of his life and sweating heavily. "He's comin' to get me! To get me! To get me!"

Len Day leapt onto the bus, his face all hot and bothered. "You've taken my blooming sandwiches!" he called to David.

Addressing the driver, who presumably thought he was about to be murdered at the wheel, Len pointed to the green attaché case in the cab.

"What's that doing there?" he demanded.

"Your son handed it in!" the driver replied, passing it over with shaking hands. Len grabbed it, and looked down the aisle at his boy. He went to say something, but found it all too much of an effort. Instead, he strode off the bus and got back into his car, while David just looked sheepishly out of the window.

The bus ploughed on in silence for a few miles. Then, apropos of nothing, the driver, who had the look of a man wrestling with some private demon, suddenly blurted out to no one in particular;

"Your son handed it in! Your son handed it in!"

Having belatedly completed the sentence in triplicate, his previously troubled countenance now took on an expression of inner calm. David got off at the next stop, miraculously remembering the portfolio, and made his way towards the 58 bus stop. The second stage of the journey somehow passed without any major incidents, and half an hour later, David was walking across town in the direction of the Victorian Art Gallery, whistling a jaunty tune. The Foundation Department shared the building, but they had their own, less-grand entrance at the back. As he walked in, he saw a large metal staircase leading to the main studios upstairs, and the woodwork rooms downstairs. A cardboard sign pointed him in the right direction for the interview room.

A gentleman with long hair, outrageous sideburns and a cowboy shirt that was open just a tad too far, told David to take a seat. David did so, bidding a cheerful good morning to a young man with long, thick black hair and round gold-rimmed glasses who was also waiting for an interview. The lad had a pleasant, friendly face, with mischievous, almost black eyes. David, who had been brought up not to lie by his parents, informed his fellow interviewee that his name was David, and the young man replied that his name was Dylan, adding that some people called him Dyl.

David told Dylan that he'd come from Brierley Bank, and Dylan said that he'd come from Stourbridge, not far away. Formalities concluded, they sat nervously in near silence, waiting to be called.

The sideburned one called David in, instructing him to sit down and place his portfolio on the table in front of him. Behind the table sat a Welshman who was introduced as John Auberton, Head of Foundation. He had more than the legal limit of toothy grin, which graced a face that David instantly took to. The sideburned man introduced himself as Bob Rosemary, before presenting the final staff member, a cheeky-faced, ginger-haired man called Ed Briers. David couldn't help but stare at his eyelashes, which were almost white.

"So far, so good," he thought. Nice people.

Mr Auberton spoke first. He asked if David had been able to find the college, as a lot of students got lost. David replied that, unfortunately, he hadn't been able to, and that he was still wandering around town looking for it. He was nervous, but still couldn't resist a touch of sarcasm, a family trait that he'd inherited from his paternal grandfather. Mr Auberton graciously admitted that it *was* rather a silly question, but also reminded David that the best time to be funny was after he'd been accepted onto the course.

"Fifteen all," grinned Ed Briers, his white eyelashes flapping wildly.

The tutors flipped through the portfolio, asking questions about David's techniques and influences. They glanced across at each other occasionally and nodded, as if to suggest that they liked what they were seeing. Mr Auberton paused at a particularly fine study done in terracotta chalks, on mottled *Ingres* paper.

"Nice bloody drawing!" Bob enthused. "It reminds me of the Italian Renaissance drawings. Michelangelo maybe?"

"Thank you," beamed David, pleased as punch. "That one's original, but do I love all that classical stuff. I often copy drawings by the Old Masters, just for fun. Some people frown upon it, but I think you can learn a lot from doing it."

"I think you're right," agreed Mr Auberton. "Learn by copying the best, eh? You certainly do have a very mature style for a young man, I must say. Anyway, we have lots of people to see. Are we agreed, folks?"

Bob Rosemary leaned over once more to look at the finer details of the Renaissance-style drawing. He sniffed, and then sniffed again.

"Sorry everybody, I seem to have a really runny nose, all of a sudden."

Suddenly, after one more sniff, a huge torrent of bright red blood gushed from his nose, and landed with a splat, all over the drawing. David looked aghast.

"My God!" said the embarrassed tutor. "I've had another bloody nose bleed!"

He took a large white handkerchief from his trouser pocket and dabbed the ruined picture. "Oops!" he said, apologetically.

"I reckon we've *got* to accept you now!" said Mr Auberton, looking askance at his friend. "Welcome on board David, and don't worry too much about your A Level results. We'll take you regardless, just on this showing. Can you send in young Dylan on your way out? And, erm, very sorry indeed about your drawing!"

"Nice bloody drawing!" mimicked Ed Briers, a barbed reference to his colleague's earlier comment, as Bob staggered off to the washrooms with his nose in the air, in search of paper towels.

CHAPTER 3

The Love Bus

David came out of the old Art School building feeling elated. His Michelangelo-style torso drawing looked as if it had been savagely butchered by a madman, but it had done its job, and he was philosophical - he could always draw another one. The important fact was that his immediate future was secure; his parents would be proud, and very happy that he wouldn't be stacking shelves at the local supermarket. After all, there was always time for that *after* he got his cap and gown. David had been far too nervous to eat before his interview, but now he realized that he was starving. It was then that he remembered the tartan attaché case, but couldn't for the life of him recall where he'd last seen it. Never mind. He had a few quid in his pocket, so a celebratory sausage roll was in order. Here was a boy whose body was a temple, albeit a ruined one. Even better, he had enough for an egg custard too.

The interview was all over by lunchtime, so he toyed with the idea of hopping on a bus to Tipperton Grammar School instead of travelling all the way home on public transport. This meant that he could catch up with Dennis, tell him the good news and hitch a free ride on the school coach at four o'clock. He jumped onto the 58 bus heading for Dudley, and sat staring out of the window, quietly pleased with his morning's work.

The bus was completely empty as it pulled away, and remained so until Sedgley, when a small Asian gentleman got on. He scrutinized the lower deck, eventually plumping for the seat immediately behind David. David thought that this was a little strange, but continued to gaze at the world through his grimy window. After a mile or so, he became aware of a hand gently stroking his bottom. The seats on the bus consisted of an upholstered vertical panel for the backrest, and a similar horizontal one for the seat, leaving around a three-inch gap between the two. David's first reaction was that the man was absent-mindedly fiddling with what he *thought* was a part of the seat, not realizing that it was, in fact, the back pocket of David's jeans.

David had a trusting nature. Less charitable types would call it *naïve*. After suffering in silence for a few minutes, he eventually turned round to the fellow, and informed him of his mistake. For a minute or two, this appeared to do the trick. Shortly afterwards, however, he became aware of hot, spicy breath in his right ear. The owner of this breath was whispering what are often referred to as 'sweet nothings', or at least that's what David presumed they were, as they were in something akin to Punjabi. He couldn't be absolutely sure. It might have been Gujarati or Hindu. He wasn't an expert.

Summoning all his *machismo*, and speaking with a voice at least an octave lower than usual, he turned around to face the man - who had a sort of dreamy, faraway look - and spoke.

"Look mate, will you pack that in?"

25

It was meant to come somewhere between Clint Eastwood and Lee Marvin on the vocal scale, with implied threats of violence in every syllable, but in reality it sounded like someone of the same sexual persuasion playing hard to get. The gentleman sat back in his chair and David resumed his forward-facing position. The situation appeared to be under control after David's assertive little outburst, and indeed remained so for fully a minute. Then he became aware of a soft finger, gently stroking the back of his neck. This, he reckoned, was the last straw.

"Stop it!" he hissed.

The gentleman responded by licking David's right ear.

David grabbed his portfolio, and thinking on his feet, rang the bell while beginning to make his way to the automatic doors next to the driver. As the bus jerked to a halt, David beckoned to the gentleman to follow him, adding a seductive little wink for good measure. The tactile little Asian bolted towards the door and alighted, whereupon David gave him an almighty shove and jumped back on again, telling the driver to step on the gas and be quick about it. The Asian man took a spectacular tumble headfirst into a privet hedge just as the doors closed, and the bus was once more on its way.

"Was that man annoying you?" asked the driver, puzzled.

"Not as much as I've just annoyed him!" replied David, deeply rattled, as he sat down and tried to compose himself. Ever the optimist, he tried to look for the silver lining. Whatever Nicole had thought of his looks, at least *someone* fancied him. He shuddered at the prospect of another encounter with the Amorous Asian, but he knew damned well that he would see the same characters night after night on that route. Was it his long hair and gentle face? Maybe

26

he was just irresistible to men, but not women. One thing was certain. This was the turning point. He was going to have to learn to drive.

He had dabbled with driving briefly before, and was already in possession of a provisional licence. His dad had taken him to the nearby Porterfields Trading Estate, which was renowned for its wide roads and lack of traffic. For this reason, thousands of learner drivers used it each weekend to practise their manoeuvres, and now it was slightly more congested than the M1 at teatime. His first-ever driving lesson had been a traumatic affair, to say the least. Len took great pride in his cars, cleaning and polishing every nook and cranny each Sunday afternoon. He would assume responsibility the general bodywork, whilst his wife, Ruby, took care of the chromium bits.

The vehicle at the time of David's inaugural lesson was a Vauxhall Cresta - a huge, pale blue affair with red vinyl seats, which looked vaguely American in design and had enough chromium to keep his mother contented. It was Len's pride and joy, and Ruby thought him a little brave, not to say foolhardy, in allowing David to get behind its enormous steering wheel. He assured her that they would only be going through the rudiments, so there was no cause for concern.

That Sunday afternoon, just after the ritual cleaning session, father and son arrived at the trading estate and swapped seats. Len went into his *spiel* about clutches, gear ratios and so on, while David feigned interest.

"In a combustible parallax compression engine," began Len, drawing diagrams on the back of his A to Z with a biro as he spoke, "the cam-shaft differential means that you have to disengage the dowelling sprockets, which intermesh with the incognito. Do you follow me?"

At least, Len might have said that. He might not have. After the first two words, David's eyes had glazed over and his brain had shut up shop. He was nodding sagely in all the right places, and pausing for effect occasionally, even asking his dad to repeat a section he wasn't clear about. Had Len asked *David* to repeat what he had been told, the game would have been up, but luckily the time for talking was over, and the time for action had begun.

David was asked to check that the car was in neutral, and then turn the ignition key. So far so good. He then depressed the clutch and selected first gear. Len was explaining about letting things out slowly and feeling the bite, or something along those lines, but David was giving virtually all of his attention to the guitar chord of B seventh, and how to form it at the seventh fret as a bar, rather than the way Ken at school had shown him. He was convinced that Ken often showed him totally bogus chord shapes just to confuse him. Perhaps he was jealous, worried that his pupil was getting better at playing guitar than he was.

Len's voice was still droning on and on about biting and clutching something or other, none of which meant a thing to David. Then he heard the words, "Let it out, come on, hurry up!" which woke him from his daydream with a start. He quickly took his foot off the clutch, accidentally flooring the accelerator at the same time.

The results were dramatic. The mighty car shot forwards like a rocket across the car park of an upholstery factory, and towards a huge brick wall with a skip full of foam rubber off-cuts in front of it. Lesson two, which dealt largely with how to stop a Vauxhall Cresta doing thirty miles per hour and heading for a solid object, had not yet been broached. Even if it had, David wouldn't have heard or remembered it anyway. Len grabbed the wheel and somehow got his right foot across the gear column, into the driver's side and onto the brake in a new Commonwealth Games record time. How he managed it he would never know. It was as if his leg had telescoped out another yard and grown a second knee. What made the manoeuvre all the more remarkable was that simultaneously he could still find time to scream the words, "Get your feet off the pedals NOW!" It was the driver's equivalent of patting your head with one hand and making circular motions on the stomach with the other, whilst counting backwards from twenty in German. Miraculously, Len's beloved car screeched to a halt, tyres smoking blue like a hotrod, a whole inch from the skip. A sandwich made with thick-sliced bread wouldn't have fitted in the gap.

Len, who had gone an interesting shade of pale grey and was breathing heavily through his nose, said that that was quite sufficient for Lesson One. He added tersely that he would get back to him in re. Lesson Two at a later date, once he had dislodged his heart from his front teeth.

This inauspicious start to David's motoring career had unnerved him a little, and he had not driven since. He had occasionally suggested having another crack at it, more to please his dad than himself, but unfortunately Len was often too busy at that precise time, so no further tuition had resulted.

This latest incident on the bus, however, had galvanized David into action once more, and he made a beeline for the Castle Hill School of Motoring, a short detour on his route to the Dudley bus terminal in Fisher Street. He booked himself twenty lessons, with a promise to send a cheque by return. His parents would have to release the necessary funds, but he couldn't see them objecting. His dad especially, he felt, would be all for it.

Once business was concluded at the driving school, he decided to head home instead of catching up with the school coach, and caught his second bus to Cradley Station, from where he walked the last mile or so. Exhausted but happy, he breezed into the house, flopped into a comfy armchair and demanded tea. He softened his parents up with the news that he'd been accepted at the art school, and slipped in the bit about the expensive driving lessons just at the right psychological moment. His argument about walking miles and catching untold buses that were full to the rafters with weirdoes had gone over big - bigger than he had dared hope for, in fact. Ruby said that they had been planning a nice surprise for his birthday, but after a brief scrum-down with Len, she announced that they had earmarked some money from his building society savings to buy him a second-hand car. They explained that it wouldn't be a stylish affair, because the insurance would be sky high at his age, but they could afford something small, practical and easy to insure and run. After a brief discussion, all three were agreed on a Mini.

After tea, David scoured the Express and Star looking for bargains. Len offered to accompany him to view the vehicles and give them the once over, when the time came. David thanked him for the offer, but said that his friend Lazlo, who was a mechanic, would gladly volunteer.

Lazlo wasn't his real name. It was Larry, and if the truth were known it was probably Laurence, but he wouldn't admit to it. His nickname used to be plain Laz, but David had amended it after watching Casablanca on T.V. one evening, and the new version stuck.

David had met him at a Blodwyn Pig Concert at the town hall in Cradley Heath, and had been impressed by this wild and exotic creature. Lazlo was eighteen years old, and already a very good guitarist. Here was a lad that could bring on David's guitar skills, in sharp contrast to Ken Stephenson, a guitar-playing acquaintance from school, who seemed less willing to share with David what he'd learnt.

Lazlo was what the polite observer would call visually 'distinctive'. The impolite observer would say 'bloody weird-looking.' He had a triangular wedge of tightly-frizzed hair and slightly Egyptian features, though his parents were of pure Black Country stock. He wore bell-bottomed trousers, stack-heeled multicoloured boots with metallic silver star motifs *à la* Marc Bolan, and an Oxford boating blazer. Ethnic bangles and necklaces would usually complement his outfits, topped off occasionally with a velvet hat. Lazlo was often cited as the difference between profit and loss when the local hippy boutique reached the end of their financial year.

On Saturdays, when he was dressed up to go to the local rock club, he would add dangly earrings to the ensemble, and, depending on his mood, a generous helping of Tutankhamun-style eyeliner. Some might think that, after David's close encounter with the Amorous Asian, this was the last person he would choose to be acquainted with. The big difference was that Lazlo was a rabid heterosexual. Eccentric of dress maybe. Three-parts mad, certainly, but definitely not a player of the pink piccolo. He just *looked* as if he might be. The first time Ruby answered the front door to him, she screamed. It was an embarrassing moment for all concerned, but she soon became acclimatized to the hair and the outfits, and was able to see the essentially decent, if slightly deranged car mechanic beneath. One presumed that he toned down the look a little at work, when he was messing with oily sumps and carburettors.

Lazlo was influential in many ways, both spiritual and practical. For a start, he drove a car, if one could call a rusty Cortina with wall-to-wall cigarette butts a car. This meant that the two could get around to the various hippy parties and rock clubs in the area, and appear cool to the opposite sex. He introduced David to strange bands that he'd never listened to before, such as Frank Zappa's Mothers of Invention and the Incredible String Band, and the pair would stay in Lazlo's bedroom for hours, teaching each other snippets of guitar and swapping ideas.

David would show him some technically challenging bit of jazz, the legacy of his clarinet-playing past, whilst Lazlo showed him how to play in the wilder and more emotionally-led styles of Hendrix or Clapton. The two were Mr Chalk and Mr Cheese, but the chemistry worked. Because Lazlo had a dirty job, which he loathed, he'd arrive back at his parents' house covered in oil and dirt, and David would turn up at eight and chat while his friend washed himself at the kitchen sink.

Lazlo could make an arm last up to two hours. By the time he was washed, changed and fully made-up, it could be nudging ten. An hour in the bedroom with the guitars took them up to eleven, at which point Lazlo would take them out for a spin in the car. The trouble was, everywhere was shut by then, so they'd end up at a motorway service station, eating revolting chicken and mushroom pies, complete with real bits of feather, but they didn't care, because it was somewhere to talk for hours about music, life and girls.

They must have looked quite incongruous amongst the regular clientèle, who favoured donkey jackets and overalls.

Once, for a dare, Lazlo had gone to the services in a dress and chandelier earrings. He ate his pie and smoked a cigarette with a straight face, as the truckers, and David, for that matter, looked on in blank amazement. After the sloppy 'death pies' had been consumed, they usually chatted about the universe and everything until the early hours, unless Lazlo had to strip a gearbox at seven-thirty the next day.

One night, after their usual excursion to the service station, David raised the subject of the new car.

"Lazlo," he said, as they pulled up outside David's house. "I'm getting driving lessons. I start on Monday night."

"Shit!" gasped Lazlo, sucking the life out of his cigarette before adding it to his priceless collection on the floor. "Let me know when you're out on the road. I'm going to stay in and wash my hair that night."

"Shit *yourself!*" riposted David wittily - he'd been reading a lot of Oscar Wilde, and it was beginning to rub off. "You've *never* washed your hair. Why start now?"

"Ha ha!" laughed Lazlo, somewhat hollowly.

"Anyway, Rube and Len said they'd crash the funds for an old car to get me started; probably a Mini, and I wondered if you'd take a look at it, to see if it's sound."

"Course," his friend assured him, as he lit up another cigarette. "Let me know when and I'll take you."

"Ta!" said David. His facial expression changed to one of concern. "You ought to pack up the fags you know. Doctors have proved beyond doubt that smoking is bad for your cigarettes. Look how nice they look, sat in that packet, and then see what they look like after you've smoked 'em -

they're ruined!" He pointed to the thousands of dog-ends that formed a noxious carpet all around them.

"I could give up any time," Lazlo assured him. "I just don't want to."

"Yeah yeah!" sneered David. "That's the fags talking, not you. They control you: they tell you what to think and what to say. I won't let you smoke in my car, for your own good."

"Christ! He can't drive yet, he hasn't got a bleeding car, and already he's laying down the law!" snorted Lazlo, blowing a puff of smoke from his newly-lit gasper into David's face. "Anyway, call me when you find a 'pap-pap'. Gotta go. Work tomorrow. You know how I love it."

David got out of the car, waved to his crazy accomplice, and tiptoed into the house so as not to wake his parents, or his six-year-old brother, Paul. This considerate gesture was rendered somewhat pointless by Lazlo's screeching tyres and the tooting of his horn, as he exited the cul-de-sac touching sixty.

The following day was to be David's last at Tipperton Grammar School, and a party was planned for the sixth form at The Shrubbery pub just across the road, from lunchtime onwards. It promised to be a raucous affair, and he needed to get his beauty sleep if he was to cope.

CHAPTER 4

La Trek to Loos

Len had gone off early to work, as usual, and David was in the kitchen with his mother and young brother, spooning in a thoughtful Weetabix as he perused the previous night's Express and Star car ads. There were several Minis for sale, but most were quite a distance away, in places such as Cannock, Hednesford and Northfield. He didn't really fancy asking Lazlo to traipse all the way over there with him after he'd done a hard day's work. Besides, the time it took him to wash both arms *and* his entire face, the bargains would be gone. Private car sellers didn't appreciate being got out of bed in the middle of the night by weirdoes with triangular hair, who smelled of fags and chicken and mushroom pies. No one needs to sell a car that badly. Besides, David knew what he was looking for - he was no fool. He'd ask about the mileage and the previous owners, why the car was for sale, and so on. Lazlo needn't come. It was a cheek asking him. He'd go on his own.

The problem was, how could he get there? One ad, for a Mini Clubman, gave the address as Pensnett, which wasn't too far away. He decided to ring them, to see if the vehicle was still for sale before he caught the coach for Tipperton. The man on the other end of the line sounded like a bit of a rough diamond, but he was friendly enough. The car was still available, so David could make his way to Pensnett after school and have a test drive. Considerably bucked by this news, he said goodbye to his mother, who was struggling with the crossword in Woman's Realm, and to his young sibling, who was busy making owl-hoot noises with the top half of his recorder.

David walked along Woodland Avenue to the spot where the coach picked the Brierley Bankers up each day. Within a few minutes it arrived, piloted, as usual, by Maurice, a toothless zombie. David hopped on and claimed his seat on the back row, which he was entitled to do as a sixth former. Dennis was already on-board, flipping through an Army careers magazine.

"Worro!" said David cheerfully.

"Worro yourself!" replied Dennis.

"I'm going to look at a car tonight - a Mini Clubman. I'm just doing it to copy my hero."

Dennis had passed his test and drove a smart Mini Clubman, which he'd paid for by doing a paper round since he was around eighteen-months old and never spending a penny, helped along by the occasional birthday bonus from his parents.

"Just one small problemette, old chap," mused Dennis. "You haven't passed your test, or even started driving yet."

"Aha!" replied David, fingering his school tie in the Oliver Hardy manner. "I begin on Monday, at the Castle School of Motoring, and with someone as talented as I, it should only be a matter of a few weeks before I hit the road. Until then I shall blag lifts off you or Lazlo, and, if I am pleased with the service you provide, toss you the very occasional quid or so to help with the petrol."

"Lord help Dudley, that's all I can say," groaned Dennis, theatrically holding his hands over his eyes in mock horror.

"Ye of little faith," sighed David, clouting him on the back of his head rather too heavily. "Anyway, what's with the magazine? You going through with the soldier boy bit?"

"Not sure. I fancy *one* of the services. I'll go to a few careers talks and chew it over."

"And you're worried about Dudley, with me driving about in my Clubman. We'll all sleep safer in our beds when *you* begin defending us from the forces of evil. Jeez!"

Dennis interrupted the conversation to point out a passing lady cyclist's enormous breasts, and as David turned to look, he received a devastating whack to the back of *his* head. "You'll be glad of my protection one day, old pal." Dennis grinned, and continued reading his careers magazine.

David stared out of the window. This was almost the last time he'd sit on the old coach with Dennis and the others. His immediate future was organized, and a whole new way of life beckoned, but most of his friends were still waiting to see how their results panned out. What would become of them all now? In a few years time, they'd probably lose all contact with each other – it was inevitable. Half of them would be grey-haired old bankers or solicitors, boring each other rigid at their golf clubs, telling awful jokes in the bar and wearing their nasty Pringle diamond-design jumpers. Dennis would be a stiff-upper-lipped Major with a posh accent. Mohammed would probably own a chain of newsagent shops. The science lads would all be doctors or chemists. Julian in his music class would surely be a professional homosexual, and David would be a professional artist - he could see it all unfolding in his daydream. What did artists do all day? How did they make a living? All this was too far ahead to worry about, and he wasn't a lad who took too much notice of the future. The main thing was that he had somewhere to go next, and he was very excited at the prospect. But he was also a sentimentalist, and it was a bittersweet day.

Six long years at Tipperton had passed and he'd forged a lot of friendships. Now they would almost certainly melt away and disappear like last year's snow, and in his heart of hearts he felt that even Dennis, his best school-mate, would be gradually prised away from him by circumstances beyond their control. Schooldays, he had been told by all and sundry, were 'the best days of one's life', and today those days were over, forever. How could anyone but the hardest, meanest individual not get a tear in the eye at the thought of leaving a school, he wondered. Luckily, he was about to move on to just about the only place that guaranteed an even better time, and better memories - not to mention the armies of naked women lying around on draped white sheets. It was this fact, and this fact alone, that prevented him from becoming seriously maudlin.

The school coach came to rest outside the front gates of Tipperton Grammar at five minutes to nine, and the mixed bag of pupils within clattered down the front steps and into the main entrance. For most, it was almost the start of a long summer holiday. For David, Dennis and Co. it was a lot more serious than that. It was the end of an era.

Lessons that day were merely token affairs. Teachers were given presents and cards, and pupils were wished all the best with their future careers. Even the head seemed less formidable than usual. Perhaps he was just relieved to see the back of them. No great consolation when he was

38

virtually guaranteed an identical bunch of urchins the following year, but hope springs eternal.

Not all the pupils were quite as sentimental as David. Ken Stephenson, David's guitar-playing friend, who had ignored the school rules and grown a beard, sat on the steps that led to the lower playing fields smoking a moody cigarette during first break. Miss Tomkinson, the P.E. mistress, who happened to be strolling that way, caught him at it and insisted he report to the headmaster - a rather futile command, considering it was the last day of school. Ken, who was leaving for good in approximately four and a half hours, told her, somewhat ungallantly, to 'shove her head up a dead bear's arse'. Incensed, she demanded that he report for punishment, and added that he must remove his beard forthwith, though exactly how he could achieve this there and then was not made clear.

The student took a long drag on his cigarette and blew the smoke into the teacher's face.

"Here's the deal," he smirked. "You shave off *your* beard, and I'll shave off mine." He then popped through a large hole in the school's wire fence and swaggered off along the canal towpath, never to darken their doors again.

Elsewhere, a carnival atmosphere was fast developing. School ties were being cut to pieces with scissors, and exercise books condemned to a watery grave, courtesy of the nearby canal. Sixth formers were wandering around with whole sleeves missing from their blazers, and several of the more streetwise girls were already plastered on low-cost cider, and had begun to weep melodramatically. Smashed eggs, not normally associated with tonsorial enhancement, were being sported in the coiffure of many of the lower school's more fashion-conscious ragamuffins. At lunchtime, the fifth and sixth formers and anyone else who could get away with it, moved the celebrations over the road to The Shrubbery, where copious quantities of Guinness were being absorbed with no thought spared for the violent sickness that would surely follow.

Dennis returned from the bar carrying two bottles, one for himself and one for David. He sat down at the old cast-iron pub table, placed the bottles onto a couple of beer mats and produced two packets of pork scratchings from his blazer pocket.

"Here," he said, "to augment your cheese sandwiches."

"How did you know that I had cheese sandwiches?" queried David, producing them from his pocket.

"Because that's all you've ever had, in the six years I've known you!" explained Dennis, unwrapping his corned beef cob.

"I like cheese," replied David, rather obviously. The Guinness was beginning to addle his speech now, and he was keeping his sentences simple, to avoid using up too much brainpower.

They munched a thoughtful sandwich.

"Look at that," said Dennis eventually. Karen Hobbins had just walked past in a tight mini-skirt, carrying a lager and lime. She had long, thick blonde hair, pneumatic breasts that pressurised her school blouse to near busting point, and a face that had forced many a spotty youth through puberty.

"Jeez!" said David, his jaw dropping to reveal a half-chewed cheese sandwich. "She's a real goer! I bet there's only me and you in the whole bloody school that hasn't been with her."

40

Dennis looked gloomily into his drink. "It's only you, old pal," he said sadly.

"How's your corned beef cob?" enquired David, apropos of nothing.

"Fine!" replied his friend, munching away at it with a determined look. "Why?"

"It's just that I put a Guinness beer-mat under the corned beef, while you were at the bar. Being round, it fitted the cob perfectly, and you appear to have virtually eaten it."

Dennis opened up his dinner and examined the beer mat. Only twenty-five percent of it remained, and it had cartoon chomp marks at the edges. "Well, it tasted okay," he replied, and discarding what was left, continued eating.

David stood up suddenly, sending the beer cascading all over the table into Dennis's lap, and staggered off to the toilets, which were at least a half-mile trek down a seedy, stale-smelling corridor, unaware that he had just marinated his best friend's groin in Ireland's finest beverage.

The lavatories at The Shrubbery were not 'five star', but usually they came up the minimum standard required by civilization, and just over the minimum for Tipperton. This particular day they had let themselves go, and it wasn't a sight for the squeamish. In fact, those who were subject to attacks of squeam had opted to relieve themselves up against a bush in the beer garden, rather than tip-toe amongst the vomit piles that were fast assembling, like pungent volcanoes emerging from a sea of urine.

David did not possess a strong stomach at the best of times, and the smell of the toilets was making him heave. While gingerly picking his way through the minefield in search of the trough, he noticed that one of the cubicle

41

lavatories had its door open, revealing the slumped figure of sixteen-year-old Hank Frill, who had retired from public life and was taking a nap with his trousers around his ankles. David, himself three-parts drunk by now, found this highly amusing and began to snort with laughter, tears rolling from his cheeks.

Hank Frill was not the boy's real name. It was Frank Hill. He was a very weedy, frail and frankly insignificant creature from the fifth form who seemed totally out of tune with the rest of his generation, since he preferred country and western music to the stuff most of his peer group were listening to.

Not for him the sublime melodies of The Beatles or Simon and Garfunkel, the heavy rock of Led Zeppelin, the bluesy guitar of Eric Clapton or the soul and funk of Stevie Wonder. Frank loved those maudlin and sentimental tales of love and death set to syrupy backing tracks that were awash with pedal steel guitars. At the previous year's end of term dance, this shy and retiring wallflower had amazed the congregation by turning up in a suede coat, complete with frilly tassels on the back, front and sleeves, offset with a huge Stetson. Dennis had looked over incredulously at David, who then coined the immortal Spoonerism, "Look out, partners! Here comes Hank Frill." and so the legend was born. Now, back in bedraggled uniform, with a one-armed blazer, a hairstyle you could have cooked chips in, and blowing a small, translucent green bubble from his right nostril, lay the peaceful remains of 'Hank – The King of Country'.

David stood at the entrance to Hank's private quarters, in order to observe him more closely. The corpse had a huge angry bump on his brow, but David, lacking the detection skills of Sherlock Holmes or Poirot, couldn't immediately ascertain the cause. What puzzled him was Hank's stance on alcohol. David knew for a fact that the boy was a strict teetotaller, so either he'd succumbed, due to 'last day pressure', or something else had floored the poor sod.

His second guess was exactly on the money. Hank, or if you prefer, Frank, had filled himself to the gills with Vimto and Smokey Bacon crisps, and decided to risk the terrors of the lavatories to relieve himself. Always a shy boy, due to the size, or rather, the lack of size, of his private parts, the private cubicles were always deemed preferable to the common trough.

The facilities at The Shrubbery were mainly of Victorian origin, which meant that the cistern was mounted on the wall high above the pan, and one flushed it by pulling a cast-iron knob attached to a long chain, which in turn was attached to a lever feeding into the cistern. The mechanism had seen better days, which meant that Frank had to yank several times, but was rewarded with only a few unsatisfying dribbles of water below - not nearly enough to disperse his waste products. Infuriated by this inefficient and antiquarian system, Hank, or if you prefer, Frank, gave a final and massive yank, releasing the knob as he did so, and turned to exit the cubicle, figuring that he'd done his best and could do no more. If it didn't flush this time, he reasoned, then so be it.

At this precise juncture, the cast-iron knob re-entered the earth's atmosphere after a brief visit to the ceiling, and crashed down onto Hank's delicate little skull, rendering him incapable of further thought.

David, who was now standing at the trough and releasing gallons of Guinness back into the wild, with a slightly cross-eyed and ecstatic look on his face, was just about sober

43

enough to realize that Frank possibly might not just be inebriated, but seriously ill. He finished his business, and placed his own meagre manhood back into his grey school trousers, releasing at least another half-pint of warm urine down the inside of his leg. Side-stepping the mounds of sick, he manhandled the unfortunate little fellow off the pan, turning him around so that he could get his arms under Hank's, and across his chest. He then dragged him backwards, through the urine and vomit, trousers still at half-mast, and slowly but surely, miles down the corridor and into the crowded public bar, leaving a snail-like trail behind him, right back to the lavatories.

The noise of the bar ceased just as surely as if a tough gunslinger had entered through swing doors to confront the crooked sheriff. There wasn't a honky-tonk pianist present, but if there had been, he would have stopped playing and scurried for cover. All eyes stared incredulously at David and his unconscious, scantily-clad patient.

"I found this chap in the toilet," he called out to those present. "I think he's had a nasty bump on the head!"

The barman quickly found his way to the scene, and covered up Hank's sorrowful little member with a beer-soaked bar towel, whilst he attempted to bring him round with a little Indian Brandy. David, mercy mission completed, returned to a hero's welcome at his table.

"Well done!" said Dennis, offering him the small amount of Guinness that had miraculously escaped landing in his crotch.

"It was nothing!" said David, modestly, taking a sip.

"No, I meant well done for showing the whole pub Frank's little todger, which he's successfully kept under

44

wraps, even during P.E., for five years, because he was so upset by its diminutive size. Well done too for allowing the barman to pour brandy down an unconscious Salvationist and teetotaller's neck."

"Oh!" replied David, stunned. "And may I add oops, for good measure."

"You may, my good man," said Dennis, hooking his arm under David's, like a couple about to take a moonlit stroll down by the Seine, "and now, if you don't mind, dearest, I would like you to escort me back to the school premises, where I fully intend to be violently sick, if that's okay with you."

"Lead on, darling," replied David, who was by now desperately trying to stop the room from spinning around like a fairground ride. "I tire of this place, and I would be alone."

CHAPTER 5

The Sweaty Vest

David woke up feeling very bad tempered and crabby at around seven-thirty that evening. He had been spark-out on the settee, much to the annoyance of his parents and his brother Paul, who were forced to use other seating arrangements. He had an awful crick in his neck, and his mouth felt as if a diseased and moribund rodent had crawled in there to decompose, some weeks previously. His first action, upon waking, was to stagger to the kitchen, put his head under the tap, and gulp down around sixteen gallons of water.

"Have you been drinking?" asked his mother. Nothing got past her.

"No," moaned David, grumpily.

"Yes he has, mommy. I just saw him in the kitchen. He's telling big fibs," added his young brother.

"Shut your face, midget," croaked David, swilling his face with water and sighing theatrically.

"If you haven't been drinking," continued his mother, "explain why you came in at a quarter-to-five, started watching Blue Peter with your brother, staggered over to the telly as if you were going to change the channels or something, and just collapsed in a heap onto the floor."

"Yeah!" said Paul, "why?"

"And then you just stayed there, with your behind up in the air and your head in the carpet for half an hour, so Paul couldn't see his programmes. Me and Len had to lift you onto the settee, and you weigh half a ton."

"And you were a dead weight!" added Len, who was washing himself at the kitchen sink.

"Bloody hell!" said David, jerking to life.

"Language, in front of your brother!" scolded Ruby.

"I've forgotten about my car," said David, panicking. "Oh sod! I was supposed to see a Mini tonight up in Pensnett. I bet I've lost it now. These bargains get snapped up in no time. That's your fault, mother."

"*My* fault?"

"You didn't wake me."

David shot upstairs to clean his teeth and smarten himself up. His head was pounding, so he took a couple of aspirin tablets with another six pints of water. Luckily, his dad was going to see a cousin not far from Pensnett and offered to drop him off at the house. As they approached the run-down council estate, Len broke the silence.

"I can't come and look at it tonight. I'm late for Wilf. You should have got Lazlo to check it out. He looks weird but he knows his cars."

"I'll be okay," replied David. "I know all the right questions to ask. Besides, if this bloke saw Laz, it might unhinge him, psychologically speaking. He has that effect on folks. He might also think we're a pair of Nancy-boys looking for a passion wagon. No, I'll be okay. I've got the deposit cheque. You'll have to trust me to make the decision."

"Well, it's your money, son," sighed Len, resignedly, letting David out of the car. "Remember, there are plenty more motors to look at. Don't rush into anything. I know that the money's burning a hole in your pocket."

With this last piece of completely unheeded advice, Len slipped into first gear and was gone into the night.

The house was scruffy. There was no other way to describe it. Other houses around and about had the good grace to screw brass or plastic numbers to their front doors, as a kind of clue for the postman, but not this one. The occupier, obviously not a follower of Ruskin or the aesthetic movement, had crudely painted '87A' with two-foot high numbers on the wall, using a three-inch brush. The front door, which must, at one time, have been green, had also in its distant past been blue, yellow, pink and brown. Piles of rubbish lay strewn across what was once a lawn and the skeletons of bicycles in various stages of decomposition were all around. David had accidentally stumbled on the mythical burial grounds where bicycles came to die.

He took a large, fortifying gulp, and knocked at the door. His tongue was stuck to the roof of his mouth, which was as dry as a bone due to the lunchtime drinking session. His head continued to gently throb. A dirty looking man in a dirtier looking vest opened the door.

"What?" he asked, aggressively.

"Er, I'm David," David replied.

"Oh, Sheila's new chap. You're early, pal. You'll have to wait. You don't look up to much, you scrawny lookin' bugger! I was led to believe you was summat special. Jesus! Wait here. She'll be down in a bit. She's cleaning herself up. She was a bit nervous, what with goin' out on a date with a chap from the posh estate, and she's gone and shit herself!"

"Er, no, I'm not your daughter's boyfriend," explained David. "I've come about the car for sale - the Mini Clubman."

"Oh, bugger me!" said the Sweaty Vest. "Sorry old pal. Come round the back. It's in the back yard."

David and the man went around the back, and were greeted by a Mini that, in the fading light, didn't look too bad, considering who owned it. It was a buff colour with a black stripe and a vinyl roof. The wheels looked decidedly sporty.

"Know anythin' about motors, pal?" asked the Sweaty Vest, lighting up a Park Drive. David noticed that his knuckles were tattooed with the words LOVE and HAIT. This was not a good sign. An illiterate psychopath with B.O.

"No, not really," answered David honestly.

"Good," said the Vest. "You get some smart-arses come round here, and they think they know it all, and they don't know shit. Know what I mean?"

David said that he did.

"Well, what do you think?" asked the Vest. "Course, I don't really want to sell it, pal - It's a great little runner. It's just that I need summat bigger, now that we've had the triplets, and we've got the two Staffies and the Rottweiler. That's them up the garden, growlin' at yer. They won't hurt yer though, as long as yer don't go near 'em or move sudden. Any questions mate?"

"Er, yes. How many miles has it done?"

"Genuine twenty-thousand pal; me missus only uses it for going to her mother's once a month. It's got a vinyl roof, which I had done, and I can't lie, it's had a respray, but it was done by the best bloke in the Midlands. He does Formula One cars as well. It's got Cosmic Wheels, see? And they ain't cheap, I can tell yer!"

David nodded, as if he knew what the man was talking about. "Is it good on petrol?" he asked, dragging himself back to the script. The question was a good one, except for the fact that the Vest probably wouldn't have given a truthful answer, and if he did, it wouldn't have meant anything to David anyway.

"You'll never have to fill it up. It's got MOT left on it, and there's a stereo radio and a partly-electric aerial. Note the deluxe leopard-skin seat covers."

David was studying the massive stickers down each side, which said Clubman, in glittery silver. He was very impressed.

"Can I have a test drive?" he asked.

The man told him it was best that he drove it, rather than let David have a go, as he was used to its gearbox, and David said that that was okay, as he couldn't drive anyway.

They got in, and the car spluttered to life. A huge blue cloud of smoke belched from the exhaust pipe.

"It's a bit slow starting because it hardly gets used," explained the Vest. "It needs a young feller like you to use it regular. Standing around ain't no good for motors, see?"

He chugged round the estate for around four minutes, enthusing with every gear change about how smooth a runner it was, and how it was breaking his heart to part with it. David had never come across anyone who loved a car quite as much, which he found touching - the big rough bear of a man revealing his softer side. By way of making conversation as they travelled, David asked if the car had been 'suped-up', as he could hear a thunderous rumble emanating from the exhaust area.

"Yeah, it's got a racing exhaust. I had that fitted to give it that special rally car sound," explained the Vest. "Throaty innit?"

David said that he liked that sound a lot, and had often wondered how it was achieved. When he enquired as to the severe grating noise that occurred when the Vest attempted a gear change, his mind was put at rest with the explanation that the gear stick was still new, and had to settle in. It sounded as if the man had spent a small fortune on new parts. How he could afford to splash out on so many items when the whole car was only on sale for a mere one hundred and seventy five pounds was beyond David, but he shrewdly kept this thought to himself, in case the Vest increased the price.

Shortly after they had set off, it began to rain, and the Vest thought it best to get back as the wipers were new and shouldn't be used till they were set properly. The test drive came to an abrupt end. They returned to the house, where the Vest turned the engine off, and applied the handbrake. He explained that it wasn't adjusted correctly, as it was also brand new, and he advised pushed a building brick under the front tyre until such time as it bedded in.

The two men got out of the car, and David took a quick look around it. It looked great in the twilight, glistening with a light sprinkle of rain, and he was very excited. The passenger door sprang open rather unexpectedly at that point, but the Vest told him this was common in Mini Clubmans, and there was an adjustment screw, which he just hadn't had time to mess with, what with one thing and another. Other than that, the car was a little gem, and several people were apparently calling to see it the next day. One man, from Sedgley, had offered him seventy pounds over the asking price to hang on to it, but the Vest said that he wasn't money motivated, and if David really liked it, it was his, subject to a deposit of fifty quid, right there and then.

Delighted and touched by the Vest's generous and altruistic spirit, David handed over the cash, after a token haggle about the price. The car was to be delivered to David's house the following evening, whereupon the balance would be handed over. Job done! He asked the Vest if he would mind just dropping him back to the bus stop, but unfortunately the man's tea was on the table, and he had to dash off.

Soaked but happy, David stood at the bus stop in the pouring rain. He'd found a good little car, all by himself, and even managed to talk the man down by eight pounds, which his dad had reminded him to do, because it was a well-known fact that people put a little extra on, fully expecting to be knocked down. Len would be proud of his shrewd business acumen.

After some time, he gave up on ever seeing the Brierley Bank bus, and resolved to walk all the way home. He was ringing wet and beginning to feel a little uncomfortable, but looking forward to seeing Lazlo, eager to show off the new car.

CHAPTER 6

Lazlo puts his foot down

"What the hell were you thinking about?"

Lazlo scratched his head in an exasperated way, as he stared at David in stark disbelief. They were sitting on the front wall of David's house, surveying his recent acquisition.

"Well…"

"Well you got so excited; you couldn't wait for me to come with you. Am I right?"

"Er…"

"Am I right, or am I right?"

"Yes. Can you stop going on about it now, do you think?" David was deeply embarrassed.

"No. I can't. Not yet. I've got to get this out of my system. You go to the seediest estate in the cosmos, and buy a car from a man with a sweaty vest and tattoos that weren't even spelt properly. Correct?"

David affected a yawn.

"He tells you that *he'll* do the driving because he's used to the gearbox. Stirling Moss couldn't use that gearbox. It's buggered - point one. Yes, I know you couldn't have driven it anyway. That's what I was coming for, remember? Point two. He didn't want to drive it in the wet. Know why? The wipers don't work. They're buggered as well. Point three. Oh, to hell with numbering the points - there's too bloody many of them to count. The passenger door didn't originally belong to this car. That's why it keeps falling open. The leopard skin seat covers are there to hide the enormous tears and filthy stains on the real seats underneath. The engine is leaking tons of oil all over the road, as we speak. The RSPCA are already on stand-by to clean up passing cormorants. Shut up and just listen. The handbrake is buggered. There's about ten minutes left on the MOT, so no need to panic about that till half-past, eh? The cosmic wheels - those beautiful alloys that sold it to you, remember? They're plastic wheel trims, stupid. The driver's-side mirror is actually very nice. Congratulations! Pity the passenger hasn't got one. The fabulous paint job - that was to cover the fact that this used to be two different cars, but now they are happily welded together in matrimony. The paint technique used is referred to, in our trade, as a 'knacker lacquer' - cheap crap designed to last a week or two before it rots, or drops off. Nice colour though, I must admit. Better than the twelve other colours it's been in its time. Oh yes, and the glorious vinyl roof. It's not vinyl. It looks like some form of tarmac. Congratulations, sucker. You are the proud owner of a car with a tarmac roof. Anybody can apply go-faster stickers. They cost a few quid, and they're great. Lovely! Why didn't you get a sun-strip, while you were at it, reading TATTOOED MORON on one side and PEROXIDE SCRUBBER on the other? Shall we get onto previous owners, or shall we deal with its Rolls

Royce-style petrol consumption first? I'm easy! Or maybe we could deal with the most important issue - the fact that it isn't a Mini Clubman. The bloody sticker says it is, but being as they were only launched last year, and this car's at least six years old, it looks like the front half is, but the back half isn't. With me so far? And finally, point seven hundred and thirty six, your Honour. That throaty, racing car sound that you're so fond of? Your man in the vest achieved that particular effect by having only half an exhaust pipe."

David, who had been doing a respectable impression of a particularly dim-witted halibut throughout this onslaught, finally found words.

"So you don't like it then?"

"Not keen, no," conceded Lazlo, confirming David's suspicion. "What did Rube and Len have to say?"

"Not much. Dad just went down to his shed and filed a piece of wood to bits. I think he does that rather than hit me. He's a gentle soul."

"Maybe he'd consider letting me hit you instead. Look, I'll take it up to the workshop next week and make it roadworthy. If you can release a few more quid, I'll make sure it doesn't kill you. Okay?"

David said it was very much okay, and thanked him profusely. All his life, he had dived head-first into situations because of his impatience, and mostly it had cost him dearly. This was just another example from a huge back-catalogue. Lazlo, sensing he had upset his *naïve* friend with his straight talking, lightened the mood by grinning at David and throwing his arm around his deflated shoulders.

"Cheer up, old pal. You can't be good at everything. At least you're good at lots of things, unlike most folks. See you later for a bit of guitar therapy and a death pie, if you're free."

"Yep," said David, sheepishly. "I've managed to get a driving lesson later, my first one. Someone cancelled, so I stepped in. I'm going to do a crash course, if you'll excuse the phrase, so that I might be in with a chance of passing in time for my new college. I'll ring you after that, if I'm not in traction in a local hospital."

"Have faith, and have confidence, my son," smiled Lazlo, "but most of all, bloody concentrate on what the poor bloke's trying to tell you. Remember what you did to Len at Porterfields. He's only just managed to quit taking Valium."

"Okay, promise," replied David, smiling at last. "And we'll put our band together, now that school is out of the way. We want to be gigging by September, latest."

"Glad you mentioned that," said Lazlo, getting up from the wall and walking towards his car. "I've fixed up a rehearsal next week at a chap called Dingo's house in Kingswinford. We've never actually met, but he was recommended by Jim, the bassist in Sweaty Betty. Dingo's folks have got a huge private house with a massive garage that's been soundproofed, so that the neighbours don't hear his drumming. He's invited a singer he vaguely knows from Dudley who he reckons is really good, and the singer's bringing a bass player with him. We'll have a knock-about and see if we gel. If we all like the same kind of stuff, and they're up to standard, we could be away. Sound good?"

David said it sounded good, and bade his friend farewell. Their plan was to find musicians who could play rock and roll and standards, so that they could earn a few pounds around the clubs and pubs on weekends. Hopefully this could run in tandem with their other project, which was to form a band that played original material, and concentrate on the college circuit. Either way, at least they'd be playing live and gaining experience, and that was the main thing. It would be no fun being stuck in a bedroom for the rest of their years. They needed to impress women while they were young enough to enjoy it.

David walked slowly up the concrete steps to his front door. Having had his ear severely bent once already that day, he wasn't looking forward to seeing his parents for more of the same.

CHAPTER 7

The Bunker

The driving lesson went well, in that no one was killed or maimed, the car got back to Dudley with no serious structural or cosmetic alteration and both parties were still on speaking terms. In fact, they got on like a house on fire, whatever that means. Bill Duffy was an amiable sixty-year-old Brummie who wore a terrible wig. Sartorially speaking, he was decidedly dodgy, with his penchant for car coats and driving gloves, not to mention the wig itself, which looked as if it had been purchased second-hand from a man with a much smaller head.

David wasn't concerned with these minor details, however. The man had a great sense of humour, (essential if one wears a bad wig with a car coat) and he was an excellent teacher. It is an unfortunate truism that, however talented the father is at any given subject, the son never takes advantage of this freely-offered knowledge and experience, preferring instead to spend untold fortunes getting exactly the same stuff from elsewhere. It was ever thus, but at least David was beginning to understand the driving process at last, and even enjoying it, now that a complete stranger was at the helm.

The Vestmobile was not used in lessons for two reasons. Firstly, Bill Duffy needed the dual controls of his own teaching car for safety reasons, and secondly, because he told David that he wouldn't be seen dead in it. In fact, he actually said that, should they ever drive the thing, they probably *would* be seen dead in it. His advice, therefore, was to sell it to some other sucker as soon as was humanly possible. David, being David, didn't think it was morally acceptable to palm it off onto some other poor sod, and reluctantly vowed to keep it until such time as it blew up or fell apart. Lazlo estimated that his friend wouldn't have to wait too long for that to happen, but duly drove it off to his place of work as promised, to set about making it as roadworthy as possible (crossing himself theatrically like some Roman Catholic cardinal as he did so).

A few days after David's first lesson, Lazlo phoned to say he'd managed to organize a rehearsal for that evening, if he could make it. He picked him up at around seven, and loaded the amps and guitars into the back of the car. They arrived at Dingo's house at seven-thirty, to find him waiting in eager anticipation by the garage doors, sticks in hand, for their arrival.

Dingo was short and extremely muscular, with the lankest, greasiest hair David had ever seen. He had been recommended, via a friend of a friend, as being a good solid, no-nonsense drummer, and though they'd spoken on the phone, they'd never actually met. He had an amiable face, light blue eyes and a set of teeth that looked like vandalized grave-stones. He wore a vest, which showed off his huge biceps, a pair of dirty Levi's and motorcycle boots. Dingo had sign-written the inside of his dad's garage door with an elaborate Germanic typeface. It read:

THE BUNKER

"Laz!" he smiled, "and you've just got to be Dave. Pleased to meet you, man. Come in. The other two are already inside, tuning up and stuff."

They carried in the equipment and dropped it down onto the oily floor. A young man who looked like a young Joe Cocker came over and introduced himself as George Jameson. He had the broadest Dudley accent that David had ever heard, and he'd heard a lot.

"Worro!" said George, a huge grin spreading across his face. "Dave, Laz, how bin yer?"

David replied that he was fine and asked him where his bassist friend was. George explained that he'd popped out to use the lavatory, and would be back shortly. Meanwhile, he gave them a hand to set up the amplifiers, having already set up his own P.A. system. Lazlo and David were impressed that he actually owned one. Most singers felt it was the duty of the band to cough up for everything, while all they had to do was arrive on time, squeal in tune, and jump around a little. With no guitars, amps, drums or pianos to buy, the singer always got off lightly, financially speaking. It was refreshing to find one so well equipped. David just hoped and prayed that he didn't sing in an incomprehensible accent too. He was already worrying about who'd introduce the songs, if they ever played outside the area.

A huge, ugly-looking, mean-spirited creature sat on a stool in the corner of the room, largely ignored by the others. David, being a courteous individual, stepped over and introduced himself.

"Hello, I'm David, who are you?"

"H."

60

"What, just an initial? Couldn't you afford the whole name?" queried David jovially.

"Are you taking the piss?" growled the mean-spirited creature, getting up from the stool to reveal his full height, which was around twelve-foot-six.

"No, no, just having a laugh," said David nervously. "No offence. What do you do?"

"Mind my own business," snarled H, staring at David with a psychopathic hatred.

Dingo hurried over. "I see you've met my mate H. He's just popped round to hear us rehearse. We work together at the haulage firm. He's all right when you get to know him. Aren't you H?"

H smirked. David was trying to understand why anyone in his or her right mind would *want* to get to know him. What were the benefits? Where were the incentives? He hurried off, back to the safety of the other end of the rehearsal room, where Lazlo and George were hanging out.

Behind him, Dingo could be seen quietly begging H to be civil. It was not unlike Doctor Frankenstein having a quiet word to his monster, after it had accidentally strangled a small blind child.

The bassist arrived back from the lavatory, Park Drive at a jaunty angle in the corner of his mouth.

"Bloody hell!" he said, astonished.

"Bloody hell yourself!" echoed David, also astonished.

"Ha Haaaaah!" chortled the bassist, his eyes streaming with laughter and smoke.

"Ha Haaaaah!" repeated David.

"Excuse me butting in, Dave," said Lazlo politely, "but have you just metamorphosed into a giant Mynah bird, or do you two actually know each other?"

"Laz, meet Ken Stephenson, my so-called friend from Tipperton Grammar. You've probably heard me mention him. He's the one who tried his hardest not to teach me the guitar. Ring a bell?"

Ken and Laz shook hands, and Ken offered him a cigarette, which was duly accepted.

"I've heard a lot about you," said Lazlo, grinning. "A bit of a character."

"You can talk!" observed Ken, also grinning, as he perused Lazlo's outfit, which was well up to par.

"Queer bastard," snarled H to himself. Dingo glared at him, and put a finger to his lips, as if to say "Shut it!"

"So what on earth are you doing here?" asked David. "The last time I saw you, you were walking off into the sunset through a hole in a wire fence, with one arm missing from your blazer. Miss Tomkinson is still in therapy. What did you say to her anyway?"

"Ah, nothing much. She's too sensitive. I'm here because my mate George told me about this new band needing a bassist. I thought I'd give it a go, if it's alright with you, that is."

"Fine by me, Ken," David assured him, "but you're a guitarist, surely!"

"I'll be anything if there's a few quid in it. I play bass as well, didn't I tell you?"

"You didn't tell me anything, where music was concerned, you git! I had to teach myself. Anyway, great news! If you're happy with it, so am I. We thought we'd learn the standards, so that we could get work in the pubs and clubs. You know, Beatles, Stones, Free, Faces, Clapton, Rock and Roll and a few of the better chart things. Does that suit you? We can have a go at original material as well, when we've got a bit more used to each other."

"Does the Beatles suit us?" asked George. "Does the Pope have a balcony?"

"The Beatles are Gods as far as I'm concerned," added Ken. Laz nodded his approval. Dingo looked a little worried.

"Okay, Dingo?" asked David, sensing the drummer's unease. He liked to be fair.

"Well yeah, if we're doing the pubs, I suppose they want to hear that shit, but I was hoping to do some heavier stuff eventually."

"The Beatles are SHIT," shouted H, and glared at them all with hatred.

"No, that's a bit unfair, H," said Dingo the Peacemaker, aware that he was entertaining first-time guests.

"You *hate* 'em, you two-faced bastard," snarled H. "You told me you were going to play lots of Sabbath and Hawkwind. That's why I came round."

"See how it goes," said Lazlo, taking his turn to play the diplomat, but secretly wishing he had a large meat cleaver at his disposal. "We'll have a go at Paranoid after, if there's time."

"H's theme tune," whispered Ken, pitching the volume an inch short of H's ears with a skill that had taken years to perfect.

"A tune he fell in love with at his Swiss finishing school," added Lazlo, with equal lightness of touch.

"How can anyone be that ugly with only one head?" asked David, as he turned away to pick up his guitar. George just smiled, maybe because he wasn't as quick with acerbic comments, but more probably because he didn't want his arm torn off and pushed down his throat.

David suggested that they run through 'All Right Now,' which was fairly easy to play, and loud enough to stop H from assaulting them. It was ragged, but not too bad for the first ever rehearsal. What came as a pleasant surprise to all was George's voice. His accent may have been incomprehensible to anyone twenty miles out of Dudley, but he had the singing voice of an angel. His pitch and range were flawless, and he was a dead ringer for McCartney. When they began to get to grips with a few simple Beatles songs later in the evening, the resemblance was uncanny, which prompted many knowing and appreciative glances between Lazlo and David.

They had the nucleus of a great little band, if they put some serious hard work into it. Dingo was a good, solid drummer who held them together well, but it was clear from the onset that he and his pet gorilla were into very different things than the others. This suspicion was confirmed when H turned on the T.V. halfway through a rendition of 'Get Back' so that he and Dingo could watch a Kung Fu film with the sound turned down. Dingo told them to carry on playing, as he could do both jobs at the same time. Obviously, he and H couldn't hear the words, but that didn't matter, since all they were interested in was the violence. This prompted more concerned glances from the others, who must have felt like the man whose wife carries on knitting a sweater whilst he is making love to her. It just isn't quite the same if both parties don't have their minds on the job.

Mainly due to this unexpected development, plus the fact that Lazlo had promised to leave early to see his latest love interest, proceedings ground to a halt. Lazlo asked David if he needed a lift home, but David said that he would pop over to the Cross Inn with Ken to spend an hour catching up, if that was all the same to him. Lazlo loaded up the guitars and amplifiers and set off, telling Dingo that he'd ring him to arrange the next rehearsal. David, Ken and George packed up their equipment, made their excuses, and legged it over to the Cross, leaving H and Dingo to cuddle up on the sofa watching Kung Fu.

As they left the garage, David noticed H's sweatshirt, which he'd taken off and left on the back of an old chair, when the old paraffin heater got too much. It had a slogan on the front, which read;

WHITE IS RIGHT.

N.F.

He tapped Ken, and made him aware of the discarded shirt's message.

"Can't wait for next time," he whispered. "Who'll be Dingo's next house guest? Hitler?"

Over at the Cross Inn, Ken was downing pints of lager and smoking Park Drives at an alarming rate of knots, while David and George chatted about music and guitars. George didn't play that well, but he had brought with him an old and valuable Gretsch 'Country Gent' guitar, which he wanted David to take a look at. It didn't seem to be working properly, and he asked if David could take it home and try it out on his amplifier. It was not in a proper hard carrying case, but just an old cardboard box, which prompted David to remark that such an instrument deserved better protection. That said, he promised to have a look and report back the following week. The conversation then turned to Dingo and his henchman.

"Did you see that sweatshirt?" asked David, shocked. Those two are National Front thugs."

"Yep!" replied Ken. "I can't see it being a bundle of laughs rehearsing there every week. That H was looking at Laz like he wanted to disembowel him. He's racist *and* homophobic, or should we say Homer-phobic?"

"Excuse me!" said David, leaping to the defence of his friend. "Laz is about as homosexual as Errol Flynn. He left early tonight to have his evil way with some new woman or other."

"That won't deter H," said George. "That bloke would kill you for wearing a lavender shirt. Lazlo's earrings must have really upset him; he just stared daggers at him all night!"

"Perhaps he fancied him," suggested Ken. "H probably wears a tutu at weekends, and covers up his leanings by dressing as a fascist thug."

"Well you two can turn up in frocks next time and see if your theories are correct," said David, shuddering at the thought. "As for me, I'll put some time into finding a replacement drummer, if it's all the same to you."

"Funny you should mention that," said George, tucking into his fourth bag of pork scratchings. "My cousin, Greg, is a good drummer. He's in a crap pop band from Tipperton. I'll ask him. He's always wanted to play with me."

"Sounds like he'd be a suitable boyfriend for H then," said Ken. "Trouble is, where could we rehearse? Dingo's got a good little place, you must admit."

"So has Lazlo's dad," said David excitedly. "He owns a factory on Porterfields Trading Estate. He said we could rehearse there, if we wanted to."

"That's it then. Goodbye Dingo and Hitler - hey! Come to think of it, I bet that's what the H stands for!"

They laughed, drank and bonded, which is always more fun when there is a common enemy to insult. A scapegoat is essential when forming new friendships. They were a tight little unit already, united in their loathing of H. David, realizing that his last bus was imminent, gathered up the guitar and made for the exit. Outside, he was greeted by torrential rain, for which he was woefully ill-prepared. He was dressed in a Levi's denim jacket and jeans and had no umbrella or hat. To make matters worse, the Gretsch guitar was housed in a makeshift cardboard box, which would surely disintegrate after about ten minutes.

He made his way to the bus stop, which conveniently didn't have a shelter, and waited - and waited - and waited some more. He now looked like a man who had been shoved into the Staffordshire and Worcester canal, or any other canal for that matter. He couldn't have got wetter - he was as wet as it was possible to get. He squelched back to the pub, but George and Ken had gone. Offering a curse to the God of Weather, he resignedly began squelching in the direction of home, which was, as the crow squelched, a good four miles.

After a while it became quite liberating to walk in such a downpour, because he was, as has been well documented, as wet as he could get, so it no longer mattered. The only problem was the guitar, which had a protective layer around it which might as well have been made of biscuit. The box was now just a few areas of mush, stuck to the lacquered finish. The electrics were probably completely ruined, and David was beginning to panic. Just at this juncture, a car pulled alongside him, with a blue flashing light on top.

"Evening sir," said a voice within.

"Evening," said David, forcing a pathetic little smile.

"Where have we been then, sir?" asked the voice.

"I don't know," replied David.

"You don't know where you've been?" asked the voice, querulously.

"Yes, I know where *I've* been. I don't know where *you've* been," said David.

"That's not what we asked you," said the voice, irritated.

"Yes you did," said David, annoyed. "You said, 'Where have we been?'"

"Are you trying to be funny, son?" asked the voice tetchily.

"No," said David.

"What's that under your arm?"

"It's a piano," said David. *Now* he was trying to be funny.

The nice policemen invited him into the car, out of the rain.

"Right, son. I can see it's a guitar. Is it yours?"

68

"No."

"Whose is it then?"

"My friend's."

"And what's his name?" asked the policeman, with mock politeness.

It's a strange thing, but sometimes, for no apparent reason, a name will just go out of one's head. Most people have, upon arriving at the fridge, wondered why they were there: especially those over fifty. Others will forget the name of a friend they shared a hire car with on a two year trip across Canada. It was like this with David. If the man had asked him slightly more slowly, he'd have remembered. Maybe the rain had affected his brain. Whatever the reason, the name of his new singer had completely escaped him. He couldn't even remember what letter it began with, though, if push came to shove, he'd have guessed P.

"Erm. I don't know," admitted David eventually.

"Do you know what kind of guitar it is then?" asked the policeman.

The other one, who was probably trying to be Mr Nice, to the speaker's Mr Nasty, a tradition amongst police officers, said nothing but insisted on smiling an irritating sickly smile.

"I can't remember, but I know it cost hundreds of pounds," said David, trying to be helpful.

"Ah, hundreds of pounds! If I had a guitar worth that much, I'd keep it in a soaking wet cardboard box too. Makes sense, eh Donald?"

Donald nodded.

"And how long have you known this friend, whose name escapes you?" asked his inquisitor.

"Erm, two hours."

"And he's given you, this nameless mate, an expensive nameless guitar in a soggy box, so you thought you'd walk the streets at eleven o'clock in the pouring rain with it, just to give it some exercise?"

"I, erm…."

"You've nicked it, haven't you, son?"

Mr Nice chewed gum energetically like a football manager on the touchline, and grinned like an idiot.

"No!" protested David. "He lent it to me so that I could sort out the electrics."

"Ah! Now we're getting somewhere. You're an electrician."

"No, but….."

"So you thought you'd sort out his electrics, but you aren't an electrician. What are you then, if you don't mind me enquiring?"

"I'm a fine artist," said David proudly. This seemed to catapult the two policemen into deep and uncharted waters. His interrogator, David sensed, was losing his patience, not to mention the plot. He feared that he might be in line for some hideous police brutality unless he clarified the situation.

"I'm a guitarist too, you see. This friend, whose name I've forgotten, because I only met him tonight at the rehearsal, trusted me to borrow it and see if I could make it work. I daresay that my chances of that are slim, now that I've put about six gallons of water into it, but never mind."

"A guitarist!" said the interrogator, clapping his hands together with glee. "Did you hear that, Donald? He's a guitarist. Scrape what's left of the box off it and give us a tune. That would be lovely, wouldn't it, Donald?"

Donald agreed. David, who was gifted with a vivid imagination, thrust a Kung Fu fist into Donald's abdomen whilst simultaneously decapitating his interrogator with a Samurai sword. Police officers, he mused, would get more respect if they'd drop the third-rate witticisms and pedestrian sarcasm, for which they were woefully ill-equipped, and get on with their tasks in a firm but civil way. He knew he had to grin and bear this nonsense, accepting that if he dared give a bit back, all he'd get for his efforts was a lot more grief. Also, he thought it unsportsmanlike to engage in a battle of wits with unarmed men. Reluctantly, he took out the guitar, sighing melodramatically.

"Play us something, Bert Weedon," demanded the copper. Donald thought this was hilarious.

David began to play a bluesy twelve-bar, with Clapton-esque lead guitar runs in between the chords. Then the style of playing became jazzier, followed by some country-style finger picking. He concluded with a spirited version of Colonel Bogey, which, for those who are not familiar with the piece, is often accompanied by extremely rude lyrics. The instrumental version, whilst less crude, still had the desired effect on the two officers.

"Very funny," said the interrogator. "Okay, sod off!"

"Thank you," said David. "Any chance of a lift to Brierley Bank? It's pouring down out there."

"Now you *are* taking the piss," frowned the officer.

"Okay, okay!" sighed David, and struggled out of the car with the remains of his box. He squelched for another mile in the diabolical torrent of rain, the box having given up the ghost back in Wordsley town centre. His only hope of salvation now was Dennis. It was about this time of night that he usually drove back from Tipperton after seeing his new girlfriend. David prayed to God for an orange Mini Clubman to pass by, and for once, his prayers were answered. The car pulled up next to him, and a grateful, totally drenched David opened the passenger door and slumped exhaustedly onto the seat with his water-logged guitar.

"Thank God for that!" he sighed, turning to face his benefactor.

A rough-looking man in a donkey jacket and swallow tattoos on his neck glared back at him. Two similar looking hoodlums were crammed into the back seats.

"Who the hell are you?" growled the Donkey Jacket.

The men had been working a night shift at the nearby Round Oak Steel Works, and Thug No.1 was dropping No.'s 2 and 3 home.

To open the car door, grab his guitar and rocket down the road was with David the work of an instant. By the time he got to Brierley Bank High Street, he was past caring, and singing the theme from 'The Woodentops' at the top of his voice, accompanying himself on the sodden and detuned guitar. In between songs, he laughed in a slightly unhinged and manic way, and began to hold brief conversations with passing alley cats. He reached Harry Kendall's Joke and Toy Shop, half-way down the street, and paused to look in the window. The rain could do nothing to hurt him now. He was soaked to the skin, the Gretsch was ruined, and he had gone gently mad.

"Aha!" he smiled, as he inspected the merchandise. "Stick-on werewolf eyebrows! I must purchase a pair first thing tomorrow - and what have we here? Why, a realistic dog turd! Essential for every home - put me down for a dozen. Yes! By Jove, wind-up chattering teeth, and if I'm not mistaken, a rubber fried egg. Fanny Craddock, you are a prat. And Barry Bucknell, television handy-man, you are too. A curse on your hardboard door panels. Now home James, and don't spare the horses. Tally Ho!"

And with this, he pretended to gallop the last few hundred yards, calling out 'Yahoo!' whenever it pleased him. Lights were going on in the High Street's terraced houses, and bedroom curtains were twitching.

Mrs Genner, in curlers and nylon dressing gown, stood at the window, tut-tutting.

She turned to her ancient, toothless husband, Stan, who was lying in bed trying to nod off.

"Thay bay all locked up, them 'as needs to be, bin 'um?" she sighed.

CHAPTER 8

The Walsall Pact

David's little brother, Paul, was sitting on his lap, learning to play the recorder through his nose. The tune, for those who find the minutiae of everyday life fascinating, was '*Frère Jacques*'. David himself had been particularly adept at this trick whilst at junior school, and had developed it into a party piece. It was important to pass down such traditional skills to future generations, he felt, and he was encouraged by how swiftly the little fellow had grasped the rudiments.

David's most impressive feat was playing the recorder behind his back, by means of a thin plastic tube leading from the recorder's mouthpiece to his own mouth. This, however, was advanced stuff, beyond the average six-year-old.

"It's toy day today!" squeaked Paul excitedly, as David squeamishly wiped his brother's dirty nose, the result of some over-enthusiastic blowing. He decided enough was enough for one day, and swilled the recorder thoroughly under the tap.

"Oh yes!" said David. "It is. Shall we have a walk up to the shop?"

David had a long-standing arrangement with the toy shop, bought about by his doing a great service for the previous owner, Mr Kettle's aunt, (followers of David's early career will be *au fait* with this) which now meant that he was entitled to a free item every month, in perpetuity. His own need for toys and jokes had diminished with his coming of age, but the present owner, true to the spirit of the agreement cast in stone by his deceased aunt, insisted that David's young brother continue the tradition. It was indeed the first day of the month, as Paul had spotted, and so the two unlikely but inseparable friends trotted up the hill to see what Mr Kettle had to offer. The boys were greeted heartily by the genial owner, who told them to feel free and mooch around until something grabbed them. It wasn't long before Paul had spotted the Werewolf Eyebrows and Joke Moustache. He was also hugely taken with the Icky Teeth.

"A good choice, if I may say so, brother," said David. "I had my eyes on those myself only last night. Had it not been peeing down with rain and half past one in the morning, I'd have probably purchased them there and then."

Mr Kettle wrapped them up and gave them to David for safekeeping. He had always felt very awkward about accepting free toys, but such were the persuasive powers of the formidable and sadly deceased Miss Kettle, that he was not allowed to say no. Remembering that some people genuinely enjoyed giving, he came to the conclusion that it would be churlish to refuse. That said, he was always sure to engineer his brother's choices, so that they never cost more than a few bob.

"Yes Paul," he would hear himself saying. "That radio-controlled boat is *okay*, but wouldn't you rather have the plastic dog turd? You'll get a hell of a lot more use out of it!"

75

Modest transaction completed, the two brothers thanked Mr Kettle profusely, and headed back home.

The summer holidays were drawing to a close, and David's life had been quite hectic. He had received his A level results (a respectable two As and a B) on the same day that he received his official acceptance letter from the Art College, together with a brief for a summer project, which had to be handed in on the first day. He was to produce finished drawings based on one of the following themes;

URBAN DECAY

CHIAROSCURO

JUXTAPOSITIONS

METAMORPHOSIS

He also had to purchase several art books and five pounds of modelling clay for a sculpture project, which would take place during the first week.

Len studied his letter closely, scratching his head.

"Can't you just do still-life and landscapes any more? I don't understand a word of it."

Luckily, David did, and he had been beavering away in his room each day, determined to create a good impression on his first morning. Quicker than he had expected, he had received notification that his driving test date had come through on the last Friday of the holidays, which meant that he could potentially be driving himself to college. This was no pipe dream. From his chaotic early adventures with Len, he had progressed in leaps and bounds, and Mr Duffy reckoned that he would pass with flying colours if his nerve held out, and he didn't do anything stupid. Anyone who knew David well would realize that these were two big 'ifs'.

Meanwhile, Lazlo had been as good as his word and had done his best to create a silk purse out of a sow's ear with the Vestmobile. It was still, ostensibly, a piece of scrap, but now it was a reasonably safe one.

Most of David's leisure time was spent either amusing his younger brother or rehearsing at Lazlo's dad's factory with his band. They were becoming quite tight and professional, and beginning to develop a sound of their own.

George's cousin, Greg, had arrived in place of Dingo, stayed for two rehearsals, and was given the push. Often, bands split up because of musical differences. In this case, it was Lazlo who put his foot down, refusing categorically to work with a drummer who wore a cardigan. This had seriously set back the band's ambition to be working by the end of the holidays. Fortunately, help came in the unlikely form of David's dad, Len, who had recommended a young, loud-mouthed but affable Brummie called Nick Chinn, the younger brother of Sammy Chinn, a steel rep who often called at Len's factory.

Some six years previously, there had been a serious disagreement between Len and Sammy, which resulted in Len trying to make him see sense by whacking him over the brow with an eighteenth century flintlock pistol, a course of action which is bound to cause a certain frostiness in any relationship. However, time - and for that matter, Germolene - is a great healer, and the necessity for a daily working relationship had eventually caused the ice to melt, which meant they were once more on speaking terms. Sammy had told Len about his brother's prowess with the sticks, hi-hats and tom-toms, and, as it turned out, he was not wrong.

Nick, like his brother, was of the market trader persuasion, viz. loud, sheepskin-clad, and prone to wearing rather too much chunky jewellery. Countered against this, he was full of amusing anecdotes, good company in small doses, and a very good drummer. Best of all, he gelled with the others, and the band was developing the essential 'us against the world' mentality which they would need, when the slings and arrows of outrageous audiences did their worst.

The line up, namely David, Lazlo, Ken, George and Nick were now as settled as any band could hope to be, and able to play around twenty songs well, with a few more in the pipeline that would do, if push came to shove, and the insatiable unwashed public demanded encores. All they needed now was a name, a roadie with a van to help hump the tons of equipment about, and a venue to play at.

The name came first. Over gallons of tea and chocolate digestives at Ruby and Len's place, the famous five threw in suggestion upon suggestion, but nothing sounded right.

"How about the Four Kinnells?" offered Ken. "We could pretend to be brothers. Imagine the laughs we'd have when some old git at a Labour Club tried to introduce us."

"Yeah, but there's five of us," said George, ever the pedant.

"How about The Shuffling Hungarians?" suggested David. "We could all shuffle on in matching rain macs, introduce each song in mock-Hungarian accents, and when we've finished, just shuffle off again."

Lazlo threw a digestive biscuit at him, Frisbee-style, which caught him squarely on the bridge of his nose.

"Be serious."

"I *was* being serious."

"How about Screaming Skull?" grinned Ken. He fell off the settee, laughing hysterically now, tears pumping from his eyes and face bright red.

"Christ!" said Nick. "You lot are barking mad. How about 'The Barrow Boys'? You know - what you buggers call me, when you think I'm not listening."

"That's a bit better," said David, wiping the remnants of chocolate from his throbbing nose. "But still not right. I know! Let's look in one of my dad's Reader's Digest books, and pick the first name we come across. That might work."

He grabbed a history book from the bookshelf and they all gathered round in eager anticipation.

"What if it says Hitler?" asked George. "I don't fancy being in a band called Hitler!"

"Or Clement Atlee," added Lazlo.

"It's only a suggestion," insisted David, "we don't have to take it. It's just that I remember from my History of Art lessons that the Dada group of painters got their name from looking in a dictionary and finding a totally random word. I think it means rocking horse, in Serbo-Croatian, or something equally crazy. Come on. It might work."

David opened the book at a chapter on World War Two. He closed his eyes and stabbed a finger on a random line.

THE WARSAW PACT.

"Well, it's better than Hitler," admitted Lazlo.

"What if we changed it to Walsall?" suggested Nick. "Make it a bit more local."

"That's good!" said David. "I like that."

"Me too!" agreed Ken. "It's as good as anything. The Beatles was a crap name really. It only became good because of the association with the music, if you think about it. It was a daft pun, just like this is."

"Okay," said Lazlo. "All agreed?"

The five friends put their hands on top of each other on Ruby's coffee table, like musketeers swearing allegiance to their king.

"I like these rituals," said David. "Shall we cut each other with a pen-knife and mix our blood together?"

"Sod off!" protested George, "But we could drink a ritual cup of tea instead!"

"RUBY!" they cried in unison, and the deal was done.

Their next problem was finding a character with a van who'd be willing to lug tons of equipment around at two o'clock in the morning for little or no reward. On the surface, it didn't seem too appealing. They dug down a little lower and it still didn't.

Lazlo suggested that they pool their resources and place an ad in the Express and Star's 'Music Shop' column. It was left to Nick to write the copy.

EXCITING NEW BAND SEEKS ROAD MANAGER.

MUST HAVE OWN TRANSIT VAN.

NO BREAD-HEADS.

"What's a bread-head?" asked George, who never read the NME, preferring the Angling Times.

"Not absolutely sure, but all the ads say that," said Nick, who didn't read anything. "I think it means don't expect payment. I've tried to make it sound a bit glamorous though.

I hope they can't have us under the trade descriptions act. What I really meant to say was;

'Thick gullible bloke with a body like a brick shithouse wanted, to hump huge, heavy boxes at unsociable times for no reward. Ability to have piss taken out of him twenty-four hours a day by five sarcastic tossers a necessity.' "

The ad, which included Lazlo's home phone number, was placed for three consecutive nights. They didn't have to wait long for a reply. Around ten minutes after the paper had hit the doormat, a young man with an Asian Black Country accent rang asking to speak to Lazlo. A meeting was set up the following day at the rehearsal room, so that the others could see what kind of sucker could possibly be interested in such a thankless task. They were all sitting on the floor at the front of the factory during a break from rehearsing, throwing pebbles at a tin can on the other side of the road, when a shabby white transit van turned into the trading estate, driven by a young gentleman of Indian appearance sporting a neat goatee beard. He was built like a weight-lifter, with more muscles than a leather Chesterfield. He also looked as if he'd been shaving since he was five years of age. The Asian man-mountain got out of his van and walked slowly towards them.

"Well I never!" said David, hastily rising to his feet and dusting off the backside of his jeans. "Mohammed, is that you?"

"Bloody hell! David Daydream. I don't believe it. How are you, pal?"

David said that he was well. Nick mouthed the word 'Daydream' to George, who smiled a wry smile. It was the perfect nick-name, and Nick, normally gifted at such things, was amazed that he hadn't thought of it himself.

"Folks, this is Mohammed, who was at school with me in Tipperton. God! It's a small world - Mohammed, look who's here." He pointed to Ken, who was sucking on a cigarette and grinning from ear to ear.

"My goodness, it's Ken! This is like an episode of 'This is Your Life.' I didn't recognize you, man. Your beard's gone."

"Yeah, well I only grew it to annoy Miss Tomkinson. Now she's not around to moan at me, it's no fun anymore."

"Look," said David, "I'll introduce you to the rest of the lads, and I'm sure we need look no further, but are you sure about this road manager malarkey? We can't pay a fortune because we've only just got the band ready for gigging. The deal is, if you're interested, and Lord knows why you should be, we split the fees six ways, equally, once you've deducted the petrol expenses and so on. How's that sound?"

"Okay by me, Dave. It's not really about money, as long as I don't lose out. I just love the idea of the rock and roll lifestyle, know what I mean? Just let me have the groupies you can't handle and I'll be happy! Anyway, when's your first gig, lads?"

The lads began to look a little sheepish. David made circles in the dirt with his baseball boot.

"Erm, well as yet...."

"Our first one is at Belton Court Sports and Social Club, Tipperton, on Saturday," said George. The others stared at him in blank amazement.

"What?" spluttered Ken, choking on his cigarette.

"Belton Court. My uncle's one of the committee members, and I was telling him about the band. They wanted to spice the place up to make it appeal to the younger crowd a bit more. It's full of old gits playing bingo most nights, and the young kids on the estate keep moaning that there's nothing for them, so Uncle Bill talked them into a band night. If we do well, he reckons they might even give us a residency there, once a month. We get sixty quid, cash, if you're interested."

"Er, just one small point," interrupted Ken. "Belton Court is a really rough place, George. There's loads of high-rise flats, with some pretty tough characters living in them. I asked a bloke the time when I was passing through there a few weeks ago, and he head-butted me."

"Serves you right!" sneered Nick. "Get a watch, you cheapskate!"

"Well, I don't fancy it, I must be honest," Ken continued, blowing a cloud of smoke heavenwards. "Even with Mohammed here looking after us."

"And he's perfectly capable of that," said David. "He's a Karate champ, aren't you, Mo?"

Mohammed nodded bashfully. He told the lads that he was the region's junior champion, which boosted their enthusiasm for taking on Belton Court considerably.

"It ain't that bad, Ken," continued George. "The social club's okay and we've got to start somewhere. It's our first gig, and we need the experience. The jobs'll get better when we get established. You don't know where it might lead. The bloody Cavern Club wasn't exactly luxury was it?"

This subtle comment was designed to bring Ken around, and it did just that.

Ken idolized the Beatles, and now that George had made the rather dubious comparison between the Belton Court Sports and Social Club and the Cavern, he could see the romance in it.

"Okay, okay! Tell Uncle Bill we'll give it a go, if it's okay with the rest of you. Everything is good for you, if it doesn't kill you, eh lads?"

They went back inside, to run through the songs for Mohammed's benefit.

CHAPTER 9

A Whole Lotta Hate

David just stared at the examiner in disbelief.

"Can you just say that last bit again?" he said. "It hasn't quite registered."

"Certainly. This is often the way you know. You look shell-shocked." His examiner smiled. "Anyway, one more time, for your benefit - congratulations, Mr Day, I have pleasure in informing you that you have passed your driving test. How's that? Sink in this time, did it?"

"Yes, er...thank you. Thank you very much," said David, still shaking. "Duffy will be very pleased. He's a great driving instructor. He's the one I must really thank for this award."

"Yes, well it isn't the Oscars, but I know what you mean. He's a very good instructor, with a high pass-rate. He regularly turns complete no-hopers into confident drivers, that man. I was talking to him over a coffee a few weeks ago, and he told me that he'd taken on a weird Art student with absolutely no skills, and a head permanently in the clouds. Nonetheless Duffy reckoned he had managed to turn him into a half-decent driver."

"Oh really?" frowned David. "I must get him to tell me about that in more detail. He's waiting in the test centre."

David thanked the examiner again, and ran over to the centre, still debating whether to hug Duffy or punch his lights out.

Later that afternoon, Lazlo popped round to offer his congratulations. It was promising to be one of the best weekends in a long time for David, what with the test result and the first gig, not to mention starting at the Art College on Monday.

"Great news, old pal," smiled Lazlo, dipping his digestive in a cup of Ruby's finest. "Just think of all the petrol that you owe me. I can't wait to be taken out every night in *your* car for a change."

David agreed that he did owe his friend more than a few favours.

"At least we'll feel safe in the Vestmobile now," Lazlo added. "It was a death trap before I worked my magic on it."

David showed his undying gratitude by flicking the end of Lazlo's biscuit, causing it to collapse into his teacup.

"Speaking of which," continued Lazlo, as he pinched his friend girlishly on the upper arm, making him squeal. "I was in the garage this morning, when this huge great Bentley pulled in. The bloke came over to me and asked me to look at his tyre, because it had a slow puncture. He was a real ponce; you know, a la-di-da upper-class type. He said that he wouldn't normally dream of going to a small garage, because everything was usually sorted out by his Bentley dealers, but this was an emergency. Cheeky bugger! I felt like telling him he could go there for his flat tyre as well, but the boss would have sacked me. Anyway, I mended his puncture, and he gave me a tip, which wasn't so bad. When we did his bill, I had to ask for his name, and you'll never guess what? He was a Lord!"

"What, like Jon Lord, from Deep Purple?" asked David, trying his best to keep a straight face.

"No cretin! Lord Hickman, of Stanmore, wherever that is. His accent was amazing. He said 'orften' instead of 'often'."

Lazlo had inadvertently strayed onto David's favourite subject.

"It's weird isn't it?" David began, "that these people can totally mangle the language, and still convince us all that *their* way is correct. The sheer arrogance of them. They turn their noses up at working-class folks with broad local accents, such as ours, and grin their supercilious grins if one of us says dinner, instead of lunch, or bath instead of barth. If God had intended bath to sound like barth, he'd have stuck an R in it."

"Yeah!" agreed Lazlo. "If it's lunch, why do kids always stay school dinners? Answer me that, Lord la-di-da Hickman?"

"The way we speak here is the nearest to the ancient Anglo Saxon dialect left in Britain. Did you know that?" asked David. "My granny Bertha still pronounces 'wasp' properly, with an A sound instead of the O sound, just like Shakespeare probably did. She calls the back yard the *fode*, which comes from 'fold'. She calls the fireplace the *suff*. Even experts studying Shakespeare didn't know what that was. They should have asked my granny. And another thing…"

Lazlo feigned a yawn.

"Yes, okay, I'm boring you to death."

"Not at all," insisted Lazlo, slumping unconscious onto the settee. He sprang back to life, sensing that David's rant had finally finished. "At least he gave me a tip," he said, "which is more than you did, you tight-fisted working class git."

They finished their tea, and headed off for the rehearsal room, where they were meeting Mo and the rest of the band. After a quick run through, they loaded the gear into the van and drove round to the chip shop, where Lazlo ordered his 'signature dish' of chicken and feather pie with chips, whilst the others went for the cod option. David, who only ever resorted to the chip shop in emergencies, was amazed by George's confession that he virtually lived there. He seemed to exist on cod and chips for breakfast, lunch, dinner and supper, which he swilled down with tea or lager, depending on whether or not the sun had gone over the yard arm. Occasionally, when he was in his adventurous, devil-may-care mood, he would have tinned roe. This restricted diet had caused his skin to erupt without warning, like an active volcano, which gave Ken and David the inspired idea to secretly run a book on where the next eruption would crop up on George's head. Lazlo had been the most recent winner, cleaning them out with his 'Back of the Neck' bet, at odds of ten to one.

Once the food had been consumed, and swilled down with copious quantities of Cresta fizzy pop, Mo set off in the direction of Tipperton. His van had two rows of grubby, moth-infested coach seats, which could just about accommodate six people, as long as they weren't too fussy about male intimacy. Immediately behind these was a plywood partition designed to stop the contents decapitating the band when Mo screeched to a halt at traffic lights.

This, unfortunately, was a real threat. Lazlo knew of a promising local band that had ended up in the aforementioned condition on mortuary slabs in mid Wales, after their driver, tired out by driving home from a gig at some ungodly hour, fell asleep and ran into the back of a parked-up oil tanker on the hard shoulder. Such was the impact on Lazlo, psychologically speaking of course, that he paid Mo out of his own pocket for the barrier to be installed, before he'd set foot inside the van.

At six-thirty that evening the van pulled into the dingy, litter-strewn car park in front of the Belton Court club, and the occupants piled out, smelling strongly of chips and Park Drive. The car park was empty, with the exception of a small, dark green van with the words WEISS BLITZ painted on the side by an unknown artist who had never let his lack of ability stop him having a go. Underneath the Germanic lettering, he (surely no woman could have been responsible for such monstrous typography) had added a couple of lightning bolts in red.

"Looks like a band's van," observed Ken, walking around it and looking for clues. "Is anyone else on tonight, George?"

"Not that I know of," replied George, puzzled.

At this point, a tall, ugly gorilla of a man came out of the club, and scowled at Ken.

"Keep away from the van, mate, or you'll be sorry." He turned, and went back from whence he had come.

"Jeez!" said David, "I don't believe it! Did you see who that was? Bloody H. What's he doing here?"

"I don't know, but I have just had a nightmare scenario pop into my head," sighed Lazlo. "Let's get the gear out and go in. Mo, you first."

Mo, followed closely by the others, pushed open the front double doors, which led to an area that would normally be called a foyer, in more salubrious venues. An elderly man sat behind a desk inside a small kiosk. He had bristly grey hair, and wore an enamelled badge bearing the word COMMITTEE.

"Can I help you lads?" he asked.

"Yes," said George. "We're the band. Can we carry the gear through and set up please?"

"Course," said the old gentleman. "The other band is already here."

"I didn't know there was another band," said George.

"Yes. We decided to get you a support act. Hope you don't mind, son. Whoever spoke to Billy Bull on the phone told him you could only manage an hour and a quarter, so we decided to fill it out a bit. These lads heard we were trying out a rock night and asked if they could play here. Billy said okay, if they wouldn't mind supporting you and they'd be happy with expenses only."

George and the others tried to put on their brave faces, but their hearts sank. Mo, who wasn't abreast, wondered what the problem was. After all, he reasoned, if they were big enough already to warrant support acts, surely that was a good thing. David explained the situation.

"This isn't great news, Mo. That bloke with the attitude was H. He's a neo-Nazi thug. A National Front gorilla. If he's here, it's almost certain that Dingo is here, and to be

90

fair, Dingo's basically okay: he's just easily led. The others, I can't vouch for. They've booked these ratbags in good faith, but they're going to be in for a shock. Plus, they almost certainly hate us, because we ditched them after one rehearsal and never went back. To cap it all, you being, well, erm…"

"Black?" suggested Mo helpfully.

"Yes. Well, we may have brought you to something that you don't deserve. They're bound to want to make life awkward. The term *support* is probably not the best word to describe what they'll do for us. Know what I mean?"

Mo smiled. "Have faith, lads," he said calmly. "Let me worry about that, and you can worry about the music."

He fastened the double doors back on their brass catches, and the lads returned to the van to begin unloading, with heavy hearts. David and Lazlo lay a large P.A. cabinet on its side, and began to carry it in between them.

"Nervous?" asked Lazlo.

"Terrified," replied David. "I've got one of those logical minds, that's the trouble. I add up how many songs there are and multiply that by how many chords and notes there are in each song. Then I multiply that figure by how many instruments there are, and then *that* figure by how many frets and strings on each instrument - oh yes, and by how many words there are in each song. That's potentially how many mistakes we can make in one night. And that's discounting the impending threat of physical violence."

"Bloody hell!" said Lazlo. "You need to calm down. Do you fancy a toot on one of my special ciggies?"

"No ta," sighed David. "I'd just forget how to play the guitar if I did that!"

They pushed through the swing doors and into the clubroom. At the far end, a group of around six or seven aggressive looking young men were clowning around on the stage. Their equipment, such as it was, was already assembled and ready to go. The drum kit, centre stage, bore the legend WEISS BLITZ, painted in the same awful typeface. Lazlo and David approached the stage with their huge speaker cabinet. Their mouths felt like blotting paper, and David had great trouble swallowing.

"Worro, you two!" said Dingo cheerfully, defusing the situation more than a little. "How have you been?"

Lazlo tried to say "Okay" but the word refused to come out of its hiding place. David smiled nervously and returned the enquiry.

"Oh, not bad," smiled Dingo. "Hey, listen, no hard feelings about the band not gelling. No problemo! We just liked different types of music. I got together with these lads not long after, so everything's cool. We play some *really* heavy stuff now. Sabbath, Hawkwind, some of our own material, a bit of Led Zeppelin."

"I bet it will go down like a Led Zeppelin here as well." whispered Lazlo, mainly to himself.

Throughout this surprisingly sociable discussion, H sat on a drum case at the back of the stage, glaring a hole through Lazlo's head. He never let a mere formality like not knowing a person get in the way of his hatred. As Lazlo and David returned to the van for more equipment, H whispered malicious nothings to the other members of the Third Reich.

One by one, The Walsall Pact arrived at the stage and were acknowledged by their rivals with a reserved lifting of the hand, or a terse "Alright, mate?"

They gave the impression that their scant greetings were veiling a seething resentment at the thought of having to play second fiddle to what they presumed were a bunch of effeminate college boys. To make matters worse, they weren't even getting paid. Things went from bad to worse when Mo arrived, carrying a huge speaker above his head as if it were a pillow. Heads turned away and the whispers began. One of the uglier Nazis spat on the linoleum floor before wandering off back stage.

Mercifully, H rallied his storm troopers at this point, and they adjourned to the pub over the road, presumably so they could draw up plans to invade Poland. This gave David and the lads a precious hour to themselves to set up behind the other band's equipment and sound-check before the punters arrived.

While the guitarists tuned their instruments, George stood in the reception area chatting to the old gentleman in the kiosk.

"What kind of music do you play?" asked the old man. "Is it waltzes and dance music or what?"

"Well, sort of," replied George. "Don't worry; we'll soon have you up dancing, old pal."

"I doubt that son," said the old man. "I've got no legs."

George peered over the counter to confirm this.

"I'll, erm, just go and help the others set up," he stammered, beating a hasty retreat.

By seven-thirty, everything was in place. The amps were switched off and the guitars propped up on their stands. David's saxophone, which he played in just one rock and roll song, stood centre stage, sparkling dramatically under the stage lights. The band members had assembled near the bar, and were looking back down the dance floor at their equipment. A simultaneous flush of pride came over them as they saw it all together for the first time under the multicoloured lighting, and they raised their glasses to The Walsall Pact.

David was experiencing a strange new emotion, comprising of pride, abject terror and exhilaration in equal measure, capped with the more physical sensation of imminent diarrhoea. He quickly excused himself and headed for the lavatory. Over the next half-hour, he managed at least eight more trips, and was spectacularly productive on each occasion. Meanwhile, the punters were beginning to trickle in, causing Lazlo to remark on their average age, which he estimated to be around ninety. As he stood aghast near the kiosk, he observed that most of them appeared to be purchasing bingo tickets, which he couldn't imagine happening at Rolling Stones concerts.

He reported back to the others with his findings.

"Have they advertised this properly?" he asked George in an exasperated voice. "They're *ancient*. I thought this was a night for the younger ones on the estate."

"It's supposed to be," said George. "It's just that the older ones like to come here as well, and they don't like to be turfed out on a Saturday night. Most of 'em have got nowhere else to go."

"Well, it's going to be an interesting mix alright. Heavy Metal White Power Anthems, followed by Bingo, Rhythm and Blues and presumably the Joe Loss Orchestra as a finale. We only need Snow White on Ice now and we've got the lot! Bloody Hell!"

"Calm down and have another lager," suggested George. "That's what Ken's doing."

"Talking of whom," said Lazlo, looking worried, "how many does he put away, in the course of an evening? He's been sinking the beer ever since we got here. If I had that many I wouldn't be able to play."

"Neither will he," George assured him.

David had returned from his latest excursion to the men's rooms. There was not an ounce of waste material left inside his intestines now, and he looked grey. He glanced at the front doors, and observed the steady trickle of regulars making their way into the hall, and reserving their favourite tables, whilst others queued at the small bar, carrying away trays full of beer and pork scratchings.

It was gratifying to see such a promising turn-out, especially as their average age had been drastically reduced by the current influx of punters. Some were pointing excitedly at the stage, with its gleaming equipment, others hanging around in small groups, smoking, drinking and admiring each others tattoos.

David was about to check the tuning on his guitar, when he saw an apparition that froze his blood. A feeling came over him, presumably similar to the one Macbeth must have experienced, when Banquo popped up and ruined his cosy dinner party.

A small man of Indian appearance sashayed into the room, wearing a lavender open-necked shirt, set off by an outrageously large belt with an enamelled Confederate flag buckle.

It was the Amorous Asian.

David immediately turned his back and pretended to tune his guitar, in order to give himself time to think. Here was someone he definitely didn't want to see that night, or any other night, come to think of it. The A.A. would almost certainly recognize him, and make a beeline for him. He'd found David irresistible just sitting on a 58 bus. Just think how he'd feel when he found out that he was a rock star. The thought of him dancing up close to the stage and winking seductively at him all through the show was too much to bear. Then there was the humiliation and the piss-taking, once the others found out. There was only one thing for it. He had to affect some form of disguise, and quick - but what? A hat would of course help, but he hadn't got one.

George had a rancid bobble hat in the van, but a night of passion with the A.A. would have seemed marvellous compared with wearing that hat for an hour. No, he had to come up with another plan. Feverishly, he searched his pockets in the vain hope that something might present itself. Inside the right pocket of his coat was a paper bag. This was strange, because he had no idea of what it could be, and David, control freak that he was, always knew exactly what lived in his pockets, down to the last penny.

He slowly extracted the bag, and looked inside.

There were two plastic bags within - one bearing the legend, WEREWOLF EYEBROWS and the other, WEREWOLF MOUSTACHE.

After a brief internal debate about whether or not werewolves wore moustaches, which eventually concluded that it was down to the personal choice of the werewolf in question, David reluctantly resigned himself to the fact that, given the circumstances, this was the best deal he was going to get. With a heavy sigh, he tore open the packages, removed the backing sheets to reveal the adhesive tapes, and applied the fake whiskers, thanking the good Lord above that his brother, who possessed a butterfly mind similar to his own, had completely forgotten about his new joke shop items the second he got home.

Turning once more towards the crowd, David sheepishly made his way towards his comrades. He discovered Ken first, ordering a pint of Lager at the bar. Two men standing in front of Ken nervously moved aside to let David in. He tapped Ken gently on the shoulder, causing him to turn round. The shock displaced at least a quarter of his beer onto the lino.

"What the f.."

"It's me - I'm in disguise," whispered David.

"Pleased to meet you, I'm pissed!" replied Ken.

"Please don't say that. I've got enough things to worry about," groaned David.

"Why are you wearing a false nose?" asked Ken.

"Oh, ha bloody ha! There's a bloke here who I don't want to see. That's all I can say. I'll explain it later, on the way home, okay? If you see the others before I do, you might just explain my situation."

Ken promised to do so, in-between doubling up with silent laughter.

An officious little man of some seventy summers took to the stage at this point, and fiddled with the microphone with a perplexed expression on his purple-tinged face. George went over to him and explained how to turn it on. A deafening howl of feedback ensued, which forced George to hurry over to the P.A. amp and begin twiddling various knobs. Eventually, he gave the officious man the thumbs up.

"Lay-gennelmun," he began. "Welcome to Belton Court Sports and Social Club. I'm Billy Bull, the Club Sekertary. We've got summat a bit diffrunt for yer tonight, lay-gennelmun. Two bands, who'm goonna play a bit of the modern jive music for yer, so without further adieu, can yer give a warm Belton Court welcome to the fust lot. What's yer name, lads?"

The band, who were on stage and ready to go, shouted out "Weiss Blitz."

Billy Bull took the microphone once more, and introduced them as 'White Bits', whereupon all musical hell broke loose.

Power chords of unspeakable volume and ferocity rained down on the helpless crowd, accompanied by a screaming demented vocalist and some truly ear-splitting feedback. Old-aged pensioners sitting next to the stage leapt back, as if some hidden force had grabbed them by the genitals. Beer glasses vibrated across the tables from one end to the other, and for a few moments, the entire room stared at the stage in a trance, as if hypnotized. Old ladies began clasping their hands to their ears and looked around them helplessly, imploring the committee members to come to their aid, and make the unearthly row stop. Several of the young men at the back of the hall, sporting skinhead hairdos and Doctor Martin's boots, began dancing around like deranged marionettes from a horror movie. The singer, who was wearing a red shirt emblazoned with a black Swastika, spat out his message of hate.

> WHITE POWER, WHITE IS GREAT,
>
> NO SURRENDER, FEEL THE HATE.
>
> DEATH CAMPS, CLEAN THE SEWER,
>
> KILL THE ENEMY, WITH A SKEWER.

Mohammed sat just to the right of the stage with the rest of the band. He put his hands either side of his mouth, like a loud-hailer, and attempted to communicate with David, above the ear-splitting noise.

"Why the facial hair?"

David shouted back across the table. "Tell you later. Long story. What d'you think?"

"They don't suit you."

"No, this band. What do you think?"

"Quite catchy, if you ask me."

"Nice lyrics. Was this originally by Nat King Cole?"

"Gershwin, I believe," shouted Lazlo, fingering his chin in mock-thoughtful fashion.

H, who appeared to be Weiss Blitz's equivalent of Mo, stood next to the stage and stared unblinkingly at David's table. He couldn't hear them, but he knew full well what they were saying.

The first 'song' came to a shambolic end, not a moment too soon for most of the audience. The space where applause should have been was left empty, but for a few pig-like grunts of encouragement from the morons in boots near the back of the hall. Outraged elderly punters shot up from their tables to confront committee members. Meanwhile, the band launched into their second offering, which sounded uncannily like their first.

Billy Bull steamed towards the stage and remonstrated with the singer as he was trying to sing, if sing was in fact the correct expression for what he was doing with his mouth. The 'song' came to an abrupt end, as Billy strode across the stage, grabbing the mike from its obnoxious owner.

"Lads, no offence, but we've had enough of that rubbish. It's too loud for a start. There's no need to play that loud - this room is rigged for sound. There's also a lot of folks in this room who fought for this country, and don't appreciate that T-shirt yo've got on, so if yer doe mind lads, it's goodnight. The bingo's on at eight-thirty, and then it's the other band, and I hope to God they'm better than yo lot."

This didn't go down big with WEISS BLITZ. Heated discussions broke out on stage, and H began to berate Billy Bull. Dingo seemed to be desperately trying to calm things down, but the arrival of the neo-Nazis from the other end of the hall wasn't helping. Mo, who had been quietly observing the *fracas*, stood up and walked into the middle of the action.

"Lads," he said calmly. "This man could have been a bit more diplomatic, and I'm sure he'll apologize for that, but this isn't the right kind of music for these old folks. If I were you, I'd take your expenses and have a nice quiet drink at the bar. We don't want any trouble. Let's just calm down, eh?"

One of the neo-Nazis stepped forward and prodded Mo heavily in the chest.

"When we want a monkey to butt in, we'll ask for one, right lads?"

It wasn't the most coherent of statements, but it was the best he could manage with his meagre I.Q.

"Come on son," said Mo, just a tad too calmly. "Don't be nasty. There's no need for that."

The little thug spat into Mo's face.

What happened next was what can only be described as a flurry of movement, accompanied by some awful crunching sound effects. Seconds later, three lifeless neo-Nazis were lying comatose on the beer soaked lino, in various stages of bodily decay. Cartoon stars circled above their heads, accompanied by the sound of twittering birdsong. Lazlo was tempted to rush over and lift their eyelids, to see if the word TILT was written underneath.

The effect this explosion of violence had on the members of Weiss Blitz was remarkable. Three of them meekly returned to their tasks, packing up equipment and gathering up electrical cabling. H quietly helped the stricken ones to recover consciousness, and dragged them off in the direction of the exit, without uttering a word. Dingo just shook his head in disbelief. Meanwhile, Billy Bull was calming the remainder of his flock, assuring them that everything was under control, nothing to see, normal service resumed.

The assembled members of The Walsall Pact stood staring in awe at their new road manager, as did a large proportion of the crowd, which pleased David especially. It made a change for people not to be staring at him.

The room now began to take on some semblance of normality, as bingo tickets were distributed, and the cockles and mussels man arrived. He flitted from table to table in his white coat, dispensing small bags of cockles, mussels, shrimps and whelks from his wicker basket. David and the band sat down at their table and took deep breaths to steady their frayed nerves. Ken returned from the bar, with a tray full of lager and a book of bingo tickets.

Lazlo was first to comment.

"Mo, that was awesome mate! I was scared stiff, to be honest. I thought World War Three was about to kick off."

Mo just smiled his best modest super-hero smile, and sipped at his Pepsi.

"He's the West Midlands under-twenties champion, or something like that, aren't you Mo?"

Mo nodded. "Something like that - that's near enough."

"Well, we all feel a lot safer with you around," said Lazlo, gratefully, "But I'm worried they might be waiting for us afterwards."

"Let me worry about them," said Mo. "You lot have enough to worry about. Have any of you noticed that it's a full moon tonight? Your lead guitarist is turning into a werewolf."

All eyes were on David, who was used to providing light relief in times of crisis. Whenever he was out with a friend there was never a problem. If two or more gathered together, he inevitably became the scapegoat, or object of fun. It was, however, fair to say that he did largely bring it upon himself.

"Yeah Dave, what with all the excitement, and Mo having to conquer the Nazis single-handedly, we haven't managed to get round to the burning question of the night, which is, what's with the fungus? Is it one of your strange Art student wheezes or what?"

"Look!" said David conspiratorially, gathering his troops toward him around the table. "There's a bloke here tonight who once travelled on my bus, and we had a disagreement, right?"

The troops nodded, to indicate that so far, they were abreast of the situation.

"So I don't want him to recognize me. That's all you need to know."

"Shall we send Mo over to kill him?" asked George, helpfully.

Mo and David politely refused this option.

"But what I don't understand is," continued Lazlo, puzzled, "and forgive me if I'm being thick here. How did you know to bring a false moustache and eyebrows with you when you didn't realize till you got here that this bloke was here as well? Do you keep an emergency disguise kit with you at all times, just in case? How many enemies do you have, Dave? I think we need to be told."

David was about to explain, when the microphone boomed out a feedback-infested message about the bingo starting in two minutes. Billy Bull had dragged the bingo machine to centre stage, and the older contingent was begging those around them to give order. Ken, true as ever to the spirit of teenage rebellion and rock and roll, got out his lucky bingo pen and began distributing the books to his colleagues. You can take the boy out of Tipperton, but you can't take Tipperton out of the boy.

Mo didn't care much for bingo, and wandered off towards the bar. The neo-Nazis had long since left, and H was also nowhere to be seen. Dingo stood on his own, nursing a pint of Guinness.

"Hi!" said Mo, guardedly, not quite knowing what reaction he would get. He had, after all, beaten up three of Dingo's friends.

"Worro!" said Dingo. "That was awesome, what you just did to those three. Listen, they were with us, but I didn't like him spitting at you like that, man."

"No problem," said Mo calmly. "Not your fault."

"Can I ask you; are you a martial arts expert or something? Karate? That wasn't just throwing your fists about and hoping for the best, it was lethal. You must have been trained to do that."

"Yeah, it's Karate. I've been doing it since I was a little boy. I was Midlands junior champion last year, but I'm over eighteen now, so I move into the senior squad."

"I'm impressed. I've just started going to Kung Fu classes in Dudley. I love all that martial arts stuff, but I'm not in the same league as you, man. Look, no hard feelings about that lot eh? They take it too far. They're a bit thick."

"Take what too far? Hating black people? No offence, but you are the drummer in a band called White Lightning. I presume it's a National Front thing."

Dingo looked embarrassed. "Well, yeah. It's the drumming I like. I love heavy rock, but I've got to be honest. Look, don't take this personally, but there are too many black people here. The white folks are getting sick of it. You're okay. You're a good bloke, and it's nothing against you, but England's turning into a black country."

"That's why we call it the Black Country," said Mo. "Look, joking aside, I sympathize with you, mate."

Dingo couldn't believe what he was hearing.

"I do, honestly. I can see your argument. You're worried that if too many of us arrive, it'll ruin the traditions and values of this country. I can see that, and I can see why you get fed up. Now you weren't expecting me to agree were you?"

Dingo didn't have to say anything. Mo was saying it all for him.

"Where I take issue with you is this. It's one thing to sort out your immigration and allow less people into your country, but it's another thing altogether to pick on individuals, and abuse them, just 'cause they don't look the same as you do. You were born white, right? Now just imagine Mother Nature had made you a black man. Would you hate blacks then?"

"I wasn't though, was I?"

"Pretend you were."

"But I wasn't."

"Use your imagination, mate."

"Okay. Then I wouldn't hate blacks, obviously."

"You might well have been born a horse or a wood louse. Do you see what I'm saying? I couldn't help being black, any more than you could help being white. My parents came to live here thirty years ago. I was born in West Brom. I couldn't help it. Jeez! I wouldn't wish that on anybody! Imagine having to support the Albion. I get race hatred from you lot, and football hatred from the Wolves lot just down the road, and I didn't ask for *any* of this crap. I just want a quiet life. In other words, disagree with the government's policies if you like, but don't pick on individuals, they can't help it!"

"Fair point." admitted Dingo, sheepishly.

"Anyway, enough of all that. Do you want a drink?" asked Mo, dipping into his pocket.

"Yeah, cheers. I'll have half of cider. Do you really support the Albion?" grinned Dingo. "You lot are scum. So are the Wolves. I'm Villa mate, through and through."

Mo gave up, sighed theatrically and ordered the drinks.

Sensing that their time was near, David had assembled the lads on stage to quickly check that everything was working, so that they could launch into their opening number dramatically, without faffing around and checking their tunings. Billy Bull stepped up to the microphone to announce that the bingo was concluded, and that it was time to introduce the main band of the evening.

"Lay-gennelmun, thay'm a nice bunch o'lads - their hair's a bit long, but it's neat. George, the singer, he's my nephew, and he's a member of Belton Court Angling Club, so give order for...what's your name, lads?"

Lazlo shouted it across, and Billy introduced them as 'The Waltz Impact', muttering to himself into the live microphone about the daft names that bands had nowadays.

No sooner had the words left his lips, than what appeared to be hundreds of elderly members got up and began a mass exodus towards the door, no doubt fearing that more from the Weiss Blitz back-catalogue was on its way. Psychologically, this was a huge blow for the band, but at least the remainder were younger, and hopefully more in tune with the music on offer.

As Billy stepped off stage, David silently counted them in for All Right Now, their explosive opener. As he hit the first power chord of A major, he became aware of a noise not unlike a huge pile of unsecured oil drums falling off the back of a lorry. Looking round, he saw Nick at his drum stool, wide-eyed with horror, and his beautiful drum kit in pieces all over the stage. Two whole chords had been played by this point, and the song had ground to a terrible and instant halt.

The audience looked on quizzically. Was this a comedy band with a novelty exploding drum kit, or had the drummer completely forgotten to tighten the many connecting brackets before commencing to knock fifty quid's worth of value out of them? Nick, looking completely nonplussed, was scratching his head in bewilderment.

H looked on, unseen, from the back of the hall and smirked sadistically, pleased with the unexpectedly dramatic results of his handiwork. George said good evening to what was left of the crowd, apologized for their eccentric start, and begged their patience whilst things were being sorted out. Several more of the younger clientèle had exited the building now, leaving it less than a third full.

Drums now firmly secured, the band decided to leave All Right Now till later, opening instead with a Beatles song entitled In My Life, which being much softer, was easier on the drum kit. After the initial traumas they would have been excused a nervous start, but surprisingly the sound emanating from the stage was quite professional, with George singing John Lennon's sentimental and beautifully crafted little ballad as well as the mop-tops ever did. As the song came to its conclusion, a polite ripple of applause echoed round the room, and the band breathed a huge sigh of relief.

When the clapping subsided, the sound of two lone fans continued to thunder enthusiastically from the bar area. Mo and Dingo were now best friends, united by their common interest, and a shared hatred of the Wolves.

George introduced their second song, and as he did so, noticed a new influx of paying guests arriving. They were a mixed bag, judging by their garb. Some sported traditional Teddy boy drapes, while others favoured motorbike leathers. The younger inhabitants of Belton Court's many blocks of flats had been getting loosened up in the pub over the road, and now they were in the mood for a spot of rock and roll.

Next on the list was 'Johnny B. Goode', an old Chuck Berry classic. The opening chords had an immediate effect on the Teddy Boys, who stampeded to the front of the stage and began dancing in energetic fashion, tossing their lady friends up in the air and under their legs. This pleased and inspired the band no end, causing them to begin cavorting around themselves and shaking off any remaining nerves.

Ken cavorted more than the rest, and several times became so enthusiastic that he fell over, and had to be helped back to his feet. By now, a real Cavern Club atmosphere had pervaded the room, with the band growing hugely in confidence and knocking out song after song without pausing for breath. The music was loud, without being ear-splitting as the previous band had been. However, the few remaining elderly members were still passing their complaints to Billy, who duly passed them on to George, who duly ignored them. One slight concern, marring David's overall euphoria, was the condition of Ken, who seemed to be fluffing a few notes, missing the odd intro and generally staggering around rather too much for David's liking. Ken's amplifier had three pints of Lager on it, which were going down fast, in-between and even during numbers. Looking on the bright side, The Amorous Asian was nowhere to be seen, and H and his cronies were also conspicuous by their absence.

The next song, the rock and roll standard Long Tall Sally, featured David's woodwind talents. He dropped his guitar back onto its stand, and grabbed his old tenor saxophone, which he had partly painted blue in order to improve its looks. This complex manoeuvre had to be completed in a few well-rehearsed seconds, because the saxophone featured in the intro to the song. Lazlo counted them in, and David raised the instrument to his lips and blew. No sound came out of the sax whatsoever, and on closer examination, this was hardly surprising. The reed was missing.

Now it was David's turn to look nonplussed. He looked in desperation to Lazlo, who luckily had realized his friend's difficulty, and was covering for him on guitar. David hastily snatched a spare reed from the sax case and screwed it in place, taking over from Laz as soon as he was able. H was nowhere to be seen, but his handiwork was once more in evidence.

A Teddy boy, having the time of his life at the front of the stage, commented to his girlfriend, "That chap's a weird-looking bugger, but he can play that sax!"

George was also having a whale of a time, and was about to introduce the next song, when a lone motorbiker stepped up to the stage for a quick word. There was something about the tattoos all over his neck and brow that convinced George that here was the kind of fellow you didn't argue with. He was, consequently, all ears, and eager to oblige in any way he could.

"Can you play Whole Lotta Love?" enquired the decorated and hirsute fellow.

"Ah, alas no!" replied George, or words to that effect.

"Play it!" snarled the biker, in a way not dissimilar to Humphrey Bogart in Casablanca, only with a lot more menace.

George called a brief meeting with his band. They were familiar with the song, of course. They all had a copy of Led Zeppelin II at home, which was prescribed listening for any self-respecting long-haired eighteen-year-old, but there was a world of difference between knowing it, and playing it. George checked with Ken.

"Tell him to bollocks!" suggested Ken, ever the diplomat.

"You tell him to bollocks!" hissed George. "It's me he'll knife to death first. Not you."

"With you in one second," said George, turning to the biker. Meanwhile, the crowd were baying for more, and some were beginning a slow handclap.

Behind him, George suddenly heard the unmistakable opening riff of Whole Lotta Love, courtesy of David, played on his beloved Gibson Les Paul, the same model that Jimmy Page used. Now it was a case of 'in for a penny, in for a pound'. For those not familiar with this rock anthem, the gist of it is thus; Jimmy Page plays a repetitive line, or riff, for the initiated, which goes something along the lines of 'Dardar-dardee-dum-dedum-dedum. This keeps going and going, whilst Robert Plant screams and cavorts over the top of it about what he's going to do to his latest lady friend, when and if he can get his hands on her. Then he tells the world that he's got a whole lot of love, from whence, presumably, the title emanates.

So far so good.

This part is easily accomplished by an adequately talented band, fronted by a versatile and enthusiastic front man, but shortly after this section of music, a strange thing happens. The band appears to go off for a well-earned tea break, leaving the drummer all by himself. He seizes this opportunity to experiment with his new drums, in order to see what strange noises he can get out of them, seemingly unaware that anyone is actually still listening. Popping back from his tea break, or possibly a trip to the lavatory, Mr Page, seeing that his friend is in experimental mode and having the time of his life, grabs the Les Paul and rubs it up and down the front door, the garden wall and what sounds like the budgie cage, in search of new sounds.

Now, one may have been wondering whether the intrepid young lads at Belton Court would be equal to such an experimental and *avant-garde* middle section. The good news was, they took to it like ducks to water. Nick, who knew the piece better than any of them, was in his element, whilst David began to rub his guitar up and down the amplifier in search of the aforementioned new sounds. Ken, by now several gallons over the legal limit, was detuning his strings and twanging them, laughing hysterically, all of which seemed to please the crowd no end. Of course, on the original recording, all this arty cacophony is soon drawn together again by a thunderous roll of the drums and some demon guitar playing, again wondrously recreated by Nick and Lazlo, who were really riding their luck. A few more furlongs now and they were home and dry.

Shortly after this lead guitar section, the whole band were back on track with the signature 'dum-dedum-dedum' motif, which, on the original record, then stops dead, presumably so that Mr Plant, (or in this case, George) could have a little go on his own.

Throwing his heart and soul into it, the singer screams;

"WOMAN, YOU NEED......."

Whereupon Jimmy Page answers with two almighty power chords, prompting Mr Plant to scream the word LOVE, in an elongated, tortured way, smothered in echo.

Now this was where it all got a little tricky. David couldn't for the life of him think which two chords they were. He looked over in desperation to Ken, who by now didn't even know which town he was in, coupled with the fact that he had completely detuned his guitar in the experimental section and was frankly incapable of restoring the status quo, *vis-à-vis* re-tuning. David turned to face Lazlo, who appeared to be working out some vastly complex mathematical equation in his head; he half expected him to produce a blackboard and chalk some Einstein-like gobbledegook on it. Meanwhile, George was stewing in his own juice. Thinking on his feet, he began to improvise with the one meagre vocal line at his disposal.

I SAID, WOMAN. WOO -WOO -WOO -WOOMAN!
YOU, I SAID YOU, WOO-WOO-WOO, NEED!

Ken had completely given up trying to find the chords by now. He stepped unsteadily towards the mike, removed it from its stand and held it tight against his backside. He then let fly with two enormous bursts of wind, the first one short, and the second long and rich with vibrato, just like Jimmy Page's two missing chords would have sounded, had they been played on a Whoopee cushion. The effect was electric, and instant. The rest of the band collapsed into near hysterics, and Ken just collapsed, in the literal sense, face down on the stage with his guitar making fittingly experimental groaning noises beneath him.

The tattooed Zeppelin fan walked up to George, and Mo, sensing danger, leapt to his feet. "Pretty good, pal. You just about got away with it," growled the biker, and offered a shaking George his hand to shake.

Billy Bull strode onto the stage and announced a short interval, promising the band would be back for a few more songs later. This gave them time to nip off to the lavatory, and also time to sober Ken up for the last half an hour.

David, as has been well documented, visited the lavatory more often than most, and he duly did so once more. He didn't fancy the main Gents near the entrance, because he knew that it would be overflowing with punters who had been waiting for a break in the proceedings to relieve themselves. Instead, he went backstage to the smaller lavatories reserved for the entertainers. Like Hank Frill, David was not keen to show off his genitalia to all and sundry, and therefore elected to give the trough a miss and wait for the only cubicle toilet, which was currently engaged. He stood there for a considerable time in silence, waiting for the occupant to conclude his business, but he appeared to be there for the night. Thinking that the door might just be stiff and the cubicle uninhabited, as had been the case on many previous occasions, David bent down to see if anyone was inside, and spotted a rather peculiar sight. The cubicle was indeed occupied, but by two sets of legs, not one. David could make nothing of this, but curiosity was getting the better of him. He made his way to the exit door, making a great play of slamming it shut, while in fact he remained inside, trying not to make a sound.

Noises were coming from inside the cubicle now. It sounded like two voices whispering to each other, punctuated occasionally by a moan, like someone straining to relieve himself whilst constipated. Surely, thought David, no one could be using the toilet while another looked on. The thought was too ghastly to contemplate. Defecation was definitely not a spectator sport. No, on reflection, the moan was more ecstasy than agony. He remained, statue-like for another minute or so, until finally the door opened. This was a shock. He hadn't thought his plan through, and had left it too late to get out of the room before the occupants emerged.

H and the Amorous Asian came out of the lavatory, to be confronted by a werewolf in a cheesecloth shirt. H jumped about a mile in the air, while the A.A. let out a frightened squeak. One suspected that H's fright was caused by guilt at being caught 'in flagrante', whereas The A.A. was just scared of werewolves.

"Ah! H, unless I'm very much mistaken," said David, divesting himself of his false facial hair as if he were Sherlock Holmes, just about to wrap up a case.

114

"Ooooh!" said the A.A., recognizing his previous love interest.

"I can explain..." spluttered H, shaking visibly. "We were...."

"I know you were," said David.

He turned his back on the odd couple, and headed back to the stage. The interval was nearly over, and the band was getting ready for the second half. All, that is, except for Ken, who was sleeping peacefully behind his amplifier.

"Laz!" said David. "I'll play bass, you play rhythm and lead. He's out of it."

They got underway with more rock and roll, which was not quite so difficult to play with one man down. During a longish guitar solo, George wandered off stage and whispered to Mo, who was close by, enjoying the show. A few moments later, Mo was on stage with a note book. He went over to David, and bellowed in his ear.

"George wants some chips. Do you want any?"

David was starving. He knew it was unprofessional, but he ordered roe and chips.

Mo sidled across to Nick, took his order, and repeated the exercise with Lazlo, who, for those who thrive on detail, ordered a predictable chicken pie and chips.

Mo disappeared, and the band continued to fire on all cylinders. Five minutes later, he was back, with six white paper parcels in his hands, which he placed one by one on the amplifiers. He'd also thoughtfully bought Ken a bag, just in case he came round. The problem was how to eat them while playing. David and Lazlo solved this by playing a Status Quo song with interminable guitar solos. Lazlo ate his supper while David showed off, and then they swapped, before David's got cold. George simply disappeared during solos to eat backstage, but Nick had more of a problem, needing both arms and both legs to do his job. Mo solved this dilemma by hand-feeding him throughout the rest of the show, prompting Nick to comment that he would insist on similar treatment if he ever became famous. George, sensing that Ken was regrettably out for the count, argued that it would be a shame to see good food wasted, and ate his portion too, causing Lazlo to win a twenty-to-one shot with his 'next zit will be on the end of the nose' prediction.

They finished their supper without missing a beat, and Mo dutifully took the wrappers away, while the lads steamed into a medley of early Beatles classics, including I'm Down, Money, and It Won't Be Long, which saw the drunken crowd become nearly berserk with enthusiasm. All was not sweetness and light, however. The few remaining elderly members were complaining bitterly to Billy Bull that they'd come out for a quiet game of bingo, and couldn't hear themselves think.

Meanwhile, the Lost City Teddy boys seemed to be annoying the motorbikers in some way, and a couple of the neo-Nazis that Mo hadn't had time to knock unconscious had re-emerged from the pub, and were getting on *everyone's* nerves. During a well-deserved encore, a chair suddenly flew across the room hitting Dingo - who had been minding his own business - on the back of the head. This caused him to send one travelling in the opposite direction, which regrettably beaned an elderly gentleman who was just trying to eat his shrimps in peace.

Now Billy Bull, who used to box for the RAF, was in the fray, swinging punches left right and centre, at anyone who wanted one. The bikers, not wishing to be left out, waded into the Teddy boys, and a glass still full of lager came screaming past David to crash onto the back wall of the stage. Never one to misread a subtle signal, he unplugged his guitar and hid behind his amp, where Ken was still sleeping peacefully. Lazlo, also never slow to catch on, did the same, which left the sound on stage a trifle thin. George sensing that all was now lost, reluctantly abandoned his mike to join them, as more missiles flew across the room.

Nick, on the other hand, seemed to be enjoying his drum solo opportunity, and played on till the end, like a stoic bandsman on the Titanic, dodging bottles with consummate ease at the same time.

* * * * *

Two hours later, they all sat crammed into Mo's coach seats, drinking frothy Cresta pop, the equipment safely stowed away in the back.

"I didn't think the police would arrest that old bloke," said Lazlo, sucking on a contemplative Park Drive.

"Nah!" agreed George. "And I thought Mo was incredible, the way he carried Ken over his shoulder like a fireman, and still managed to flatten that Teddy boy."

"How about our David then?" asked Mo, patting him on the shoulder. "Did anyone see what happened? That H character was just about to give Lazlo a good kicking, when Dave just walked up to him, stared him straight in the eye and told him to disappear, or he'd sort him out. H ran a mile!"

"My bloody hero!" said Lazlo, hugging his friend. "I didn't know you had it in you."

"Anyway, what did we all think?" asked Nick.

"Bloody marvellous!" said Lazlo. "I can't wait for the next one."

Ken woke up with a start, like a dormouse at a tea party.

"Christ! My bloody neck's stiff. Sorry folks. I got a bit pissed. Did I miss anything?"

CHAPTER 10

David and the Old Banger

David turned the ignition key, watched proudly by his mom and dad from the front steps. Remarkably, it started first time. He put his portfolio full of holiday work on the back seat, together with his five-pound bag of modelling clay and his lunch box. He had driven his car for the first time only the day before, and it still felt very strange to be in it by himself - a heady mixture of excitement and trepidation.

He glanced down at his rev counter, and realized that there was just a hole in the dashboard where it should have been. The actual item was still on his back seat, waiting for Lazlo to put it back. It didn't matter - he never referred to it anyway. Slowly and with great caution, he pulled away, and out of the little *cul-de-sac* where they lived. He rounded the corner, and was gone.

Ruby waved goodbye, but it wasn't reciprocated. He was far too busy navigating.

"I hope he'll be okay, Len," she said. "Does he know the way?"

"He'll be fine," said Len. "He'll be fine."

Three quarters of an hour and several wrong turns later, he kangarooed into the road that ran alongside the front doors of the college, and parked up. He wasn't sure if there were parking restrictions, so he left everything in the car, locked the doors, and crossed the road to enquire at the college. The foyer was alive with activity. Bright-eyed and excited, the new students were heading up the stairs to reception, with huge black portfolios under their arms and plastic bags full of modelling clay swinging at their sides.

David couldn't see anyone he recognized downstairs, so he vaulted upstairs three steps at a time in the hope of coming across a tutor who could fill him in on the parking regulations. He pushed open the shabby, paint-stained blue double doors, and found himself in the main studio, where several of the new intake had already gathered. It was a large whitewashed room with Victorian skylights, designed to give the artists as much natural light as possible. The studio was equipped with large easels, wooden stools and oak plan chests, and at the far end was a low platform, covered in loose white sheets. Next to it stood an old-fashioned log burning stove with a pipe coming from it that disappeared into the ceiling, to let the fumes escape.

The room was quickly filling up with students, who were sitting in a loose circular arrangement in the middle of the room, waiting for John Auberton to appear. David spotted Dylan, the lad he'd seen at his interview, and waved at him. He also saw Bob Rosemary, who had emptied the contents of his nose all over his renaissance drawing. He attracted his attention by raising a hand.

"Ah! The master forger!" said Bob, smiling. "Sorry about the nosebleed at your interview, David. I'll look at your work from a safe distance this term."

David asked him if his car was okay where he'd parked it, so Bob walked over to the window to take a look. It was possible to see most of the street from the studio windows, which was handy for keeping an eye on parked vehicles, and a recent spate of car thefts in the area had forced the college to become more vigilant. On being told that David's was the buff coloured Mini by the lamppost, Bob assured him that it legally parked and fine where it was.

He asked his new tutor if he should return to the car to collect his work, and the clay, but he was told to remain in the studio for the time being, as Bob and John Auberton wanted to introduce themselves and welcome the students. He assured him that they wouldn't need to see any holiday work till after lunch, so David grabbed a stool and sat down with the others.

The double doors swung open, and a beautiful, dark-haired girl walked in, carrying the regulation portfolio and clay, and accompanied by a girlfriend. She briefly scanned the room, looking for an empty stool and noticed the tall, long-haired young man with his mouth half open, gazing into space.

Her eyes continued to sweep the room in search of vacant stools, stopping suddenly as she jerked her head back in David's direction. He was still staring blankly at nothing in particular, soaking up the atmosphere and completely oblivious to her presence. She walked over to him, and prodded him on the shoulder, causing him to jump about four feet into the air.

"Nice to see you have put some clothes on for your first day at college," she smirked.

"My God!" he exclaimed, snapping out of his reverie. "You're the girl from France - the Youth Hostel trip."

He could feel his cheeks reddening, which he hated. It made him feel about eleven years old. He recognized her friend, Suzanne too, hovering in the background. She gave him a little wave.

"What on earth are you doing here?" asked Nicole, in a tone that implied he'd be better off in a secure unit.

"Oh, the same as you - the Foundation course. I didn't realize you were an artist."

"I didn't realize you were an artist either," she replied coldly. "I thought you were perhaps ze life model, knowing how fond you are of taking your clothes off."

"Look, I couldn't help it, okay? They played a nasty trick on me. It wasn't my doing."

By now, eighty-percent of David's blood had migrated north to his face, leaving precious little to operate his legs, but Nicole hadn't quite finished. There was more humiliation left to drag out of him yet. She wasn't the kind of opponent to cease hostilities until her enemy was flat out on the floor, begging for mercy. Even then, she had been known to have one last kick.

"I 'ad to 'ave a rabies shot when I got home. You were frothing at ze mouth. I didn't want to catch it!"

John Auberton strode into the room with his customary grin, just in time to save David from Nicole's knockout punch, or at least delay it.

"Well, are we all here?" he asked, in his beautifully musical Welsh accent. "Welcome to the Foundation department. I'm John Auberton, and I'm in charge of this lunatic asylum. This is my colleague, Bob Rosemary, who'll be taking you for life drawing, amongst other things. The

122

gentleman over by the wall is Ed Briers, who is in charge of all the three-dimensional stuff. He's based downstairs in the woodwork rooms, and the man in the grey overall by the door is Alf, who is our printing technician. The only other man you need to be aware of is Ron, who is the stores technician, but he only comes in on Monday afternoons and all day Wednesdays. He's situated on the ground floor, and that's where you can buy paper, paints, canvases and most other basic items, at a heavily-discounted price - we're far too good to you! The working day is from nine a.m. till around five p.m. but you are encouraged to work late when you need to. We don't close the doors till nine, or the Benny Hill show, depending on the day. Take a few minutes to introduce yourselves to each other, and then grab a work space. There are allocated, numbered spaces around the room. You'll each get a locker and a key for your personal belongings. Can you all be ready to begin at ten? Bob will get you started on your first pieces of work."

He milled around the room for a while, renewing acquaintance with students he'd remembered from the interviews and sorting out any little problems that had arisen. He then went back to his office to do a bit of administration, and leaving Bob in charge.

Flinging his coat on the back of a chair in order to officially commandeer space nine, David was delighted to discover that Dylan had earmarked space ten.

He was less pleased to see that Nicole had taken space eight, given her ability to make him feel less important than an earthworm with an inferiority complex. Physically, she was a joy to behold, but after their earlier encounter he would have preferred to view her from afar.

A brief look around the room revealed to him that Art students came in all shapes and sizes. There was a tall thin freckly fellow in a kaftan, with long, thick ginger hair that was kept in place by a leather string affair around his brow. David shuddered momentarily and moved on. Around half of the inmates were of the opposite sex, two or three of whom were exceedingly easy on the eye.

There was a pre-Raphaelite vision with waist-length golden curls, fully equipped with the standard issue unworldly, wistful face and long flowing velvet skirt. He could imagine her floating in a brook, strewing flowers that she had gathered in the meadow, all the while singing folk songs with a deranged and plaintive little voice, before sinking, broken-hearted to her muddy death. In reality, she probably came from Wednesbury and worked part-time in a fishing tackle shop.

Next to her was another wistful and pitifully thin creation, who almost certainly would never eat of her own volition, and if she were forced to, would probably regurgitate it when no one was looking. Every new intake had a girl such as this. Perhaps it was part and parcel of the artistic temperament. By way of stark contrast was the earth-mother to her left, squinting nervously around the room nervously from behind huge, black-framed spectacles, and clad in a loose-fitting shapeless floor-length outfit, which shrouded her giant, bra-less udders.

Sat by the front windows was an altogether more attractive proposition, a curvy girl dressed entirely in black, which perfectly complemented her mass of curly blonde hair - a thousand baby snakes writhing on her head. She ran a hand through her curls as she looked out of the window, her face lit like a girl in a Vermeer painting, causing an audible whimper of desire from David's quivering lips.

124

For the sake of his sanity, he moved on. There was a jovial character with a Groucho Marx eyebrows, glasses and moustache ensemble that could have been purchased from Mr Kettle's toyshop. He was chatting to an intense, pug-nosed young man in paint-spattered overalls, who looked as if he'd got to nineteen without ever smiling. Suzanne, Nicole's friend, sat next to her. David hadn't given her much thought, but she too had an extremely pretty face, in a 'girl-next-door' kind of way. He began to imagine a scenario whereby Miss World was living next door to him, which would of course make a nonsense of his awful 'girl-next-door' cliché. Taking his ridiculous idea to extremes, he then imagined that some hideously ugly, moustachioed woman was living on the other side.

Some of the students in the room patently believed that they had to *look* like artists, regardless of whether they could paint like them. One sported a hairstyle that covered his eyes almost entirely, like a sheepdog's. David wondered how that could possibly be the hairstyle of choice for one whose career was based on being able to see. Others looked more like bank clerks, who'd somehow found their way into the wrong room, and really should have been at a lecture on the exchange-rate mechanism two doors away. It would be interesting, he thought to himself, to see if they adjusted their garb as the term progressed.

That said, on balance, he slightly preferred them to the ones who actually looked like artists. Though he was himself a student, David wasn't overly enamoured with students, as a breed.

Bob Rosemary addressed the class. He told them that they would be thrown in at the deep end with a life drawing class, so that he could assess their basic drawing skills. Everyone had to find an easel and arrange themselves around the draped plinth by the heater. Bob handed out drawing boards and cartridge paper, and gave them all a stick of charcoal. David noticed a dumpy little lady in a dressing gown hovering at the back of the room, and he rightly guessed that she was the model. Any hope he might have had that drawing a naked woman would be a sexual experience was immediately dashed when he saw what was on offer.

Cynthia walked up to the plinth and removed her gown. The students looked nervously at each other, as she slowly lay down, facing the ceiling, and clasped both arms around the back of her head. She was all of four feet eleven inches tall, with a massive shock of violent red hair which had been pulled back into a bun that appeared to be secured with a piece of rough old leather and two knitting needles. She wore pebble glasses, which were perched on top of a nose so hooked that she could have opened a bottle of Pepsi on it. All these details, however, paled into complete insignificance, compared to her breasts.

There are large breasts, and there are very large breasts, but these defied description. Each one weighed at least a ton, and completely obliterated her entire stomach. As she lay on her back, they changed their shape completely, with the result that she now resembled a cadaverous pygmy on a mortuary slab, who appeared to have been crushed to death by two giant Edam cheeses. Looks of horror spread around the class. Many had been told that drawing naked women, and for that matter, men, was commonplace, but they had expected someone built along the lines of a Greek Goddess, or Michelangelo's David. No one had warned them about Cynthia.

Bob clapped his hands, and spoke to his shell-shocked charges.

126

"Okay, listen up. I want you to produce a drawing of Cynthia, which must be completed in fifteen minutes. I've deliberately set a short time limit, because I want to see a bold, quickly executed drawing. After fifteen minutes, we'll swap positions and Cynth will change her pose. Everyone understand? Good. Off you go."

The students began sketching. Some looked nervously at others, unsure of what was expected of them, whilst others appeared smugly self-assured. Each of them had been the cream of their respective schools, but now they were thrown together with people of similar or better abilities, and they would have to prove themselves all over again.

Bob wandered over to the window that overlooked the street.

"David," he called. "Did you say that yours was the buff coloured Mini?"

David looked up from his drawing. "Yes, why?"

"Well, all the other cars in the street have gone now, but yours is still there."

"Pleased to hear it!" said David, sketching furiously as he spoke.

"The only thing is, it's got traffic cones around it, and there are two policemen looking at it."

"I thought you said it was okay to park there," said David, frowning with concern.

"You can! I park there myself. One of them is talking through a megaphone. Come and look."

David set down his charcoal and began to walk over to the window.

"Oh, it's okay, they've gone now," said Bob. "Maybe they thought it was a stolen car. We get a lot of that."

David got to the window just in time to hear the explosion, which shook the college windows. His car lifted off the ground, and came back to earth a second later, smoke billowing from its interior, and all the windows shattered. It was still rocking gently from side to side, and a constable with an extinguisher was dealing with a small fire which had started under the dashboard.

"Bloody Hell!" gasped David. The entire class, stunned by the blast, had ceased to draw. Cynthia, sensing that she was no longer the centre of attention, got up and stretched her legs.

"Ah, now they've come back. I think they've just carried out what is known as a controlled explosion," explained Bob helpfully. "Can you think of any reason why they'd have done that?"

David dashed through the double doors and leapt down the stairs, six at a time, his personal best. He fell through the front entrance into the arms of two policemen, who prevented him from crossing the road.

"I don't believe it!" said one of them. "Look who it is, Donald."

Donald, chewing gum, smiled a sarcastic smile. "Well I never! Johnny Guitar!"

"You've just blown my bloody car up. What did you do that for, you, you, you morons?" sobbed David brokenly.

"Now now, steady on son. Is that your car then?"

"No! It *was* my bloody car, but now it's a bloody burnt-out bloody shell. I've only done twelve miles in it, and

128

you've bloody exploded it. What's my mother going to say? Eh? Eh?"

"Calm down, son. We had a phone call from a man using an official I.R.A. codeword, so we knew it wasn't a hoax. He said that they'd planted a bomb in a shit-coloured Mini parked outside the Art Gallery."

"I prefer to call it buff, actually," protested David indignantly. "Anyway, this isn't the bloody Art Gallery, it's the bloody Art College. The bloody Art Gallery is over bloody there." He was gesturing wildly and in imminent danger of succumbing to a stroke.

"Well how do you explain the plastic explosives wired up to the clock, which we saw in the back of your car?" demanded the officer, through gritted teeth.

"What?" yelled David, exasperated, his arms waving round like a demented windmill. Then a look of realization swept across his face.

"That was my bloody modelling clay, and the bloody rev counter from my bloody car!" he screamed, his arms still flailing and imploring, Italian style. He studied the burnt-out remains of his nylon leopard-skin interior. "Congratulations, you complete pair of tossers. You've just ruined my car, which I've only had for ten minutes, exploded my holiday project and blown my sandwiches to pieces. Now what am I going to do?"

"There's a bakery on Queen Street that does nice sandwiches," suggested Donald helpfully.

David looked around him. His destroyed car was smouldering gently. Hundreds of onlookers were gawping at him from behind red security tapes at each end of the street. Two constables in body armour had left their armour-plated car and were walking towards him. Up on the first floor of the college, a line of students looked down in disbelief at one of their fellow students, wondering if he was a terrorist. He picked out Nicole, and could have sworn that she was laughing, behind her cupped hands.

"Need any help with him, lads?" asked the armoured officer, whilst his colleague guided a small tank-like vehicle back towards their police car with the aid of a remote control hand-set.

"No, we're okay," said the officer. "He's just a bit upset. No problem - we know the lad."

"Just one small point," interjected David, fuming. "Forgetting for a second, my bloody problems, if my car wasn't the right one, don't you think you ought to go and find the shit-coloured one by the Art Gallery?"

"Bloody hell!" said Donald.

"Oh Christ!" said his partner.

Somewhere behind them, a huge bang seemed to shake the whole of Wolverhampton.

CHAPTER 11

The Larger than Life Model

"It's a wonder nobody was badly injured," said David to the bus driver.

"A miracle. A miracle. A miracle."

"We all dashed round there as quick as we could. If you cut through by the Church and across that grassy bit where the park benches are, it was parked there - a brown Mini. Normally there are folks walking across the grass, or sitting eating their sandwiches, folks queuing for buses. It could have been mayhem."

"I know what you mean. I know what you mean. I know what you mean."

"The police said that flying glass had cut a few people, and the windows of the pub across the road caved in, but it could have been much worse. Apparently it wasn't a big bomb - just a nasty wake-up call. I hope to God they don't start doing this in all our big towns now. We won't be so lucky next time."

"No we won't. No we won't. No we won't."

David sat down and stared out of the window. All he needed now was the bloody Amorous Asian to cap a perfect day. Mercifully he was spared that one. He mused upon his first day at college. Certainly not one he'd forget in a hurry. Bob had been very understanding, and excused him from the holiday project. He'd also let him off the day's life-drawing, as his hand was shaking too much to hold the charcoal. He'd kindly sat him down in the office, made him a cup of tea, and tried to make him laugh a little, which was nice of him.

He explained to him that Cynthia was a bit of a stopgap until a more suitable lady could be found. Apparently their regular model, who was by all accounts gorgeous, had succumbed to the advances of one of the students that drew her regularly, and had fallen pregnant. That left them desperate for a replacement and Cynthia had volunteered. In the absence of any other takers, they had to be grateful, though Bob admitted that she wasn't ideal.

"The trouble is," he said, "the drawings that the students do of Cynth go into their portfolios, which are shown at interviews for Bachelor of Arts colleges elsewhere in the country. The interviewer takes one look at them and marks the student down as either someone who patently can't draw, or a sexual pervert, or both. It could potentially ruin their careers. You can imagine them being dragged out of their interview, kicking and screaming, 'but she really *did* look like that, honest!' Lord knows where they all go, these failed students. They're probably sitting on park benches drinking bottles of cider out of brown paper bags and ranting 'I could have been a successful artist, if it wasn't for that bloody big-titted dwarf!'"

David had asked if there were male models, and whether the girl students feel cheated because it was always women that they had to draw. Bob said that they sometimes employed men, but that, too, was often fraught with difficulties.

132

"We had one chap," he began, "who seemed flattered by the attention. The students would begin to draw his naked torso only to find that certain parts of his anatomy - how can I put this - had changed shape. They'd reach for the erasers, rub it out and draw a longer one. Then he'd cool off, fearing that he was about to make an exhibition of himself, and out would come the erasers once more. That bloke had more rubbers on the end of his willy than Casanova!"

David forced a wry smile, but in truth his head was in turmoil. It had been a strange first day. Nicole was now totally convinced that he was a complete lunatic, and Heaven only knew what he would say to his parents that evening. At least the police assured him that he would be compensated for their cock-up. That was the light at the end of the tunnel. Perhaps it was all for the best, and the compensation would be enough to buy another car, but this time, with Lazlo's help, one that people wouldn't laugh at as he drove by.

David got off the bus at Cradley Station, and shouted goodbye to the driver, who shouted back goodbye twice, and immediately embarked on a series of facial tics whilst punching the steering wheel. Mentally and physically drained, David staggered up the front steps and into the kitchen, where his mom was preparing the evening meal. His dad was relaxing on the settee reading the newspaper, after a hard day's graft.

"How did you get on?" asked his mom. "Good first day? Lazlo phoned. He wanted to ask how you'd got on too."

"Interesting and eventful, I would say," sighed David, helping himself to a bite of his dad's bread and butter.

"How'd the car go?" called his dad from the other room.

"Like a bomb!" replied his weary son, quickly disappearing upstairs to his room for a lie down.

CHAPTER 12

Alf, Patron of the Arts

Several weeks had passed since the exploding car incident, and thankfully, life had become a touch quieter since. David had settled into his new way of life and loved the college, though the daily grind of catching two buses and walking a mile home every night was wearing a bit thin. The police had been in touch with David's insurance company, and agreed to compensate him to the tune of three hundred pounds, which was good news, considering his old car had been worth around four pounds eighty.

This time, Lazlo was put in charge of finding the replacement vehicle, and he was not rushing into it. Whilst David approved of his friend's thoroughness, he wished he'd hurry it up a bit. After all of three quarters of an hour behind the wheel, and the exquisite feeling of freedom it provided, it was hell going back to public transport. College life though, was as good, if not better than he had expected, and he was making many new friends. Nicole was still sending shivers down his spine whenever he gazed upon her swan-like neck, but she was as cold and aloof as ever, which was like a red rag to a bull as far as David was concerned. He was determined to convince her that he was the dashing and witty man-about-town, but so far he'd failed at every hurdle. Katie, the girl in black, was helping to comfort him in his darkest hours though, which helped. She would often sidle over to his workspace and chat, and she was funny and cute, which made him feel at ease around her. He'd never felt that before with other girls, possibly because he'd been trying too hard to impress. He thought of girls as formidable and impregnable castles, with himself cast as Don Quixote, perched on a knackered old donkey, trying to storm them, and always failing miserably. Katie was more of a cosy, picturesque cottage with the front door open, and a nice coconut door-mat saying WELCOME.

Unfortunately, this promising relationship seemed doomed to fail, with Katie destined to join the ranks of the many girls who liked him 'just as a friend'. She had mentioned quite early on that she already had a long-standing boyfriend, and you didn't own up to that that if you were looking for romance. David was so lacking in confidence that she could have turned up at college wearing a T shirt with 'Shag me, Dave' on the front, and he wouldn't have spotted the subtle body language. The news that she was already spoken for completely put the kybosh on any plans he might have had to storm her portcullis, welcome mat or no welcome mat.

Whatever the outcome, he was very happy to have made friends with her, and seeing her popping over for a coffee break at his desk always lightened his spirits.

Dylan, his next-door neighbour, was also becoming close, and their friendly artistic rivalry helped both of them to improve.

If Dyl had drawn a decent picture, David had to draw a better one, which in turn inspired Dyl to greater heights. There is a common belief that competition belongs only in sport or business, and has no place in art, but this is simply untrue. Artists have always hated the thought of anyone being better than them. Michelangelo and Leonardo went to the same school, vied for the same commissions, and hated each other's guts. At least David and Dylan were friends, and David couldn't see that changing.

Occasionally, he would feel very guilty about not keeping in touch with his school friends, but with the exception of Dennis, he wasn't really missing them as much as he'd feared. The people he was with now were much more his kind of people, with shared interests and attitudes. It had been the same when he left his junior school. His best friend Mally had not passed for Grammar School, and they had been separated. Each had promised faithfully to keep in touch, but they had barely spoken since they went to their new schools. It was nothing to do with being fickle or aloof. It was simply life moving on. There would be time enough for sentimentality when he was older. Life was too exciting at that moment to worry too much about the old days. He had his college each day, and his band at night and weekends, and that was more than enough to be getting on with, thank you very much.

David was hard at work on his first major project, set by John Auberton. Initially, he had to produce several working sketches based on the theme of Metamorphosis. He'd approached the thing from several angles, but nothing was setting him alight, so he gazed dreamily across the room at Nicole, who was looking her usual gorgeous self. He tried to imagine what she would look like naked, and asked himself why they had to draw human gargoyles in life class when creatures like Nicole were available.

He couldn't imagine laughing his head off at the sight of her naked body, as she had at his. Tortured by the memory, he tried to reel in his mind and concentrate on the task in hand. He stared at the ginger-haired freckly lad with the horrible leather string round his head. It was the kind of contraption that the Mona Lisa made famous, but the effect was not comparable. It made freckle-face look like a complete fool.

David was at his best when daydreaming. It was how he solved his problems, and came up with his best ideas. One had popped into his mind now, and he quickly began sketching it out, before he forgot it.

The Headband came across as one of those vacuous characters with minimal talent, who knew all the correct words and phrases. He probably smoked wacky baccy whilst sitting astride a giant mushroom in a room full of Indian artefacts and scented candles. His dialogue was littered with phrases like 'far out', 'spacey' and 'cosmic', and he infuriated David by referring to people who didn't smoke marijuana as 'Straights'. In short, he was a phoney hippy from Aberystwyth, and therefore fair game for a bit of satire.

David decided to metamorphose him into a teapot.

In frame one, he would draw this fool as he looked in real life. In the second frame, the area above the headband could become more pronounced, and the nose more upturned. The third frame would see his skin take on a slightly more metallic look, and a stray clump of hair begin to curve into a handle. By frame four, the face would be very metallic indeed, and the nose would become spout-like. In frame five, the neck would have thickened to form a base, and the handle, spout and lid would be fully formed. Frame six, the final frame, would show a completed silver teapot. The headband would have become the rim of the lid, which would now be slightly opened at the hinge, and tea would be seen pouring from the nose-cum-spout.

Perfect!

David began surreptitiously sketching his victim, whilst affecting an air of nonchalance and guarding his drawing with his forearm when anyone passed by, like a child in junior school who has caught his neighbour copying.

* * * * *

Alf the print technician was having five minutes in the staff room with a fag and a cup of coffee. He was around sixty years old, with wavy, grey Brylcreemed hair and yellow eyes. His fingers were stained brown with years of Woodbine abuse.

"John," he called to his boss, slyly, "any decent prospects amongst 'em this year?"

John Auberton looked up from his paperwork.

"Yes, actually Alf, there are. It depends what kind of decent you're talking about though. The French girl, Nicole is a talented all-rounder, and so is Dylan, the Stourbridge lad with the round glasses – he's done some nice work. David Day, the lad with long brown hair and the dreamy expression, he's extremely good, and he can turn his hand to a lot of styles too. At his interview he showed us a Renaissance-style drawing, which was nothing short of superb. Could have been a Michelangelo - I'm not kidding. Pity Bob had another one of his bloody nosebleeds all over it. That kid could be a forger, Alf. You should get him doing banknotes for you. With your printing press, you'd be well away!"

Alf nodded in agreement and smiled. A great plume of smoke wafted into his eyes, which made them water. He wiped his face with his handkerchief.

"Then there's Katie Black. She's the blonde curly-haired one who's always dressed in black, funnily enough. She's a good future printmaker for you to nurture and guide, in your inimitable fashion. Why do you ask?"

"I've got a little commission for one of them," explained Alf. "I've got a holiday cottage in Wales, and I want a nice drawing done of it, realistic and very detailed."

"If you want realism and detail, I'd probably recommend David Day, but don't you get tying him up with your private stuff, you bugger. He's got college work to get done. He's already a summer project short, thanks to Sergeant Plod and his explosives boys."

"It won't take him long boss, and he'll need a bit of cash, to help pay for a new car!"

Alf, a sly and cunning man, returned to his print room, and inked up the press, ready for his next job. He liked to collect work by the students, and frequently borrowed pictures on a permanent basis, if they had been left behind in plan chests. He would often flatter students into parting with pieces by telling them how much he admired their work, and how he would treasure them. He also promised them little favours, such as preferential treatment when they were queuing for the presses, in return for a little something for his wall. At home he had a huge collection of work, begged, borrowed and stolen from everyone who had passed through his hands that had half a chance of making it big.

Alf was a patron of the arts.

David, totally engrossed in sketching out his finished Metamorphosis piece, didn't immediately realize that someone had been watching him working for a few minutes. When Alf finally spoke, it made him jump.

"David, isn't it?" he asked.

David turned and said hello.

"John Auberton said I should have a word with you about a little job I need doing. Are you in the market for a bit of extra cash?"

David said that he certainly was, as long as the job was suitable, and he felt up to it.

"I've got a holiday home right next to Harlech castle," said Alf, perching himself on the edge of David's work desk. "I'd love a pencil drawing of the castle, from the angle where you can also see my place - something around A3 or a bit bigger perhaps. Not a sketchy thing mind. I was thinking of one of these drawings where you can see every brick. Do you follow me?"

David said that he specialized in that kind of detail, but he was dependent on a really good piece of reference to work from. Alf assured him that the photos he possessed were of superior quality, as he'd commissioned one of the best photography students to travel to Harlech and take a series of snaps from several angles.

"Why not frame the student's photos?" asked David.

"Well, good as they are," explained Alf, "you can't beat a real drawing on the wall."

David had to agree.

141

"I hope you won't think I'm being cheeky," said David, who genuinely hated talking about money, and found it deeply embarrassing, "but these things take ages to do, if you want lots of detail. It's not something I could do in a night, and…"

"Don't worry son," Alf assured him, "I'll see you alright. You needn't worry about that side of it. There's no deadline either - just when you can fit it in."

David agreed to undertake the drawing, and Alf just happened to have the photographs with him. They were good, sharp reference, and David felt he could do a decent job. He placed them into his new portfolio, thanking the printer for giving him his first official art commission; hopefully the first of many.

Later that afternoon, David and Dylan went downstairs to the small refectory to get a cup of tea, and give their eyes a rest from four hours of drawing. It was Dylan's turn to pay, so he queued up while David stood by the cork notice board, which was full of exhibition posters, college news, wanted ads and lonely hearts messages.

He noticed a small card that read;

ARTIST REQUIRED FOR PROJECT.
DISCRETION ESSENTIAL.

The card had a phone number with a Staffordshire code. When Dylan came back with the tea, David pointed it out to him.

"Strange!" remarked Dylan. "Why would an artist have to promise discretion, I wonder?"

"Perhaps it's a woman who wants a nude portrait. She's put this up in colleges, hoping to get a young, virile student round," said David, ever the optimist.

"Maybe it's for the government, and you have to sign the official secrets act," suggested Dylan.

"I might just phone it," said David, who was convinced it was a nymphomaniac housewife, "just out of curiosity."

"You've got enough to do, what with replacing your exploded summer project and doing creepy Alf's castle," said Dylan. "I'll ring it. I need a bit of excitement."

"Sounds a bit weird to me," said David. "You're right. I don't think I'll bother."

"Maybe you're right. We'll have enough on our plates with John's new project. Shall we give it a miss?"

They drank their tea and walked out of the refectory.

"You go on," said David, "I need the loo."

Dylan quickly nipped back into the refectory and jotted down the number on a scrap of paper, before returning to his desk. David, having made sure Dylan had gone, popped back into the refectory and did likewise.

CHAPTER 13

The Sound Hole

"I reckon it's buggered!"

Bobby Burns, joint proprietor of The Sound Hole, the music shop for the *cognoscenti*, opposite Dudley Zoo and Castle, was a man who spoke his mind.

"What think you, Jack?"

Jack McCartney, (no relation to the Beatle) his business partner, and legendary jazz guitarist, shook his head. He looked uncannily like Glenn Miller, but stockier of build, and a few of the musicians that frequented the place were convinced that it *was* him. Quite why he'd chosen to abandon the United States Air Force Band, settle in Dudley, disguise his accent and ditch the trombone in favour of a guitar they couldn't say. Maybe they were just being flippant.

"It might be some use as a decorative ashtray, but its playing days may well be over. The neck's so warped; you could use it as a bow and arrow. Well, a bow anyway. You'd have to get an arrow for it of course, and we don't sell those."

Bobby ruffled his unkempt mess of brown hair, and stared at the neck closely through spectacles that hadn't been cleaned since nineteen-sixty-six.

"Shame though. That's a proper guitar, that is. I'll have it for a week and see if I can straighten it out and get it working again. Tell me again why you threw it in the canal, young Dave."

David explained that, whilst the effect was broadly similar, it was in fact rain damage. Not just a light sprinkling of rain, but two hours of the kind of deluge that convinced Noah to build an Ark. Lazlo, meanwhile, sat on an old speaker cabinet, trying out a Gibson SG that he had no intention of buying until his solitary premium bond came up.

"Sounds like it's shagged to me," he added cheerfully. "Better start saving for another one, or George will kill you."

"Never say die," said Bobby, who had the mannerisms of a slightly eccentric and unworldly boffin, rather than the jazz clarinet player he actually was.

"I've had much worse in here, and mended it. Jack'll be getting a tune out of this by Friday, or I'm a Dutchman."

He wandered into the back room carrying the stricken instrument and singing 'Tulips from Amsterdam'.

Lazlo and David bade them good luck and farewell, and jumped into Lazlo's car. Next stop was a house in Netherton, where Laz had located a Mini that sounded promising. The owner scored highly on his patented 'Car Seller's Test'.

Lady teacher, respectable bank manager husband with Rover on the drive. One owner from new, full service history and genuine reason for sale. It all felt right. The car was clean, well looked after and had low mileage, and there wasn't a nasty car sticker in sight, with the exception of a little thing on the back window about an Owl Sanctuary, which was easily removed. It was even a nice bright red, which beat 'shitty beige', or 'buff', as David preferred to call it, hands down.

Lazlo drove it around the block, looked under the bonnet, in the boot and underneath it, and declared it a worthwhile investment. After the customary Moroccan market-style price haggle, which involved Lazlo knocking off the token fifty pounds which they'd added on specifically for that purpose, the deal was done, and David had a new car. He hoped and prayed that it would last him longer than the previous one. They drove in tandem back to David's house, and coerced Ruby into making the tea. She told Lazlo that she liked the new car very much, thanked him for looking after her idiot son, and rewarded him with a slab of home-made bread pudding. He asked her, rather ungratefully, whether he should consume it or use it to stop his car from rolling down the hill until he'd fixed his dodgy handbrake.

"No matter how fed up you are at the time," she continued, ignoring the slight on her culinary skills, "Sometimes it's all for a reason, the way things work out. You were so depressed when your first car was blown up, but then you were given enough money to buy a far better one."

"Yeah," spluttered Lazlo through a mouthful of edible concrete, "now we'll try and get this one blown up. If we keep it up, we'll have you a Ferrari by next month!"

David thanked his friend profusely and saw him to the door. He wanted to get cracking on his Harlech Castle commission, and the light was fading. Lazlo reminded him that they had a gig the following week in Stafford, at the Dale's Best Butter Sports and Social Club in Stoke on Trent, and they'd need a rehearsal mid-week to go over a few new songs. They said goodbye and David went up to his bedroom to lay a sheet of best quality cartridge onto his drawing board. He traced out the scene, and began meticulously drawing in the castle in minute detail. He was eager to impress Alf, but he also knew that John Auberton was bound to see the finished piece too, which wouldn't do him any harm at all.

He drew virtually uninterrupted for the rest of the evening, completing around a quarter of the drawing. Sensing that his concentration was waning, he covered the picture with a dustsheet and put it away until the next evening. An artist can often, in the last, tired ten minutes, do untold damage which can take hours the following day to rectify. David knew, to the exact brush or pencil stroke, just when to stop for the day, which was a skill in itself. He also knew exactly when a picture was finished, which other students found difficult. They would either stop far too early, fearful of spoiling it, or fiddle with it until it was completely overdone. He had a deftness of touch and a maturity of technique that was rare in one so young.

He staggered downstairs at nine-thirty, rubbing his eyes, and toyed with the idea of phoning the number on the college notice board, but thought that it might appear rude, phoning so late. He resolved to ring first thing in the morning instead.

He had expected that he would have to do four years at college before anyone offered him work, and yet, here he was already, working on one commission and another one in prospect just a phone call away. Life was getting better, at last. He had a great new car, another gig with his band coming up, and paid work. All he needed now was a girlfriend.

CHAPTER 14

Nigel to Teapot in six moves

"Okay, we'll begin with Bessie," said John Auberton. "Take us through your thought processes, if any, and tell the room which of the four subjects you chose for your project, the rationale behind your choice, and how you set about the task in hand. Also, are you satisfied with the end result, and do you feel it answered the brief that I set you, and if not, how would you improve it next time."

The Earth Mother stood up, her enormous udders swinging around unchecked beneath the baggy home-knit jumper with the fluffy chicken motif.

"Erm, well, I looked at your brief, and to be honest, I didn't really want to do Metamorphosis. I don't even know what it is. Well, I do sort of, but…"

"Right," said John, closing his eyes, as if trying desperately to control himself.

"So you ignored the brief, and did what?"

"Well, I like kittens, so I painted a kitten. You told us that we should always take advice from the tutors, but what they said wasn't gospel. You said that it was highly likely that *you* might tell me one thing, but Bob or Ed might suggest something different, and it wasn't like maths, where two and two always equals four."

"I see," said John, gazing at the ceiling fan.

"So I was assertive, like you told me I ought to be in my tutorial, and I did what I wanted to do."

There was so much that John wanted to say to Bessie that he didn't know where to begin, and a feeling of complete hopelessness came over him. Thankfully she was only treading water by being at college, until some poor farm labourer gave her twelve babies, so she could do what she did best, and knock out the odd kitten drawing in between breast feeding. He bit his lip and moved on.

"Nigel. Tell us about your project."

The Headband rose and addressed the class.

"Oh, right on. Well, as you can see, I haven't got much to show you today, yeah? Because I've been working quite hard on this back at the flat, but I prefer to, you know, play with initial concepts in my head first, because I find that actual drawing can restrict you in many ways and…"

"You haven't done anything have you?"

"No."

"Have you seen David's six panel piece here, where he has taken an image and staged a gradual metamorphosis, so that a human being becomes a teapot?"

"Yeah. Tosser!"

"Don't you think that's answered the brief perfectly, in a witty and clever way? Don't you reckon the drawings are beautifully executed too?"

"Well, yes, and I was going to do something similar to that, yeah? But, like, my head's been so spaced lately, what with…"

"Dylan, I feel yours has been very successful too, in a different way to David's piece. Talk us through your thinking."

* * * * *

The session went on for most of the morning, with students being encouraged to criticise each other's efforts. They had never had to do this at school, and some plainly found it uncomfortable. However, after half an hour they were tearing into each other like vultures around a road-kill goat. Quite soon there were so many tit-for-tat insults flying around, that John had to reel them in before it came to blows. Nigel's tactics were to attack everyone willy-nilly, presumably to save face after being exposed as a lazy sod.

The exercise was invaluable to John Auberton, because it allowed him to categorise the students. Top of the list were the talented hard workers, followed by the talented but lazy. Then came the talentless hard workers, the talentless *and* lazy and finally Bessie, who defied categorization.

Another marked difference to the old school regime was how the staff dealt with discipline, time-keeping and quality of work. The college had such an air of freedom compared to school, that students imagined they could get away with murder. There was no headmaster to put the fear of God into them on a daily basis, but come the end of term, the slackers would be invited for a cosy chat in John's office and given a few weeks to put their house in order. If they didn't, the next time they would meet was when the student was serving John with his lunchtime hamburger.

The criticism finished at twelve-thirty, which gave David just enough time to use the payphone in the reception area before he snatched himself some lunch in the refectory. The Foundation students were to spend the afternoon over at the Bachelor of Arts College, a short walk away, where some of them would end up, if they decided to stay in the area. The idea of Foundation was to do a crash course in the various aspects of art, such as photography, sculpture, graphic design and so on, before choosing their specialist subject at degree level. Some would apply to their own degree course, whilst others might prefer to move on. They were being given a guided tour of the various departments that afternoon, so that they could get a taste of what was to come.

David took the crumpled piece of paper from his denim jacket and dialled the number. A plummy voice answered.

"Good afternoon, Stanmore Castle. How may I help you?"

David told the receptionist he was calling about the advertisement, and she asked him to hold. An even plummier male voice took over.

"Hello, Lord Hickman speaking."

David was very impressed. A real Lord, in a real stately home by the sound of it. Something in the deepest recesses of his mind told him that the name was familiar.

"Hello, it's David Day here," he said, suddenly conscious of his Black Country accent. "I saw your ad on the Art college notice board, so I thought I'd give you a ring."

"Excellent! Now listen, I'm looking for someone who is extremely good at copying different styles of art convincingly for a project of mine at the castle. You need to be a bit of a craftsman, do you follow me? I don't want any of that conceptual nonsense."

David told him that he had come to the right lad. He mentioned the renaissance drawing he'd done that had impressed the tutors, and Lord Hickman said that was jolly good, and exactly the kind of thing he was thinking about. An appointment was made for him to call at Stanmore Castle, South Staffordshire for an interview on Sunday the third of October at ten in the morning for an interview. The Lord also reminded him that discretion was all-important, warning him not to mention his project to others - not even his fellow students. Walls have ears, he said, and he promised to explain the need for secrecy when they met on the third. David thanked him, and replaced the receiver.

After lunch, David walked over to the main college with Dylan and Katie. First stop was the seventh floor, which was the fine art department. Ed Briers, who was in charge of the guided tour, told them that the air up there was rarefied, which often resulted in the long-term inmates speaking gobbledegook. He reckoned it was caused by the lack of oxygen to the brain.

They were met by a little man in a black polo-neck with a pair of gold half-rimmed glasses perched so close to the tip of his nose that David feared they would drop off at any minute.

Kieron Hastings, graduate of the Royal Academy, painted abstracts, which he sold in London for the price of a small bungalow in Poole. His work hung in the homes of people who had foreign *au pairs* and nannies, and only ever saw their children for five minutes of quality time just before bed. Each painting would come with a thousand-page manifesto, explaining the deep thinking behind why Mr

Hastings had elected to paint the eight-foot-square canvas pure black, with one red stripe.

He took over the tour, taking them through the various studios on the top floor, or astral plane, as John liked to call it. He pointed out what he called an 'installation' piece by one of his third-year degree students, Lemuel Ronsflob. At least, that's what David thought he said. He was only half listening. The 'piece' in question was an old picture frame in the middle of the floor, covered in wood shavings and splattered paint.

"Lemuel is quite brilliant," Kieron gushed. "He's in line for a first, in spite of his setback. The cleaner came in one weekend recently and swept away all of his installations. The stupid woman thought they were just a pile of old frames and rubbish. Can you believe that?"

"Yes," said David, trying to be sociable. Mr Hastings gave him a withering look that would have felled a buffalo. They wandered into another room, where an outline of a man was marked out on the floor in white tape. At the place where the heart would have been, there was a vivid splash of what looked like real blood. Bessie the Earth Mother blanched and had to grab onto an easel for support. Mr Hastings dashed forwards and said "Oh my God!" Several of the Foundation students looked uneasy. Katie whispered to David that she'd heard Fine Art students were highly strung, and prone to suicide. She clutched his arm for comfort, and felt him shiver with what she erroneously assumed was horror.

"This is a final degree piece by one of our overseas students, Spatula Christian, which examines human mortality. What on earth has happened here? Someone has added this red splash. It wasn't here a few minutes ago!"

Bob Rosemary, looking very sheepish, appeared at the back of the room.

"Er, sorry Kieron. That's my fault. I was taking a look around the degree work when I had a sudden nosebleed. It's okay though. I had a word with Spatula, and he likes it, so he's decided to keep it."

David wondered if Bob had a serious medical problem, or just had an art critic for a nose. The tour moved on to the department two floors below, which housed the three dimensional design students. Dylan noticed immediately that the air had improved, and the students here looked healthier and spoke plain English. They also had a really good view of most of the Wolverhampton Wanderers football pitch, which solved the mystery of why Fine Art and 3D Design always put in a good deal of overtime each Saturday, whilst the lazy Graphic Design lot down on the third floor just got drunk and went to the match instead.

Further down still were the printing rooms, soft materials and finally, deep in the basement, photography. The Foundation students would have to go over to the big building for specialist courses during the year, to help them decide which of the many aspects of the Art College appealed to them most, so it was useful to know where everything was. When the official tour was concluded, the students adjourned to the refectory, which was much bigger and better equipped than Doris's humble tearoom over at the Foundation department, with its cardboard box full of assorted stale biscuits. David treated himself to a sausage roll and the inevitable cup of tea, whilst Dylan favoured the wagon-wheel biscuit and coffee combination.

"Interesting place," said David.

"Very," agreed Dylan.

"Did you ever get round to phoning about that ad in the tearoom?" asked David, a little too casually.

"No, I couldn't be bothered. Did you?" asked Dylan.

"No, me neither," his friend replied.

CHAPTER 15

The Big Interview

It was about eleven o'clock in the morning, mid October, and the ground was wet after a recent downpour. David Day was wearing his powder blue suit, with dark blue shirt and tie, black brogues and black wool socks with little paintbrush motifs. He was neat, clean, shaved and sober, and he didn't care who knew it. He was everything the well-dressed young artist about town ought to have been. He was calling on twenty million pounds.

David had initially not known the whereabouts of Stanmore Castle, but was pleasantly surprised to find that it was in Kinver, only a few miles from his house. He had often seen the place, looming majestically out of the trees behind the old oak gates on the Bridgnorth Road, without realizing who owned it or what it was called.

The castle had its own square church tower, dating back to the fourteenth century, from which the flag of Saint George was flying. The place had been constantly added to since those early days and now the majority of it was Victorian. All around was farmland, dotted with the odd expensive property here and there. At the back of the castle was a small river, the Stour, which dropped a few feet as it approached the property to create an impressive weir. Running parallel with it was James Bindley's Staffordshire and Worcestershire canal, which led south to Stourport and the River Severn, and North to Wolverhampton or Birmingham, and eventually Wales.

As David drove his new car across the crisp gravel to the visitor's car park, his heart pounded with excitement. He reckoned the place must have around three hundred bedrooms, and conservatively, at least a million windows. A felon could get seriously wealthy just by nicking the lead from the roofs. He parked up, grabbed his portfolio and crunched his way to the front door. He felt a tad disappointed that there wasn't a drawbridge or a moat, and toyed for a while about withdrawing his services in protest. It was all a long way from his council house in Brierley Bank. Pausing at the front door, he examined his once shiny shoes, now covered in cream dust and mud from the gravel. He polished them on the backs of his trouser legs, which did the trick, but left the back of his suit filthy.

He rang the polished brass doorbell and waited. A minute or so later, a well-kept and attractive lady in her mid-forties wearing a smart blue suit and pearls answered the door. David felt sure he knew her from somewhere, but couldn't think where. She asked his name and business, telling him to come in and wait in the hall for a few seconds, while she told His Lordship. She had a lovely, upper-crust French accent, a little like Nicole's, but less pronounced, which again reminded him how awful his own sounded.

He gazed around the hall in awe. Huge old oil paintings shared the wall space with stuffed animal heads mounted on mahogany shields. He wondered what kind of person could get pleasure from that kind of thing. How could they make the giant mental leap from admiring a creature for its beauty, to then wanting to kill it? It made little sense. They were the same people who felt they *had* to have children, but then sent them away to boarding school so that they didn't actually have to see them too often. The strangest thing was that the children, having cried themselves to sleep each night in some horrible dormitory, grew up and inflicted the exact same torture on *their* children.

A funny lot, these toffs, thought David, smiling ruefully.

Then there was the name thing. It seemed to him that the lower-to-middle classes had the best choice of names, whereas the toffs appeared to be strictly limited. As far as he could make out, one only had a choice of about three or four for each sex. Everyone seemed to be called Charles or Henry, unless they were eighteen years old, in which case they were Nick, Hugo or at a pinch Tarquin, if the family was *really* posh. The women were always called Caroline, Henrietta, Camilla or Arabella. As far as he knew, there were no toffs called Brett, Wayne or Sharon.

Americans, he mused, had taken the whole name thing too far the *other* way. At heart, he was a traditionalist, and he didn't approve of the American habit of just inventing names. Sometimes it got darned silly. He imagined, with horror, the thought of being christened Autumn Tomahawk, or Chutney J. Wildebeest III.

No, for all its faults, the English way was still preferable.

Further speculation on what loony Americans could possibly christen their offspring was interrupted by the front door bell chiming. The well dressed French lady came out of her office, assured David that His Lordship was almost finished on the phone, and walked over to the front door with a natural poise that had no doubt learnt at a Swiss finishing school, at enormous expense to her parents.

159

She opened the door and spoke to someone for a few seconds before inviting him inside. David watched, intrigued, as a large black portfolio poked its nose into the hall, closely followed by a puffing and panting Dylan Weldon. For a few seconds the two students just stared at one another, each looking like finalists in a sheep impersonator's competition, and the result was a dead heat. John Auberton had often lectured the students about having a healthy competitive streak, reminding them that they would be vying for the same few jobs, once college was finished. Neither David nor Dylan dreamt that they'd have to compete this early on.

Mercifully, the sheepish expressions soon turned to big grins, as the two culprits realized that they were equally guilty of subterfuge, and neither could occupy the moral high ground. Dylan sat down, sweating (to use an expression coined in the locality) like a glassblower's backside.

"Couldn't be bothered eh?" he said.

"No. You neither?"

"Well, I thought about it, decided not to bother, and then I thought about it again, and I thought…."

"Nothing ventured?"

"Exactly!"

"Well, here we both are. It looks like you walked all the way from Stourbridge Park."

"I did! I can't drive, remember? I kept walking from bus stop to bus stop, waiting for one to arrive. They did, eventually, but I was always between bus stops, and the buggers wouldn't pick me up."

"Ever tried just waiting at the bus stop for a bit longer?"

"I get bored with it."

"I see. Well, hang around and I'll take you home in my new car. We can compare interviews. Besides that, you'll need someone to be consoled after your disappointment."

"Ha ha!" laughed Dylan, a bit short of heartily.

The French lady interrupted their catfight.

"Would either of you like a drink?"

"Coffee for me please," replied Dylan, "and a saucer of milk for my friend."

The French lady affected a strained smile. She looked as if she were about to say, "Please keep your puerile jokes to yourself. I'm very busy." but refrained. David mumbled something about preferring tea. She told him that Lord Hickman was ready to see him now, so she'd bring the tea into his office. She showed him where to go, and he picked up his portfolio.

"I'll wait for you. See you here," he said to his friend, and went in search of His Lordship.

David knocked on the heavy oak door and a voice within said "Enter."

Lord Hickman sat behind a large desk, which had the unfortunate effect of making a smallish man look even smaller. He was good looking in a Lord Lucan kind of way, and sported a similar moustache. His hair was brown, with grey around the temples, and he wore an open necked shirt with a Paisley cravat, topped off with a lemon yellow pullover.

161

As David entered, Lord Hickman rose to his full height, which wasn't an awful lot, and proffered a beautifully manicured hand. David wasn't sure whether to kiss it or shake it. He wisely chose the latter.

"Charles Hickman," he said. "Pleased to meet you."

"He's a Charles - I bloody well knew it!" thought David, triumphantly - and out loud, "David Day. Pleased to meet you too, erm, Lord."

"Yes, best call me Charles. We don't need to stand on ceremony, dear boy. I see you've brought some of your work. Good show! Let's have a quick look, shall we?"

David put his portfolio onto the table and unzipped it. He displayed his renaissance style drawings and some photographs of paintings he'd done in various styles, from Pre-Raphaelite to Impressionist, and Lord Charles was quick to realize that David was no slouch with a paint brush. He appeared both surprised and impressed by such precocious talent in one so young.

"Excellent. This is perfect for what I had in mind. It's your versatility that's interesting me, David. I need to know though; can I rely on total discretion from you? That aspect is as important as your artistic skills are. I'll explain."

Just as he was about to get to what is commonly known as the 'nitty-gritty' or 'nittoi-grittoi', as the people of Birmingham would have it, the French lady breezed into the room with a coffee and a tea on a silver tray that looked to be worth as much as Len and Ruby's house.

"Ah, merci, Brigitte," he said, and gave her a crocodile smile that suggested he'd like to know her better, if he didn't already. She smiled sweetly back and sashayed,

162

catwalk model-style to the door. Charles savoured every second until the door closed, and then resumed.

"As I was saying, before we were beautifully interrupted," he said, winking a revolting wink in David's direction. "Discretion, dear boy. I must have your absolute word."

David assured him that he could be the very soul of discretion. He almost convinced himself.

"I have many works of art scattered around the castle. You are welcome to join me on a guided tour later, if you wish, and I'll show you. I occasionally open the rooms to the public in the summer months, and one can't be too careful. My insurers are worried about how stealable a lot of these treasures are, so they're charging me a bloody fortune. I want someone who is, for want of a better term, a bit of a forger, David. I want you to copy certain pictures for the castle, so that the real things can be stored in a vault, or secure room. Your forgeries will hang in the castle, purporting to be the real McCoy. Most people won't be able to tell the difference. If we do get the odd smart-arse who knows his stuff, we'll quietly give him a deluxe tour and show him the real thing, as long as he's not an international art thief - do you follow me?"

David said that he did, but was worried that he might not be up to the job.

"Listen, old thing," said Lord Hickman, "I have learnt a lot about art over the years, and one thing is certain. Most people haven't the foggiest idea. If you tell them it's a Monet, they accept that it's a Monet. They might question it if it was in a council house in Dudley, but they wouldn't dream of doing so here. One presumes they are the real thing, in such a setting. *Capisco?*"

"I'm not familiar with his work," admitted David.

"Never mind," said Lord Hickman, looking heavenwards. "Follow me."

He rose from his chair, and took David for a wander round the castle's rooms, pointing out various family portraits as they walked.

"None of this stuff is important, in terms of what we spoke about," he said. "Thieves wouldn't target that kind of thing. "Now here!" he said, pausing at a small terracotta drawing in a gilt frame.

"This is a renaissance drawing by Gozzoli. Doesn't look much, does it David? It's worth a small fortune. This is the kind of thing I need replacing. Could you handle it?"

David studied it closely.

"I'd need to antique the paper. I've done it before. You use tea to stain it, and coffee granules to create the foxing effects. It's incredibly convincing. The drawing is red chalk. I reckon I could forge that so as you'd hardly tell the difference."

"Excellent. What about this old oil painting here?"

"No real problem, but you'd need to get a canvas that was of a similar age. That's the difficult bit," said David.

"I have an attic full of crap from the same era. You could simply over-paint one of them."

David was warming to the task. "Superb! Then it's do-able. I can even add a crackled glaze on top to age the paint finish. You can buy it!"

"I'm impressed with your knowledge, young man. Remember, you are not fooling Christies or Sotheby's here.

No disrespect, but you're probably nowhere near good enough for that. All I want is for you to fool the man in the street. Understood?"

David nodded, notching up a mark against His Lordship's debit column for the slight. They continued to a room that Lord Hickman had to open with a key.

"No one other than my special guests is allowed in here." he said. "I want you to see something special."

They entered a small but grandly furnished room which was decorated in a rich red colour, with drapes that went from the ornate high ceiling to the floor, and made from material that must have cost around ten thousand pounds per square foot. There were only two or three paintings in the room, and the space they were allowed on the wall suggested that they were extra special. Lord Hickman took David over to an Impressionist landscape.

"This is what I wanted you to see, young man. Recognize the style?"

"Maybe Sisley?" guessed David. "Where's the signature? - jeez, it's a Monet!"

"Absolutely, and it's worth a fortune. Could you copy it, do you think?"

"To be truthful," replied David, with all the arrogance of youth, "it's far easier to copy a Monet than some of that other stuff you've got scattered around. The renaissance stuff is much more difficult."

"Just what I wanted to hear, old boy. You don't suffer from modesty do you?"

"That's unfair!" frowned David, mortally wounded. "I *am* modest, and I've got a lot to be modest about, but I hate *false* modesty. There's nothing worse than a pretty girl telling you how ugly she is, just so you can assure her that she's beautiful. It's revolting. It is quite easy to fake a Monet, relatively speaking, but he was a pioneer. He was one of the painters who invented the style, whereas mere mortals like me can just copy it. There! A bit of modesty for you."

"Don't apologize, dear boy. I like your confidence. Now - the big question. When?"

David knew this was coming. He explained that his college work was very important, and he couldn't overstretch himself. He could do a little each weekend, and during any holidays. Maybe, if His Lordship were desperate, he could even take a few days off here and there, but he had to be careful. His new patron weighed this, and offered a solution.

"Begin with the renaissance drawings. There are three I'd particularly like reproduced. That'll ease you in, before you tackle any oil painting.

Obviously, these pictures are not allowed off the premises, so I propose to set you up here. I'll set aside a room for your studio, which you must keep locked at all times. I don't want anyone knowing what you're doing in there, and that includes my wife. The only people who are to be a party to this are you, the insurance company boss, and myself. We can rely on the discretion of their M.D. We went to Eton and Cambridge together. Where did you go to school, incidentally?"

"Tipperton Grammar."

"Oh, I *am* sorry. Anyway, feel your way with the drawings. They shouldn't take you all that long. The Monet

166

is the most important picture, and the one most at risk from thieves. Hardly anyone knows that I have it, and as you can see, it's not in a public room. My secretary and my wife are aware of it, as is Jean Jacques, the manager of my vineyards. You'll no doubt bump into him. Any questions so far?"

David asked how he would explain the paintings being removed from the walls, should anyone ask. Lord Hickman suggested that they could be being restored, and David's presence could be explained in the same way. He could be the young but gifted restorer, sent from an old and respected firm to work 'in-situ'. David agreed that this sounded convincing.

"I still have two more things to discuss," said His Lordship, flinging a patronly arm around David's shoulder. "We'll begin with the more prosaic of the two items - money. I propose to pay you fifty quid each for the drawings, and two hundred each for the oils, but you must assure me that they will be top quality. I will pay two hundred and fifty for the Monet. How's that with you?"

David was delighted, and more than a little taken aback. He currently existed on ten pounds a week pocket money, and had no income whatsoever, if he discounted the band's very occasional outings. To him, this was a small fortune.

"That sum not only buys me the best you can achieve, but also your complete discretion. Now for the perks of the job. Have you ever been to Florence, my good fellow?"

David said that he hadn't, but would love to go.

"Well that's very convenient," said Lord Hickman, "because I have another job for you. I have an apartment in the heart of that wonderful city, and it too contains art treasures, mainly old renaissance drawings, as you have seen here, and a painting or two. My insurers are equally worried about my Italian place, though of course the public are not allowed in. Florence is full of thieves, dear boy, and the drawings are worth a lot of money. I want you to go there, armed with your pencils, tea bags and coffee granules, copy the three most expensive pictures, and put your copies into the existing frames. Then, if you are willing of course, wrap the originals and bring them here for me. I wish to place them in the vault with the Monet and the other stuff, for safekeeping. While you're over there, you may stay at the apartment and enjoy the city. How does that sound?"

David was reeling. He was a working class lad of nineteen from a council house in Brierley Bank. Things like this just didn't happen to people like him. They happened to James Bond.

"It sounds flipping marvellous!" he said, shaking the Lord's hand. "I can't believe it's happening."

"David, I've taken a liking to you, and I think I'm a good judge of character. I trust you, so you'd better not bloody well let me down, do you hear? There's another young man waiting outside, and I've decided that I'm going to have to let *him* down. Don't make me wish I'd chosen him instead of you."

"He's a friend of mine. He'll be disappointed, of course." David sounded heartbroken.

"Friend or not, you tell him nothing, do you understand? People tell other people, and before you know it, someone's jemmied open a window and the lot's gone!"

David promised that what had been discussed would go no further, and they strolled back to the office. Lord Hickman asked for a phone number, so David borrowed a gold-plated fountain pen and scribbled it on the back of one of his band cards which Alf had printed for them, at what he assured David was a knock-down price.

Lord Hickman studied the card before putting it into his wallet.

"You *are* a talented chap. Play in a rock band too eh?"

"Yes, we play around the clubs locally. We could do with more work though."

"Interesting! I'll keep this - it may come in useful. Well David, I'll be in touch."

They said their goodbyes and David returned to Dylan, who was fast asleep in his chair. He woke him gently by kicking him on the shin, and told him that Lord Hickman would see him now. Meanwhile, David took a quick walk round the grounds, knowing that Dylan wouldn't be detained for too long. The gardens were beautiful, with Elizabethan style walks and topiary. Behind the house was a stable block, which had been converted into the Vineyard offices, and another larger building, which was presumably the actual winemaking and bottling area. Immediately behind these were fields full of vines, stretching as far as the eye could see.

Eventually, Dylan returned to the Mini, and called over to David to say that he was ready to leave. They jumped into the car, and headed for Stourbridge.

"How did you get on then?" asked Dylan.

"Waste of time," replied David, somewhat dishonestly. "He wanted someone with more experience. What about you?"

"He didn't give me the job either," said Dylan, "presumably for the same reason. Did you get to meet his wife?"

"Oh, the French lady? That was his assistant."

"No," said Dylan. "It was definitely his wife that I saw. I met the French one, but his wife is English. She came in while we were talking and threw a silver picture frame at his head, followed by a small bust of Mozart. At least, I think it was Mozart. It was travelling too fast to be sure. Then she let him have it with a cut glass goblet."

"She sounds lovely. Shame about the bust though. I noticed that. It was very nice."

"Yes. Well, it's buggered now, and it buggered up my interview, I'm telling you. I had half a mind to lob that stuffed perch in the glass box at him, just to be sociable. It seemed to be the done thing."

"It's very curious though. Behaving like that in front of a stranger. Maybe they'd just had a huge row."

"God! Nothing gets past you, Dave, you're incredibly astute, the way you pick up on hidden little signals like that. You could be the next Phillip Marlowe - especially in that awful Oxfam shop double-breasted suit."

"Bollocks!" replied David, wounded.

They arrived at Dylan's house.

"Thanks for the lift," he said, lugging out his gigantic portfolio from the tiny car with some difficulty. I'm knackered now. I could do with a big sleep before I hit the pub tonight. Anyway, sorry it was all a waste of time."

"Ah well!" said David. "You win some, you lose some."

CHAPTER 16

A dish best eaten cold

David arrived at college on Monday morning much buoyed by the events of the weekend. There were several things to be very cheerful about. His interview with Lord Hickman couldn't have gone better, and he couldn't wait to get cracking on the first of the renaissance drawings.

It was a shame that Dylan couldn't have given him a hand. He was more than capable, but the secretive Lord had stressed that this whole adventure had to be kept under wraps, and that was how David intended to play it. Another cause for optimism was the band's recent gig, at the Dale's Best Butter Sports and Social Club. It had gone down very well, generally speaking, though there were a few little niggles that he wanted to iron out. For a start, Ken had persevered with his one-man quest to drink every pint of lager in the world, an unrealistic ambition that seemed doomed to fail. He'd recorded a new personal best by surviving until the encore, but was unable to participate after that for largely technical reasons. He had managed to remain awake, but had no memory of how to play his instrument, or what his name was. On returning to the parental home at three in the morning, he slept but fitfully, and woke to relieve himself. Turning right onto the landing instead of left, he entered his parent's bedroom, opened his father's wardrobe door and emptied his distended bladder all over the old man's best suit and collection of brogue shoes.

There was also growing unrest about the band's name. Compères struggled with its pronunciation, as did Ken after the first few drinks, and so a board meeting was called in Mohammed's van after the gig, to vote on a new name.

Nick opened the proceedings.

"Listen, listen!" he began suddenly, laughing like a deranged fool. "I've got it! A stroke of bloody genius. It's obvious what we *have* to call the band, right? First, the facts. Dave here formed the band, correct?"

The others nodded in agreement.

"Right, agreed. Ken's always falling asleep when he's pissed. No problems so far?"

This was indisputable. Ken smiled one of his 'I'm about to have the mickey taken out of me,' weak smiles.

"Laz has got a great big snout, you must admit, Laz."

Laz looked less than pleased with the way this was going, but he reluctantly waved Nick on.

"Okay! Now, as you know, my name is Nick, right?" he continued, chortling at his inventiveness. The others stared at him blankly.

"And George, I hope you don't mind me saying, it's nothing personal, but you've got a bit of a facial tic that you do when you get tired. You know the one I mean?" Nick did his best impersonation of it, in case George hadn't been aware of his own affliction.

"How come, when somebody says 'Nothing personal', they always come out with something really personal?" asked George indignantly. "Anyway, where's all this leading Nick? You're just talking bollocks as usual."

If Nick had possessed a bugle, he would have blown a fanfare at this point to herald his big idea. This not being an option, he got down to business.

"How about 'Dave Day, Dozy, Beaky, Nick and Twitch?'"

* * * * *

And so it was that 'The Stubbles' was chosen, courtesy of Lazlo, a reference to the fact that none of them could usually be bothered to shave. The name also had a vague resemblance to the one chosen by four lovable moptops from Liverpool, which pleased all concerned. Even Nick was happy, once they had tactfully persuaded him that, whilst his suggestion certainly drew the best laugh of the evening, there was no way they could envisage it becoming a reality. David liked the new name, but was worried about the now obsolete cards he had had printed at enormous expense, courtesy of Alf.

Mo, childlike in his enthusiasm, vowed to get the new name sign-written on his van as soon as possible, and warned the lads that he would take a dim view should they have another change of heart. Lazlo suggested a new system of lettering that his boss used on their commercial vehicles, which consisted of highly adhesive plastic letters, rather than actual paint. Apparently these could be accurately machine-cut to any typeface, and should Mo wish to sell his van, they could be removed by heating them up with a hair dryer. Lazlo was duly put in charge of the sign-writing project, and this caused great mirth when David, who had originally christened him after remembering the name of Ingrid Bergman's screen husband in Casablanca, realized that Lazlo would be in possession of the 'letters of transit'.

* * * * *

David was very pleased that he had finally completed the drawing of Harlech Castle, which had seemed to drag on interminably. He estimated that it had taken at least forty hours in total, and he was glad to be now handing it over and collecting the reward. He felt sure that Alf would be delighted, but couldn't resist running it past John Auberton first. He deliberately avoided Bob, fearful of what his nose might think of it.

David knocked on his office door and went in. John, as usual, was knee-deep in administrative turmoil. David took the artwork from his portfolio and placed it on the desk.

"That's a lovely piece of drawing," beamed his tutor. "Excellent! If Alf doesn't like that, he deserves to be horse-whipped on the steps of his club."

"Thank you!" said David proudly. "Er, John, can I ask your advice please?"

John sat him down and offered him a green Opal Fruit, the one he didn't care for.

"I've had an opportunity come my way that I don't want to pass by. A wealthy person that I know has commissioned me to produce some paintings for him in the Italian Renaissance style. He's also asked me if I'd like to work in

Florence for a few weeks, at his holiday apartment. Obviously, this is a dream come true for me. I never dreamt that I'd be commissioned until after college, and he's offered me hundreds of pounds worth of work. I'm going to struggle to do it, *and* do my college work, if I proceed. I'm getting very stressed about it all, because I love the college, and I wouldn't give it up at any price, but this is such an opportunity, don't you think?"

John pondered as he sucked on a strawberry flavoured Opal Fruit - his favourite.

"This is a tough one, David. I'm pleased you came to see me, rather than struggle through and risk cocking up both your college work *and* the commissions. My first question to you is this; does this man fancy you in any way? He's not another Amorous Asian is he?"

"How do you know about that?" demanded David, reddening around the cheeks.

"You told Ed Briers one day when you were doing that woodwork project. If you want a rumour to spread across town, tell Briers that it's a secret. We call him Radio Wolverhampton."

"The bugger!" snarled David indignantly. "I'll get him back for that. Anyway, no, this bloke's not after my body. He looks to have enough on his plate with the women in his life."

"Good. And you say he's wealthy?"

"As in stately home wealthy, but I can't tell you who it is. He's one of these reclusive types who shuns publicity."

"Like Howard Hughes?" asked John, intrigued.

"Exactly!" agreed David, wondering who the hell Howard Hughes was.

"And how long would you need to complete these commissions?" asked John. "A month? More?"

David estimated that a month would be more than adequate. If not, he always had weekends and nights.

"Look David," said John, thinking it over as he spoke. "Look! I'll tell you what I'll do. Firstly, a trip to Florence is a golden opportunity. We'd all go there on a college trip if we could afford it, so I regard that as educational. I'd expect you to visit all the museums while you were there, or I'd be disappointed in you."

"Of course!"

"You want to be an illustrator or maybe a fine artist when you leave college don't you? What could be better than producing work of that quality, and studying the masters? I think I could justify time out for such a prestige project, as long as you have something to show for it at the end. Could you take pictures of your commissions perhaps?"

"I'm not sure if he'd let me, but I'd have time to produce work of my own while I was there. It's such an inspiring place, after all. When would I ever get that kind of chance again?" asked David, selling it big.

"Right," said John. "I'm going to stick my neck out here, so I don't want you to disappoint me. You're a talented lad, and I don't want you leaving college bitter and twisted because I refused you. This bloke's work won't last forever, and you need your degree. However, I agree that this is out of the ordinary, so I'm going to set you a special project. Take a month out and work on my brief, which I will formalize this afternoon, on Renaissance art. Mind you, I'll want it on my desk before the Christmas holidays. Drawings, photos, paintings - the whole shooting match. You'll have to work hard, but hard work never killed anyone."

"Tell that to those who built the flipping Siam Railway," grinned David ruefully.

"Very funny! Okay, I'll type up a brief today. You have one month to paint your commissions and visit Florence. I want you back here with something spectacular by the end of November. Agreed?"

David was ecstatic. He thanked John profusely, and shook his hand.

"Right, that's a huge weight off my mind," he said. "Now I have two things to do. I must give Alf his drawing, and then find Ed Briers, in order to kill him."

He skipped down the corridor to the print room, where he found Alf studying the Daily Mirror.

"Ah, David, how's my drawing coming on?" he enquired, closing his newspaper quickly to protect the modesty of the scantily clad model he had been focussed on.

"It's finished. There you are."

Alf opened the folder and studied the pencil drawing. It gave him just as much pleasure as the girl in the Mirror had, but in a different way.

"That's marvellous! Bloody marvellous! There's so much detail. You've shown every brick in the wall, and every blade of bloody grass. Thank you. That's just what I'd hoped it would be."

He fumbled around in his back pocket for his wallet. David felt awkward, and pretended to study the etching plates on the press. Alf took a five pound note from the wallet and pressed it into David's hand, as if it were the Crown Jewels.

"Here. I told you I'd see you alright. I know it's tough for you students, and a bit of cash is always welcome, eh Dave? Now shush, before you say anything. I want you to take it. No arguments. You deserve it. Now, if you don't mind, I must press on."

David staggered out of the print room. He had learnt a valuable lesson in life, for which he needed to thank Alf. It's just that he couldn't find the right words at that juncture. He had wanted to ask about some new business cards for the band, but concluded that now was probably not the right time. Instead, he went to see Ed Briers.

Ed was busy sawing out a piece of Perspex for one of the students when David arrived, and he seemed in some discomfort. David was disappointed, because he wanted to see him in a lot more.

"Hi!" he said. "Sawing out a piece of Perspex eh?"

"No, I'm playing football in a bloody pink tutu," replied the lecturer somewhat tetchily, in between rubbing his groin and moaning.

"What's up? You look in pain."

"I'd rather not say, thank you," said Ed, looking unusually embarrassed.

"Come on. You can't just leave it there -it's too teasy!" begged David, making himself comfortable on the edge of the woodwork bench.

178

"Look, between you and me, I went to the pub last night in our village, and I got a bit pissed, I must admit. I decided to take the short cut home across the fields, and I tried to vault this barbed wire fence. Trouble is, I left half of my right bollock attached to it. I was at the hospital until three, having stitches. I'm in agony."

David expressed his concern, and left him to his sawing. Perhaps now was not the time to tell him off. After all, he believed it was wrong to kick a man while he was down. He returned to the studio and carried on quietly with his project, even refusing a lunch date with Dylan and Katie, in order to continue on working. At five o'clock, he packed away his equipment and asked Dylan if he needed a lift home. The two lads walked to the door, and David asked Dylan to hang around for a second, as he had something to do. He opened his portfolio from which he produced a large A1-sized piece of cartridge paper with a perfect caricature of Ed Briers in a hospital bed, having an unfeasibly large pair of testicles stitched back on by a buxom nurse. A doctor looked on, amused, with a newspaper in his hand. The headline read;

LECTURER IN BIZARRE BARBED-WIRE KNACKERS INJURY.

He pinned it onto the college notice board.

"Okay Dyl. Now I'm ready."

CHAPTER 17

A Monet-making venture

Lord Hickman was helping his glamorous French assistant to tidy up. She picked bits of Stuart Crystal goblet from his greying locks, while he gathered together Mozart's shattered facial features with the dustpan and brush. It would have taken an archaeologist from the British Museum ten years to reassemble it. A thousand piece jigsaw depicting a foggy night in West Bromwich would have been easier.

"She really doesn't like you, does she?" observed Brigitte.

"That was her being caring," winced Charles. "You should see her when we have a real go."

They stood up and he went back to his desk. Brigitte walked over, swivelling her hips like crazy, and sat on his lap. She removed her spectacles, Miss Moneypenny style, and gently lowered her fulsome lips onto his. Had this been a scene from one of those Romance paperbacks that plague airport bookshops, the author would probably have described her kiss as moist and lingering.

"Does that make you feel a little better?" she purred, in her lovely French accent.

"Oh yes!" he moaned. "All that crawling about on the floor at my age. It's made me a little stiff."

"I've noticed," she whispered in his ear. "Maybe you just need a little lie down, my love."

"That sounds like an excellent idea," he drooled, "but we'll have to wait till Her Ladyship goes out for her daily spot of retail therapy. She'll need fresh stuff to throw at me, after all."

Brigitte removed her curvy bottom from his lap and sat on the chair erstwhile occupied by David.

"How did the interview with the students go?" she asked, stroking his hand across the desk.

"Well, apart from my having to dodge flying busts halfway through the second one, excellent. Both chappies were very good, but the first one is also marvellously naïve, which is ideal for our purposes. I offered him a paltry sum for copying the stuff, and he seemed to think it was a king's ransom! I'd have cheerfully given him three times that, but you've got to try it on, and the silly bugger went for it. In fairness, I suppose it's a lot of money for a penniless art student, after all."

"Do you think he bought the line about the insurance company?"

"Absolutely - hook, line and sinker," sniggered Charles. "I can't believe my luck. That bitch I married has no idea about art. Never has had. All she understands is what it's worth. I'm telling you, she won't even notice. Those pictures will be hanging on the walls of this bloody castle for years after we disappear, and she'll show the Yanks around boasting, 'that's a Monet,' and the silly buggers will gasp in appreciation and waddle on to the next fake. It's perfect!"

"What if she does find out, somehow?" asked Brigitte.

"Then all I have to do is say that they were bought in good faith, and *we* must have been duped, years ago. We've had some of those renaissance pictures for ten or more years - the trail's gone cold. Besides, I always buy the art, not her. She wouldn't even know who to ask. Trust me. It's virtually foolproof."

Lord Charles Hickman liked to fly by the seat of his pants. Now fifty years old, he had met his wife, Caroline, at a hunt ball, and swept her off her feet. She came from an extremely wealthy family, and he knew what he was doing. He had lost most of his money on failed business ventures with less than scrupulous partners, and lost the rest, quite literally, on wine and women. The vineyard he had planted was a disaster, and the meagre supply of rancid vinegar that he generated was so awful that no shops wanted it. He had been having affairs with unsuitable women before, during and after he became engaged, and they had bled him dry. His wooing of Caroline was not borne out of love, but out of survival. He had heard that she had the stuff by the sackful, and he desperately needed to get his paws on it. It was a relatively simple task for the smooth, good-looking Lord to sweet-talk her into his bedroom, and her parents saw it as a good thing, to be encouraged. The family were Black Country folk who had made a fortune out of metal bashing, thereafter moving to the countryside to live in a gaudy, architect-designed nightmare full of Russell Flint and David Shepherd prints. Had there been an enterprising young artist in the locality who specialized in naked Spanish women riding on the backs of majestic tigers or noble elephants, he would have made a small fortune from their patronage.

They also splashed out on fleets of cars, golf club memberships and private schools, where their spoilt little brats were taught to speak properly and sneer at their embarrassing parents. To have a daughter called Lady Caroline was something money couldn't buy, and these were people for whom acceptance by the aristocracy of England meant an awful lot. They would now be able to thumb their noses at the *Nouveau Riche*, without the slightest idea that they themselves fell into that much maligned category.

Charles, desperate for money, was all but bankrupt when he met Caroline, but they each had what the other needed, and wedding bells chimed with unseemly haste. Within weeks of their marriage the happy couple didn't much care for each other. After a year this mutual antipathy had disintegrated into virulent hate, and remained so. The castle belonged to Charles, but it was so dilapidated that Caroline had virtually rebuilt it. On his many excursions abroad, frequently accompanied by his current 'secretary', Charles procured works of art, for which Caroline paid the bills. Now, after far too many years, fights and affairs, she had at last realized that happiness was worth more than titles, and she was divorcing him, citing infidelity as the official reason, though she could easily think of many more.

Charles was worried, to say the least, because the courts would surely find in her favour, which meant that, if all went to her plan, he would be a Lord without a bean. This was galling in the extreme, because the house was now splendid and full of priceless art, while the vineyard had been turned around, thanks to Caroline employing a knowledgeable Frenchman called Jean Jacques. (The couple were rather fond of having French staff. It gave the place an air of sophistication.)

She had poached him from a famous French wine producer and set him up in the stable block. Now, thanks to his expertise, the castle was bottling and selling large quantities of decent quality wine to the large supermarkets, in the process making a lot of money.

It was Jean Jacques who was also responsible for supplying Charles's current love interest, the shapely Brigitte. When Charles had suggested that he could do with a good P.A., Jean-Jacques recommended Brigitte, who was his old boss's P.A. at the French vineyard. He described her in such glowing terms that his new boss interviewed her the following week. He found her not only extremely efficient, but very easy on the eye. He therefore made her an offer she couldn't refuse (using Caroline's money of course) and had her crated and shipped over double-quick to help with the now thriving wine business and the general running of the castle.

To the public, he was Lord of the manor, but on paper it was Caroline who held the purse strings. Charles didn't even own the apartment in Florence. That too was in Caroline's name. If his wife divorced him, and he reckoned that it was fairly imminent, he would need a few bits and pieces to sell, so that he and Brigitte could start a new life in Australia. A Monet and a few renaissance drawings would come in very handy.

Charles had not been totally forthcoming with his new love, however. Despite being currently in the midst of love's early passion, but he was also a pragmatic man who had taken that path many times before, and realized that things could and did go wrong, even with partnerships that appeared to be made in heaven. In him there lurked a caution, borne out of experience, and a reluctance to put all his eggs in one basket, just in case. After all, unlike puppies, which are (so the advertising slogan informs us) for life, and not just for Christmas, women and fast cars were transient things with a sell-by date. To this end, he was not entirely truthful when Brigitte brought up the subject of Florence. When she had asked Charles if David was going to copy any artworks at the apartment, he had told her that this wasn't worth the effort, as the drawings there were mainly by obscure painters, and not of great value. This wasn't strictly true. The Florentine apartment had a drawing by an Italian artist named Sandro Filipepi, which Charles carelessly hadn't bothered to mention to anyone. Filipepi, confusingly, was not known by his real name, but as Botticelli. Quite how Charles had managed to come by this picture, or, for that matter, the Monet, was shrouded in mystery. The drawing was worth a fortune and out of his league, even backed by his wife's money. It was this that Charles particularly wanted copied, so that he could leave his artistically ignorant wife a genuine David Day in its place.

CHAPTER 18

The Disappearing Students

Nicole sat in John Auberton's cramped little office, waiting for him to get off the phone. He kept making silly faces at her and winding gestures with his free hand, as if to speed up the boring old vice-principal on the other end of the line. Eventually he wrapped up the call and placed the receiver back on its cradle.

"Sorry Nicole. God, that man does go on. Now, what can I do for you?"

"I'ave ze bad news," she said, looking up cutely at him from under her fringe. "It's my grond muzzair."

"Your which did what?" asked John, perplexed.

"My grond muzzair. She is all but dead."

"Oh, your grandmother, I'm sorry," he said, trying his hardest to look sombre, which was difficult for a man who had been born with a permanent grin and more teeth than the legal limit.

"I must return to Paris for a while, to comfort air on air dess-bed."

"I see, compassionate leave, kind of thing?" he asked.

186

"Oui. I may be gone for a couple of weeks. Of course, I will do my best to catch up wiz my projects, once I return."

Assuring her that this was okay, John saw her out of the office. He may have even added, "Keep your chin up!"

"If they keep disappearing like this, there won't be any left by Christmas," he thought to himself ruefully, as he continued marking his student's latest projects. When the phone rang once more, he feared it might be the vice-principal again, but a voice at the end of the line announced itself as belonging to Lady Caroline Hickman. She wished to speak to a Dylan Weldon in confidence.

John Auberton was beginning to think that most of his students were in the pay of the aristocracy or the filthy rich, and only attended his humble art college to amuse themselves between commissions. He walked out of his office and called Dylan, who was hard at work in the main studio. As he stepped into the office, John informed him of the caller's name. Dylan picked up the phone.

"To whom am I speaking?" asked Lady Caroline.

"This is Dylan Weldon."

"Are you alone? What I have to say is private," she said. Dylan put his left hand over the mouthpiece, and gestured to John, who was so dumbstruck by the request for him to vacate his own office, that he did.

"Right," she continued. "Firstly young man, I offer my sincere apologies for bursting in on your interview and throwing things around. My behaviour was totally unacceptable, and I apologize."

"No problem whatsoever," replied Dylan graciously. "We all get a bit heated sometimes. I was very impressed with

187

your technique. The way you copped him on the back of the head with that cut glass goblet was superb. He wasn't an easy target. It reminded me of playing Cracky Crabs."

"What on earth, if anything, are you talking about?" asked Her Ladyship.

"You know…. well, I suppose you don't. It's a game you play at seaside amusement arcades. The crab pops up and you whack it with a club, but there are several crabs, popping up at random, and you have to be quick. He was a moving target, because he was trying to duck down behind his desk, but you got him a treat!"

"Thank you. I must have ruined your interview. I'm sorry."

"Well," said Dylan, "I must admit, it went downhill after the bust hit him. He kind of gave up interviewing me, and I still don't know what I was actually being interviewed for."

"Well, his P.A., that French thing, told me that he was trying to find an artist to finish the mural in our swimming pool room. The previous chappie had a nervous breakdown, as I believe a lot of artists do, so he left the job half-done and went to live in Wales."

"God!" exclaimed Dylan. "He must have been seriously depressed if he thought Wales would cheer him up!"

"Exactly!" she replied. "Anyway, I hear that he didn't offer you the job. The French thing explained that you were very talented indeed, but my husband didn't feel that your style would have fitted in with the previous fellow's."

"Ah! We didn't get that far with our interview. He seemed disorientated at that point, and he kept his explanations a little on the brief side."

"I'm sorry. Anyway, I may have a little job you can do for me, by way of making up for your wasted trip, if you're interested."

Dylan replied that he was extremely interested, whereupon she arranged to see him the following evening at a country pub near the castle. He replaced the receiver and informed John Auberton that he could now return to his office, for which Dylan was humbly thanked. The student returned to his duties, whereas the lecturer, who had rather hoped to return to his, was subjected to yet another interruption, in the form of Nigel the Headband.

"Er, John, can I see you for a second, man?" he asked.

With a heavy sigh, John invited him in.

"John, yeah?" he began, " I was wondering if, like, I could take a week off, right, because there's this really heavy festival in Holland, and I really want to go, right, because, like, The Incredible String Band are on, and that's where my head is right now, musically, and I feel it would inspire me to paint. In fact, right, I've got this idea for a concept piece, based on the poetry of..."

"Nigel," interrupted John. "You can go. Go with my blessing. Go to your festival. Produce your concept piece. Smoke as much dope as you like. Just don't come back here afterwards. I may as well tell you now. We had a staff meeting yesterday. You're off the course. Sorry."

CHAPTER 19

A cup of tea and a fake

David's Mini rolled into the castle's car park at nine-thirty a.m. the following Monday morning. The three unoccupied seats were full to overflowing with artist's equipment, his tartan sandwich box and a matching thermos flask. Ruby liked to make sure he was well fed when he was at work, and openly admitted to spoiling both of her sons. David had reached the age of nineteen during his first term at college without ever making so much as a sandwich for himself. He probably didn't understand how to.

Brigitte walked out to his car, helped him in with everything and set him up in his room. She'd laid white sheets over the wooden flooring and set up a trestle table and an old easel near the French windows. She'd also left him a tea caddy, an electric kettle and a tin of biscuits. Thank goodness he'd discovered how to make tea the previous year, when Ruby was forced to bed with a bout of flu.

"There's a country pub just up the lane, if you want a cooked lunch," she suggested. "It's called The Fox Inn. Oh yes, and the toilets are just down the corridor on the left."

David thanked her. She told him where she would be if he needed anything, and wiggled out of the room. He was still sorting out his equipment when he heard a polite knock on his door. Lord Charles Hickman entered, and offered his hand for shaking purposes.

"Morning David. Good to have you here. I'm so pleased that your college saw sense and let you off for a few weeks. You'll probably learn more here than at that mad house, eh?"

David reckoned that His Lordship was about right.

"Now, old son. Here is a key for the room, which must be locked at all times when you aren't in here. I can't stress that enough. No one, not even my wife, must know what you are doing. She and my P.A. think you are here to restore the drawings. I told Lady Caroline that it had to be done every so often, due to their age, and she believed every word. Thank God she didn't see you when you came for the interview with your mate, Mr Weldon. She thought that he was being interviewed about finishing off the swimming pool mural, but she cut it short rather by beaning me with a bust of Mozart. Bit of a tiff; nothing serious. Between you and me, she hasn't a clue about art. If I told her the paintings had to be washed and ironed every week she wouldn't bat an eyelid. I know this seems a bit cloak and dagger, but I have my reasons. She's a bit of a gossip, you see. Within weeks, half of Staffordshire would know they weren't real, including the thieves, and then they'd start looking elsewhere in the house for the pictures, understand?"

"Of course," replied David, "But where am I supposed to be from, if anyone should ask?"

"Well, we'll make something up. How about Novac and Goode Limited, of London - fine art restorers by appointment to the Queen?"

"That sounds posh!" said David, impressed. "I hope I can remember that if I get flustered."

"Don't worry, old son. Just remember, 'I'm David the picture restorer – and I'm Novac and Goode.' Repeat it like a mantra. You'll have it by this afternoon. Now, the French windows overlook the gardens, but hardly anyone comes near this room. You shouldn't be disturbed, but to be on the safe side, throw a cover over the easel each night. We can't be too careful."

He went back to his office and left David to get started. Firstly, David lifted one of the renaissance drawings down from the wall and laid it on the trestle table, where he began to remove the picture tape and nails at the back of the frame. Very carefully, he took out the drawing. It was strange to think that some Italian artist had touched that same paper over five hundred years before him. He felt a shudder of first day nerves surge through his body as he laid it onto a sheet of fresh white paper. Making sure his hands were clean, and more importantly, dry, he overlaid a sheet of tracing paper, which he taped lightly to the edges of the old drawing, and began tracing the image with a technical pen, being careful not to bear down heavily for fear of scoring the image beneath. Once this was done, he lifted off the tracing, and sketched on the back of it with a 2B pencil, until it was liberally covered.

He then screwed up a piece of kitchen roll and rubbed the graphite in a circular motion, until the entire back was covered in a smooth layer and any excess was removed. Now he opened his portfolio and took out a sheet of heavyweight handmade paper, which he laid onto a sheet of polythene on the trestle table. Removing the top from his thermos, he poured a weak solution of tea over the paper and gently coaxed it around the page with a piece of natural sponge, until it was evenly distributed.

He repeated the process with four other sheets of paper, and laid them aside to dry. While he waited, he poured more of the same fluid into a cup, added a drop of milk, and sipped at it. He opened the biscuit barrel and took a chocolate digestive.

"Life doesn't get much better than this!" he said to no one in particular, and strolled over to the window to look at the peacocks. He sprinkled a few crumbled coffee granules over the almost-dry sheets, to simulate the 'foxing' marks which often affect old paper, and because he had always been the impatient type, gave them all the once-over with his portable hair-dryer to speed the process up a bit. He then placed the tracing carefully onto his antiqued paper and began lightly tracing down the image by going over his technical pen lines with a very hard and sharp 9H pencil. A few minutes later, he lifted the tracing paper to reveal an incredibly accurate ghost image of the drawing. He tested a few terracotta pencils on some scrap paper, and chose the one that most closely matched the original. Taking a deep breath and blowing the air out noisily through his mouth, he began.

No one disturbed David throughout the day, which meant that he was able to progress at a remarkable rate. He had always been quick at drawing, because he usually had an image in his mind of exactly what he wanted, and he didn't linger for hours, pondering his next mark, as more cautious artists did. When he copied pictures, he became quicker still, because all the really tough decisions about composition, line and tone had already been resolved by the original artist.

He was drinking his final cup of tea, and gazing critically over his day's work when Lord Hickman tapped the door with his 'signature' knock. David turned the key and let him in, to be confronted by two identical renaissance drawings on easels, side by side.

"Well well well!" he said, rubbing his chin. "It's incredible! *I'd* know the difference, with my trained eye, just about, but she - I mean, most folks - wouldn't have a clue. You are a remarkable young man."

"Thank you very much," said David, blushing.

"Are you going to put that one into the original frame now, and let me have this one for the vault?" asked Lord Hickman, as he picked up his precious drawing.

"If you like," said David, "But I think you'll find that you're actually holding the fake."

CHAPTER 20

First the good news

David had been at the castle all week, and had copied three renaissance drawings, all of which had impressed His Lordship. This gave his employer not only immense satisfaction, but also cause for concern. The pictures were so convincing that he had already mistaken one of them for an original, which might conceivably prove both embarrassing and expensive. He went to David's studio to ask him how this potential problem could be solved.

"Don't get me wrong, it's a jolly nice problem to have, old boy," he smiled, "but it would be nice to have some way of positively identifying the bloody real ones!"

"Don't think I haven't thought of that," replied David, sagely. "I have added a tiny, almost imperceptible mark on everything I've done so that you know it's my handiwork."

He showed Charles a minute dot which featured on all of the pictures at the bottom right corner. No one would give it a second glance if they weren't specifically looking for it.

"Excellent!" said Charles. "Can you make sure you use the same system for everything? You're too damned good, that's your trouble!"

He retired to his study to go over the yearly accounts with Brigitte, and left David to his tasks.

* * * * *

The Stubbles had no gigs planned for the weekend, which was just as well, because Lazlo had injured himself at work, and couldn't play his guitar for a while.

His boss had asked him to shin up a ladder to change a light bulb in the workshop. He had become the victim of a freak accident when his old purple loon pants, the ones he worked in, got wrapped around the step ladder's mechanism, causing him to fall (to use his own delightful expression) 'arse over tit' into the nearby inspection pit. He eventually emerged covered in oil and moaning, like some exotic Egyptian zombie rising from its tomb, with a gash above his right eye and a badly cut hand.

He was currently at Ruby and Len's house, retelling the gory details of his heroic fall for the umpteenth time. By now the story had been embellished considerably, and it was a miracle that he wasn't dead. After all, most people who had fallen thirty feet from a roof and had their fall broken by a Land Rover *en-route* to a bottomless pit had no right to survive. Ruby 'there-there'd' a lot and fed him up with chocolate biscuits, which he held awkwardly in his left hand, and nipped at pathetically. The phone rang, and David answered it. It was Bobby, at the Sound Hole.

"Is that Dave?" he asked sheepishly. "Listen, I've got some good news and some bad news. You know that Gretsch guitar? Well, I managed to rescue it, and it didn't look half bad when I'd finished either."

"Fantastic!" said David. "What's the bad news? The bill?"

"Not exactly. You know young Dave Lowe who works here of a Saturday? He's sold it."

"What?" yelled David, pulling the phone from his ear, and quickly jerking it back into position.

"He thought it was a second-hand one that Jack had bought in, and this chap who came in the shop was dead keen to buy it. He collects 'em, apparently. He asked how much and Dave told him three hundred quid, so he bought it."

"Who is he? What's his name? I've *got* to get it back. George'll kill me."

"Funny you should say that. This bloke's name was George too!" said Bobby.

A few moments later, David returned to the living room, where Lazlo was helping himself to another biscuit.

"I'm in trouble, Laz. George lent me a guitar so I could have a go at mending it. Instead I drowned it and took it to be mended by a shop that has just sold it to George. It could only happen to me."

"What are the ramifications of that?" asked Lazlo, baffled. "I'd need a slide rule to work it out."

"I'm not going to think about it just yet," groaned David.

CHAPTER 21

Froggy went a'courting

It was Monday, which meant it was Monet. The big day had arrived, and David stood in his makeshift studio, teacup in hand, waiting for His Lordship to bring the picture in, so that he could begin work. The hour produced the man, and with him an old gilt frame that he placed carefully onto the easel. Both men stood and stared at it in silence for what must have been a minute. Finally, David spoke.

"It's weird. It's just an old painting. Nothing special really, just a few trees and a cottage with a field in front of it and a woman in a hat. It looks as if it could have been completed in a day, and yet it's worth a fortune. Just being next to it makes me feel strange."

"It makes one wonder doesn't it?" asked Lord Hickman. "Does one feel that something is extra special, just because some expert told us all that it was, or can one sense it for one's self? If I told you that this wasn't a Monet, but one of those old bits of tat from my attic, would you feel more comfortable doing your job?"

"Yes," replied David. "For a start, I'd be handling it a bit more freely. Having to lay tracing paper over this and have it so close to paints and thinners and the like is nerve-wracking. It's the best cure for constipation I can think of!"

"Just be careful. That's all I can ask of you. Allow no one in, and make sure you're not holding your palette knife when you take a close look at it. Now, I'm going to leave you to get started," said his patron. "This is the big one. Take your time and get it spot on, there's a love."

David pondered and fretted. He walked around it, up to it and behind it. He was trying to work out how the picture had been under-painted and what colours and brushes had been used. He had already selected an old Victorian canvas from the castle attic, which was perfect for size. This was a real stroke of luck, because he feared that he might have to get a larger stretcher cut down, which was the devil of a job. His dad had been primed to perform the operation, as it was beyond David's woodworking knowledge. Not only did complex corner joints need to be restructured, they also had to be aged. The discovery of a same-sized canvas was a good omen. It boded well for the rest of the project.

He sanded the old canvas to remove the lumps of paint from the original picture, which was a leaden portrait of a young boy in a sailor suit. As he did so, David felt a tremendous sense of guilt. Some Victorian artist had laboured over the painting, and it was not a nice feeling, having to erase it from the canvas. However, he reasoned that he or she was now just a pile of bones, and as such wouldn't give a toss one way or the other. This cheered him up somewhat.

When all the impasto brush strokes had been levelled, he dusted it off and coated it with white primer twice, to cover all remnants of colour, before staining the stark white area with a thin coat of Burnt Umber to age it.

Next, he traced the basic lines of composition from the Monet itself, breathing heavily as he did so. If he bore down too strongly he would leave lines on the original, which would be disastrous. An hour later it was done, and he applied a layer of graphite to the back, as he had done with the renaissance drawings. The tracing was then transferred to his canvas, which meant all the hard preparatory work was done.

Now all he had to do was paint it.

He squeezed out little dollops of colour in a neat circle around his favourite palette, filled his dippers with linseed oil and distilled turpentine and selected his brush. He was ready, all except for his pre-painting ritual, which he adhered to strictly. He put the kettle on, and made a cup of tea.

Elsewhere in the castle, it was business as usual. Charles was in his study, reading the Tatler. Brigitte was working on the vineyard's accounts, and needed to consult Jean Jacques. She left her office and walked across the yard to the old stable block where her fellow countryman was in his lair, sampling his own product and spitting it into a bin by his desk.

"Ah, bonjour!" he said, in between gargles. "Comment ça va?"

"English please J.J," insisted Brigitte. It appears rude to the English staff. They think we are plotting."

"That's because we are," he said, squirting more of the company's product into the bin. "I can't believe that he's got an artist in. Is this going to wreck our plans?"

"Absolutely not. Why should it? Think about it! We have the real Monet already. What does it matter if he gets his copy copied? It couldn't be better. The best scams of all are when you are conning someone who is far too busy trying to con someone else to even notice. C'est incroyable! This whole thing is such a crazy coincidence. We copy his picture, and then he returns from holiday in Florence having conceived a plan to do exactly the same."

"And what about Florence?" asked J.J. "Has he got anything there that we should know about?"

"According to him, no," said Brigitte. "Just some average drawings by third-division renaissance artists, or so he says. I've sent Nicole to the apartment, just to be sure. According to his diary, there's no one scheduled to be there for a few weeks, so she's given the art college some cock and bull story about her grandmother, and borrowed my keys to the place. If there's anything of interest, she'll copy it, like she did with the Monet."

"Our little girl has a great talent. We should be proud of her." smiled J.J.

"Yes, she's just as ruthless as her dad too," replied Brigitte. "She'll go far. It's a pity that she didn't have time to fake the renaissance stuff that's here, but Charles would know straightaway if it were to go missing now, so we've missed a trick there. At least in Florence, if there is anything, she'll be able to work uninterrupted."

"True. I agree about the renaissance pictures, and there's no way she could work from photographs. It's just not the same, and he'd spot the differences - I'm sure of it. Anyway, let's not get greedy, my dear. One Monet is more than enough to set us up. Herr Grunstrasse is a fanatic. He wants that picture badly, and he'll pay through the nose."

Brigitte helped herself to a glass of red.

"Then, we can disappear in our own sweet time," continued J.J. "The beauty of the scheme is, we don't have to go as soon as the painting is sold. We can bide our time. Charles thinks the picture that he's probably looking at right now is real, which is quite funny, considering he fancies himself as a connoisseur. He came back from a month in Florence, walked into his room to look at it and saw Nicole's masterwork instead. I was hovering in the background, shitting myself with nerves, and all he says is 'Just as beautiful as ever. Daddy's home, my little darling!' It was *so* funny. I'm telling you. My daughter is a genius."

"Yes, funny how she's *your* daughter when she does something good, and mine when she stays out all night with a boy and comes home drunk."

"She follows her mother in that respect. You were always flirty. That's how you landed me," smirked J.J., "and talking of flirting, is it necessary to be quite as intimate with that short-arsed toff? It's getting on my nerves. I'll be glad when we're out of here."

"Listen," said Brigitte angrily, "you were the one who set this scheme up in the first place. It wasn't my idea. You said that I had to use my charm on him, and become intimate. Pretending to be in love with him was the only way that I could be trusted with his secrets. He'd hardly plan to leave his wife and run away with someone who never made love to him would he? I've done no more than I had to, to become his *confidante*. I don't see why you're so jealous. You're not interested in me yourself! You just hate when others become interested in me. I'm like a possession you don't want, but you don't want to give away either. Anyway, relax. It's purely physical. There's nothing for you to worry about."

"Okay, okay! You are right," conceded J.J. "I've neglected you. I'll make it up, when we are living in luxury on the Côte d'Azur."

* * * * *

Dylan sat in the snug, nursing his pint of Guinness. He saw Lady Hickman walking furtively towards him, and he rose to shake her hand. He asked her if she needed a drink, but she politely refused. She had with her a small portfolio that she duly unzipped, once the formalities were concluded. It contained a set of photographs, which he studied intently.

"Mr Weldon," she began, "I must apologize once more for my outrageous behaviour the other day. It was completely out of character. That man has turned me into something I'm not proud of."

Dylan assured her yet again that he fully understood.

"These pictures are of an original Monet, which I own," she continued. "The quality is very good in terms of colour. I've written exact sizes on the back, and I've also included some blow-ups for detail. I hope that's enough for you to go on. I'm a complete ignoramus when it comes to art, so please excuse me, but I would like you, if possible, to copy this picture onto canvas, as accurately as you can. I will pay you five hundred pounds, if you do a good job. I intend to switch your fake for the real thing, as I suspect that Charles will attempt to steal it, once the divorce comes through. He is in debt up to his eyes, in spite of the fact my money that has supported him all these years. It wouldn't surprise me if he pulls a stunt like this on me, so just in case, it's worth five hundred to get my retaliation in first."

Dylan was virtually salivating at the thought of the money. It was more than he'd ever seen.

"Here is a deposit of one hundred, Mr Weldon. You must assure me that what we have discussed will go no further, not even to your closest friends. Do you understand?"

Dylan said that he did. They shook hands once more, and agreed to meet in a week's time, he with the painting, and she with the remainder of the money. Dylan then bade her farewell and stayed at the pub, in order to finish his pint.

"Christ!" he said to no one in particular. "It won't even be *dry* by then."

CHAPTER 22

Jethro

If Lord Hickman had been impressed with David's renaissance work, it was nothing to what he felt now. He grabbed him around the shoulders and shook him up and down. He pinched his cheek in that irritating way that the Italians have made their own. His Lordship had become very tactile that morning, and the reason for all this exuberance was the oil painting in the old gilt frame, hanging on the wall. He looked at it from the other end of the room. He looked right up close, causing David to yelp, "Don't touch, it's wet!"

From wherever he viewed it, it was perfection.

"Bellissimo!" he said, continuing the Italian theme and beaming at David like a deranged Cheshire cat. "Molto bene! Grazie!"

David didn't want to risk spoiling His Lordship's moment of euphoria by being pedantic, but he would have liked to point out that Monet was French.

"Come on then David," said Lord Hickman, finally slipping into his native tongue. "Where's the bit you've added, so that we know this is your copy, and not the original?"

"Ah!" replied David smugly. "Can you see these poppies, just here, in the foreground? The Monet has ten. Mine has eleven."

"No one would ever spot that, but it's good that we are aware of it," said Lord Hickman. "I'd hate to mix them up. Let me get this straight. Monet – ten, Day - eleven."

"Correct," said David. "David Day goes on to meet Da Vinci F.C. in the cup final."

"What are you talking about, boy?" asked Lord Hickman, who wasn't the sharpest palette-knife in the box when it came to jokes. "You are obviously barking mad, as all artists are, but I'm very pleased with your work, nonetheless. Now, here are your air tickets for Monday. Don't lose them. You catch the plane from Birmingham to Pisa, where you can get a train to Florence. The Santa Maria Novello station is two minutes walk from my apartment. Here's a map of the city, and some spending money. You can stay in the master bedroom - there's no one else there. Here's a list of three pictures I want copying, and I've added photostats so there will be no confusion. They're all drawings, so you won't need paints, and to save lugging your equipment to Italy, you can get all you need from the art shop, which is excellent, and just a street away. When you are finished, simply bring the originals back in your portfolio, and keep them with you at all times. Put them in the cabin, not in the hold. Those luggage buggers throw things about. Listen to me David, you're dreaming again. Is everything clear?"

"Absolutely," David assured him. "I can't wait. I've never been on a plane before. I've conned my mate Lazlo into taking me to Brum. He's flown lots of times, so he'll show me where to go and what to do."

It was too late to do any more work, so David treated himself to a walk in the gardens to finish off his Friday afternoon. He came across Jethro, the young gardener, who was lugging a wheelbarrow laden with manure across the lawn. He was around twenty-five years old, with a blond skinhead hairstyle and large sideburns. His real name was James. He just looked like a Jethro, so the other estate workers had re-named him.

Jethro had the demeanour of someone who had never had to worry about thinking too much. His Lordship would say, "Fetch a barrowful of shit," and he fetched a barrowful of shit. His Lordship said, "Go home now, Jethro," and he went home. Each day was the same, and that was how he liked it.

"Afternoon," he said, in his country bumpkin accent. All he needed was a straw in the mouth for the image to be complete. At first, David thought that he was putting it on, but soon realized that the poor sod really did speak like that. He felt tempted to ask him to rush off home, so as not to deprive some village of an idiot. It had long fascinated him that farmers throughout the land always had the same accents and big sideburns. Surely, he reasoned, a Birmingham farmer would have a Birmingham accent, but it was not so. Perhaps they were all bred in some special barn in Somerset and shipped out to their postings afterwards.

The trouble with David was that he had a mind that concerned itself with trivia. He also had a disposition to frivolity, which continued to land him in trouble.

"Afternoon," he replied. "I see you've got a barrowful of shit."

"Ar! His Lordship told me to get it, and put it down by the roses. Who are you then? You that picture cleaner they told me about?"

David said that he was.

"Oi bet you sees the world then, loik His Lordship. He catches a plane loik most folk catches a train."

"Really?" asked David, bored rigid.

"Only, I ain't ever been on a train."

"Have you not?" asked David, trying his damnedest not to smirk.

"No. I went to Evesham once. My uncle Les took me in his car, but we didn't go on the motorway. Oi've never been on the motorway."

"Goodness," said David. "Is that the time? My dinner will be ready!"

"His Lordship can fly a plane. He's got one down the road, at Twopenny Green. He asked me if oi wanted to go up in it, but oi told him no."

"You should give it a try, you might just like it!" said David, with the smug superiority of one who was embarking on his own maiden flight the following Monday. "Anyway, I must go now, I have to get back to the twentieth century."

* * * * *

It was a typical autumn late afternoon. An inky black curtain was enveloping the cobalt blue sky and there was a chill in the air, as David crunched his way back across the courtyard to his car. The natural light was fading fast, so he wasn't able to continue working, and besides, when one had just knocked off a quick Monet, he reasoned, one didn't feel inclined to begin a new painting on the same day.

He felt sure that Monet must have felt the same way.

He turned to take his last look at the castle for a week or so. The whole thing had been such an adventure, with the best was surely still to come. An unashamed sentimentalist, he began to think over what had happened to him since he had left school. It felt as if he'd crammed ten years of living into a few months. As he opened the car door, he began laughing out loud, as he recalled the Youth Hostel, Hank Frill, the exploding Mini, his band's first gig and now the castle adventure. David wondered what Dennis was doing, and vowed to ring him on his return. He turned the ignition key and rolled off the gravel drive and into the night. Stiff-necked and tired from a hard day's work, he planned to take a long, hot bath and listen to his favourite band, Free's 'Fire and Water' album on his brand new stereo.

David had borrowed the money from his dad, Len, on the strength of his recent commissions, so that he could at long last hear his vast and comprehensive collection of three L.Ps. After his bath he vowed to phone Laz, and ask how his cuts and bruises were doing. He also had to grasp the nettle and make a rather more difficult call to George, but after further thought, he decided to postpone that one till he got back from Italy.

David was beginning to feel excitement and apprehension in equal measures about his trip on Monday. He had always wanted to go to Italy, but the thought of flying terrified him. There he was, looking down on poor old Jethro the gardener, when he was hardly the world traveller and

209

sophisticate himself. Most family holidays were taken in Tenbury Wells in an old caravan owned by his grandmother. His parents never had enough money to go abroad when he was a child, even if they had the inclination, and Granny Bertha still hadn't ever been to the seaside. She'd never used a phone, and didn't have a fridge. Italy would have seemed like a foreign country to her. Now here was her grandson, off on his first adventure abroad, and not having a clue what to expect. He had no grasp of the language whatsoever, and his only brush with the native food was when Ruby did him spaghetti hoops on toast. He thought about his new college friends, wondering what they'd be doing while he was away. Could Katie cope without him? Might she fall into Alf's evil clutches? Would Dylan have enough competition to stimulate him without his archrival?

He pondered Katie's pert breasts beneath her black top, bouncing around unhampered by brassieres. Italy was reportedly crawling with such women, with bags of style and sunglasses on the tops of their heads. Perhaps one of them would take a shine to him in some café or Ristorante, become fascinated by his cute English accent, and accept his invitation to go back to the apartment to see his renaissance drawings. He'd pour her a glass of Chianti and seduce her, to the tune of plaintive mandolins coming from the cobbled street below. Yes, he was getting very enthused now, and though it was wishing his life away, he couldn't wait until Monday morning.

CHAPTER 23

Leaving on a Jet plane

It was Monday morning, and not a moment too soon. David's small black case was packed, and his passport, wallet and portfolio were propped up against it, near the front door. Ruby had made him some cheese sandwiches for the journey, and Len, who had left much earlier to go to work, had left him a note on the breakfast bar to wish him good luck.

The doorbell rang, and David opened the door to greet Lazlo. Normally he would have been at work himself, but his boss had given him a week off on full pay, which seemed cheaper than a law suit for sending an employee up a wonky step ladder next to an inspection pit. They said goodbye to Ruby, and walked down the front steps to Lazlo's Cortina. She called after them, "Drive carefully!" in the vain hope that it might make a difference.

"Oh, right ho, Rube!" shouted Lazlo. "I was going to drive like a complete nutter and get us both killed until you reminded me."

"You're catching that sarcasm from David," she shouted back. "I bet you won't be sarcastic next time you want a chocolate digestive and a cup of tea, you cheeky bugger!"

The car flew off with its wheels screaming for a few yards, before settling down to a more sedate pace. Lazlo waved at Ruby and laughed. He could see her through his rear view mirror, smiling and shaking her fist. David was precious cargo, and the plane trip was worrying her already. She didn't need Lazlo's driving to worry about too.

She needn't have worried; he drove at what, by his standards, was a reasonable speed all the way to the airport, parked up, and showed David where to go and what to do. The two friends shook hands, and David promised to ring, if he could fathom out how Italian phones worked and which coins to insert. David turned to walk away and, remembering something, called back to Lazlo.

"Oh, can I be really cheeky? If you're heading through Wolverhampton, could you drop something off at my college? There's a girl on my course called Katie Black. I borrowed her small easel to use at the castle. Could you return it for me? I'll get you a stick of rock from Italy. She needs it for the next project and I forgot to return it on Friday. It's at Rube's. You can pop in for a cup of tea and thirty-five biscuits!"

Lazlo asked David what his last slave had died of, and assured him that he'd do it that afternoon. He was bored with being at home, and it would give him something to do.

Thanking him profusely, David disappeared through security.

CHAPTER 24

Pooh Sticks at the Ponte Vecchio

Santa Maria Novello train station was like all train stations - noisy, chaotic and bustling. Outside it was pouring with rain, and inside, a thousand Italians were smoking, arguing, kissing, chatting and waving their arms around like crazy. David had never seen so many gestures. He had once heard a joke about two burglars who were robbing an Italian man at his house.

"Tie his arms together," said one of them, "To stop him talking."

Only now did he realize how funny that was. He sat down on a bench for a few minutes to rest. It had been a long day. His first aeroplane trip had been wonderful, and after the take off, which made his palms sweat and inspired him to have a few quiet words with his maker, he settled into it very nicely. For most of the trip, he just sat in awe, looking out at the world above the clouds, and sipping on a nerve-restoring gin and tonic. The stewardess handed him his lunch, which was comprised of a lump of chicken with some mysterious red slop on top of it, a bun, a slice of weird-tasting angel cake and a cup of coffee. He rounded this feast off with a small bottle of Chianti, followed by another one.

Visibly mellowed, he continued to gaze on God's creation, whilst refreshing his sweating face and neck with his complimentary wipe. He wished someone had had the presence of mind to warn him about turbulence. He was roused from his meditations by a brief period of bumpy air that frightened the life out of him, but after a kindly stewardess assured him that this was common he withdrew his request for a commode seat.

The train ride was less fun, as he had no reserved place, which meant he was forced to sit on his luggage next to the foul-smelling toilet for an hour, in a carriage rammed full of people. As he was the only one in the toilet area lucky enough to be seated, his field of vision was largely restricted to crotches and fat stomachs. Whenever the train lurched to a halt, the huge man in front of him would fall forward, knocking David's head into the toilet door. He wasn't sure what part of the fat man was pulverising his head, but he hoped and prayed that it was just his stomach. Each time the man would say *"Scusi Senor!"* By the time they pulled into Florence, David was delirious.

Now all he wanted to do was walk to the apartment and rest. The red wine had taken its toll, and he was wishing that he'd listened to his dad's advice about drinking during the daytime. He walked out of the station into torrential rain and cursed himself for not bringing an umbrella. Lugging his heavy case with one hand, and carrying the portfolio with the other, he struggled across the shining cobble-stoned street in the direction of Via della Scala.

He consulted his map, but within seconds he and it were sodden with rain, not for the first time in his life. Luckily he was standing at the entrance of the very street he was looking for - Via de'Canacci.

Just to his left he could see the small art shop that Lord Hickman had mentioned. He decided to purchase his materials there and then to get it over with, so that he could relax, take a hot shower and have everything ready to begin work the next day. He walked in, and was greeted by a friendly gentleman in a bow-tie, with hair like a mad scientist's. He didn't speak a word of English, so David endeavoured to explain what he was after by speaking loudly in English with a strange Italian accent, and miming like Marcel Marceau.

Eventually, after the proprietor had put back the multitude of items that he wrongly presumed his wet young customer wanted, and had laid the correct ones on the counter, David thanked him with his best Spanish 'Gracias' and shelled out the necessary funds. He put his wallet back into his trouser pocket and loaded the various papers and pencils into his portfolio along with his passport and travel tickets to save them from getting wet. He staggered back out into the torrential downpour and squelched the hundred yards or so to his new front door.

From the outside, it didn't look much. He had imagined something far more palatial, but this was an old brown door set into a crumbling mustard-coloured wall, in a fairly dingy side street. Up above him he could see a small balcony with potted geraniums and a small breakfast table. If the rain ever stopped it would be nice to sit there and eat croissants, watching the world go by.

In spite of the rain, the temperature felt warm, which was surprising, given that winter was fast approaching. He pulled his wallet out of his trousers once more and found the small gold key, inserted it in the lock, and breathed a sigh of relief when the door opened.

Inside was no better. It was pitch black, but Lord Hickman had told him about the light switch just to the right of the door, which he duly located, thus illuminating the hallway with what looked like a twenty-watt bulb. In front of him were two storeys of old stone steps with a metal balustrade, and by the time he reached the inner door at the top, he was exhausted. He turned the key in its lock, pushed open the door and again clicked on the lights. This time the effect was rather more pleasing.

He had heard that Italian houses could look very ordinary from the outside whilst they were often beautiful within, and this one didn't disappoint. The switch activated a splendid chandelier, which lit up a hallway lined with expensive old furniture and oil paintings. There was a dark oak floor, strewn with Persian rugs, and a *Chaise Longue* upholstered in lemon yellow and white. He opened the door immediately in front of him. It led into a lovely large sitting room with two old leather chesterfields facing each other, and separated by a low antique table. All round the mustard-coloured walls were old paintings and drawings with individual brass picture lights. Sideboards heavily decorated with marquetry lined the room, displaying what seemed like hundreds of antique silver frames, teapots and jugs. A giant renaissance painting hung on the far wall, virtually filling it, and heavy floor to ceiling drapes added the finishing touch. He recognized the curtain material from Stanmore Castle's drawing room.

The room next door was a small but luxuriously appointed kitchen, with old panelled doors at one end. David presumed that these were the ones that led to the small balcony that he'd seen from the street.

Setting his sodden belongings down, he located the two bedrooms. The larger of the two was decorated in a rich red colour with an antique brass bed and the usual array of opulent fixtures and fittings, while the other, smaller one had a single bed, and was decorated in a tasteful turquoise. The bathroom, which was off the master bedroom, was again small, but to the usual high standard.

David was beginning to feel very uncomfortable in his wet clothes, so he took them off and looked for a suitable place to dry them. Dressed only in his Y fronts, he wandered into the kitchen and opened the panelled doors. His initial guess had been correct - they led to the balcony. He poked his head outside, and was pleased to see that the rain had stopped and a warm air was blowing through the alleyway.

The night air now felt almost tropical. He walked back inside, grabbed his clothes and arranged them neatly on the balustrade in the hope that they would dry out a little. Meanwhile, he found the all-important kettle, and began to make a pot of tea, helping himself to Lord Hickman's best Earl Grey, even though, as a good Black Country lad, he couldn't usually stick the stuff at any price. Beggars, after all, couldn't be choosers. It would suffice.

There was a small cooker, which gave him an idea. He lit the oven section with a match, and set the temperature on low. Rather than let his sodden clothing air outside, he would put everything in the cooker for a few minutes. Meanwhile, he could then open his luggage and find a clean shirt and another pair of jeans to wear after his shower. With this plan in mind, he returned to the balcony.

His clothing, which he had left hanging over the balcony rail, had vanished.

For a second, David couldn't work out what had happened. Were there two balconies, he wondered, and had he just walked onto the wrong one? Had a notorious cat burglar climbed up the sheer wall from below just to steal his wet shirt? By now, panic had set in, and his head was reeling. He looked down into the street below, but they were not there. At this point his panic level rose by around five hundred percent.

His wallet, with all his Italian money inside, was in the back pocket of his jeans. For a bleak moment, he presumed that the passport and air tickets were with it, but by way of scant consolation, he remembered putting them in his portfolio. David's first instinct was to go downstairs straightaway, on the premise that the clothes had blown off the balcony in the wind. Maybe someone had picked them up and handed them in to the restaurant next door, or perhaps they were still in the gutter below, hidden from view by the shadows. He dashed back into the sitting room and found his luggage, and as he bent down to open the suitcase, a thought hit him like a blackjack to the back of his head.

The keys to his case were in his wallet.

He tried the catches in the vain hope that he'd left them unlocked, but they were secure. After a mouthful of heartfelt expletives, he dashed back to the kitchen and began ransacking the drawers. He found a large screwdriver and a carving knife, with which he attacked the case. First the locks, which politely refused to budge, and then the canvas sides, which were less stubborn in their devotion to duty. Having destroyed Ruby's best travel case, he peeled open the gaping flap he had created. What met his eyes caused him to emit a deranged scream.

Delving into the ruined case, he pulled out a bra.

David looked at the bra with a crazed expression for a few seconds, as if he was desperately willing it not to be a bra, but a bra it was. He dipped his hand once more into the bag, and pulled out a dress - size twelve, summery and floral. He dived back into the bag in a frenzy now, tearing out panties, stockings and high heels, still hoping against hope that somehow, somewhere his clothes would also be in there.

They weren't.

Then he noticed the small tag with the maker's name, welded onto the side panel of the case. It said 'Reindeer Bags.' David knew beyond a shadow of a doubt that his mother's had said 'O'Dell and Co.' It was one of those stupid things he always remembered, because he had a school friend called Rob O'Dell.

A thought was slowly percolating through his razor-sharp mind, like the espresso in the restaurant next door.

He'd picked up the wrong case at Pisa airport.

Letting out a few more choice Anglo Saxon oaths, he ran into the bedroom to see if Lord Hickman had left any clothes in the wardrobes. He might have done, or he might not have done. They were locked.

"What kind of cretin locks wardrobes?" he screamed aloud in desperation. He looked through the drawers and in every possible place he could think of, but there were no keys. When one's suits cost more than David could earn in a year, one felt justified in locking them away.

Releasing a strangled 'Gnah!' from somewhere deep in his bowels, David returned to the case. Maybe the lady owner had left a phone number or a name in the case, so that he could get in touch. There was nothing. Somewhere in Florence, a lady would be sitting in her hotel room, contemplating having to go to dinner in a cheesecloth shirt and loon pants.

He shot downstairs in his soaking wet Y Fronts and poked his head round the front door. His clothing had quite simply disappeared. There was no way he could stroll into a Pizzeria semi-naked and ask the waiter if anyone had handed in his garments. For a start, if the art shop were anything to go by, the man wouldn't have a clue what he was on about. They'd probably call the Carabinieri.

It was hopeless. He resigned himself to the fact that he could go nowhere that evening. He would have to take a shower and go to bed. With a lot of luck, the next day, with the benefit of better lighting, he should be able to locate the wardrobe keys, or if not, hack at the wardrobe doors with his carving knife and screwdriver. He walked into the shower room with the weight of the world on his shoulders, and pulled the cubicle door shut behind him. The hot shower felt good after the miserable rain, and it helped him to marshal his thoughts. He could perhaps ring the castle and explain his predicament. Lord Hickman probably had a secret stash of money somewhere for emergencies, or he maybe had a friend nearby who could lend him some. Just as David was adopting a more optimistic approach, he heard the phone ring in the sitting room. He grabbed the towel hanging inside the cubicle on a peg, and wiped the soap from his eyes. Leaping from the shower like a startled gazelle, he threw down the towel and ran naked to the phone.

It was Ruby, Len and Paul, asking how his first aeroplane trip had been. It was lovely to hear voices from home, but he spared them the details of the disastrous situation he found himself in. He sat on the chesterfield chatting to them for around twenty minutes, trying to act as nonchalantly as he could. He was glad he'd had the presence of mind to give them the apartment number in case of problems, but given that there was no way that they could help him with his money or clothing, he couldn't see the point of worrying them. Assuring them that everything was okay, he asked them to ring him the next morning to let him have the castle's telephone number. He then had to listen to Paul playing 'Frère Jacques' on the recorder through his nose, until Len butted in to remind everyone that he was paying for the call. David was just wrapping things up, saying lengthy goodbyes to each in turn, when he glanced down at his bare feet, and realized that they were swimming around in half an inch of water.

"Gotta go!" he yelled, and shot up like a rocketing pheasant from the settee. A huge pool of water was surging ever onward through the beautiful sitting room. Presumably emanating from the shower, it seemed intent on taking over the entire apartment. David ran back into the steaming bathroom, and saw, to his absolute horror, what had caused the flood. In his haste to get to the phone, he had dropped the towel onto the shower floor and blocked the plughole, causing the water to rise to the rim of the cubicle and cascade over, making its way quickly across the ceramic tiles and into the sitting room. He turned off the shower and surveyed the damage. Everywhere was well and truly soaked.

He got down onto the floor and grabbed a large towel, which he dropped into the lake of water. When it was saturated, he got up and squeezed it as dry as he could into the sink. By repeating this laborious method for the next three hours, he dried out the apartment, hoping to God that not too much had seeped through the oak flooring and through the roof of the flat below.

An Italian mosquito on the wall would have seen him gently sobbing to himself as he did so, until, exhausted beyond belief, he sank, still naked, into a chair and dozed off, hungry, cold and aching from head to foot. An hour or so later, he woke with a start. It was late, and he needed to get to bed. He located some weird Italian-style cornflakes in the kitchen cupboard, but couldn't find any milk. He ate as many as he could face, to stave off the hunger pangs, and feeling very sorry for himself, shuffled back into the steamy, damp bathroom to clean his teeth.

Some form of central heating had automatically come on, which was helping to dry the rooms a little, but the Persian rugs were still sodden. He was in the final throes of his rigorous dental hygiene routine, a chore made more than usually difficult by the masses of stubborn dried cornflake residue, when he heard a noise in the hall.

Fearing that the burglars who had stolen his trousers were back for more, he ran through into the sitting room and grabbed the knife and screwdriver that he'd left on the floor *en-route*. Heart pounding, he yanked open the hall door to confront his assailants, and came face to face with a young woman who leapt about ten feet in the air as he burst out at her.

"What is it about you that you always have to run round naked and frothing?" asked Nicole angrily.

"What the bloody hell are *you* doing here?" he asked, grabbing a miniature silver picture frame from the sideboard to cover himself up.

"What ze bloody 'ell am I doing here? Ze question is what ze bloody 'ell are *you* doing 'ere? I sink you would be better off in an asylum. And put zose weapons down. You are making me nervous, you madman!"

"Listen!" said David indignantly. "I am here by request of Lord Hickman, who owns the place, as it happens. I'm borrowing the apartment so that I can study the renaissance painters."

"Well so was I. My mozzair is his personal assistant, and she told me that no one was using the place, so I took advantage of it. I've been 'ere a week already. I go home tomorrow afternoon."

"Well well well!" he replied, sounding a little like his bus driver friend. "Look, can I get a bath towel?"

He ran off to the bathroom, giving her an excellent view of his bottom in motion. He came back a few seconds later, suitably wrapped, and asked her if she cared to come in.

"Zis floor is wet," she observed. "What 'ave you been doing, madman?"

"Listen, I am *not* a madman. It's just that you always seem to catch me in, well, untypical situations," he argued.

She sat down on one of the chesterfields.

"Untypical you say? I'm from Paris, so forgive my grasp of your language. I know sometimes I struggle, but I thought that meant *not* typical. Every time I see you something is going crazy wiz you. Every time! You 'ave been naked and frothy twice, and your car was exploded to pieces. That's three crazy incidents out of three meetings. I'd call zat typical. Wouldn't you?"

David tried to change the subject.

"Look, Nicole. Have you got any money you could lend me? I've been robbed. All my clothes are gone, and my wallet too."

"Ha!" she cried triumphantly. "Four out of bloody four!"

She told him that she had just enough for lunch and her taxi to the airport, and couldn't help him. He doubted that she would have put herself out even had she had sackfuls of the stuff. Ringing Lord Hickman the next day was still his best bet. He mentioned his plan to Nicole, whereupon her face registered concern.

"Look!" she said. "I would appreciate it if you didn't mention that I was 'ere. My mozzair let me 'ave the keys, but she didn't exactly tell 'im. It might cause an argument, and I would 'ate for 'er to lose 'er job. Do you understand?"

David assured her that it would go no further. Nicole relaxed visibly, and asked him how he knew Lord Hickman, adding something about it being a small world. He told her that he had been interviewed about finishing the swimming pool mural, and the man had taken a shine to him. He hadn't actually landed the swimming pool job, but they'd kept in touch. Nicole smiled the smile of a girl that recognized a load of lies when she heard them.

You must excuse me," she yawned, "I 'ave to go to bed now. Which room are you sleeping in?"

"Yours?" he asked hopefully.

"You must be joking," she replied frostily. "I'll let you take ze master room and I'll take ze small single, being as it's your turn to stay 'ere."

"Very decent of you," he replied, and shuffled off to bed, wondering how to take his mind off the gorgeous naked French girl who would be sleeping next door to him in his own private luxury apartment.

* * * * *

Meanwhile, seated on a riverside wall next to the Ponte Vecchio, two young ragamuffins of around eleven years of age were sharing out the *lire* from the wallet that had fallen from above. The taller of the two was convinced that God had answered his prayers. Only a minute before, he had asked God for enough money to buy a bike, because his mother was so poor that she couldn't afford one. The smaller boy said that he had also prayed to God that Sunday for a guinea pig. As they walked through Via de' Canacci, a shirt and a pair of jeans had landed on their heads, with exactly the right amount of cash within to get what they had asked for.

"It is a miracle," said the taller boy.

"But why did God send us a big shirt and a pair of old trousers?" asked the little one.

"I don't know. Father Vincento said that God moved in mysterious ways, and we could never understand everything that he did. They are no good to us though, Marco, and my older brother wouldn't wear such rubbish. Why don't we offer them to the River Arno in thanks?"

He threw them into the water, and they both ran to the other side of the Ponte Vecchio to see which item came out first. It was touching to see that, whilst the Italian and English cultures were quite different in many respects, the universal language of 'Pooh sticks' was understood by all.

CHAPTER 25

Life's a drag sometimes

David slept but fitfully that night. He dreamt that an irate and dripping wet Italian had come upstairs from the flat below, and attacked him with a screwdriver. He also dreamt about Nicole. He had been in what is best referred to as an intimate situation with her, but whenever he had tried to progress the union, strange things kept happening to thwart him. As a result of this, he had awoken at seven-thirty with a thin white sheet over him that had taken on the appearance of a small tent. He rose to take a cold shower, in the hope of subduing his passion a little, wary of bumping into the object of his desires. He couldn't risk her seeing him doing anything strange ever again. A girl could maybe forgive two bouts of naked frothing, but not three.

Draped in his bath towel, he gingerly explored the sitting room and bathroom, but she wasn't there. He tapped on her bedroom door, and receiving no answer, he gently pushed the door open, only to be met by an empty bed. She had gone. There was a note on the kitchen work surface by the kettle, saying that she'd got up early to do some last minute sightseeing, and would go straight to the airport from there. She had signed it, and added a postscript, which read;

See you back at college, Madman.

What's next? I can't wait.

He took a shower and put on his old pair of Y Fronts, which frankly needed to be rested in favour of a fresh pair, but he currently had no such luxury. He phoned his parents, who gave him the castle's number, but Lord Hickman was away on business, and he didn't want to discuss anything with Brigitte.

Then an idea floated into his head. It was bizarre, but feasible. He dismissed it after a few moments consideration, but then, unable to find a viable alternative, he allowed it to float back, albeit with extreme reluctance. David wandered into the sitting room to examine the battered suitcase. He removed all of the items inside it and laid them out neatly on the floor. There were a couple of dresses, stockings, suspender belt, two pairs of shoes, (one comfortable and one high-heeled) and a bra. A leather bag contained lipsticks, foundation, mascara and eye makeup, and, glory be, a Ladyshave. Grabbing the garments that he thought would go well together, and it has to be said, which he thought would suit him, he proceeded to the bathroom. He was more than a little worried that he was finding it all very exciting, but he kept trying to convince himself that it was a case of needs must, rather than a hitherto unacknowledged tendency to deviance.

He thought about Lazlo, wondering how he'd have approached things. For a start, he'd probably have loved it, plus he had the added advantage of having nicely shaped hairless legs, whereas David's were stick-thin and hirsute, like a spider's. He shut the bathroom door behind him, and set to work.

An hour later, a vision emerged from the steaming bathroom. Six foot tall and willowy, she wore a floral patterned knee-length dress and a pearl necklace. Her long brown shoulder-length hair had been curled, Lauren Bacall-style, with the help of the heated rollers from the suitcase. Smoothly shaved and immaculately made-up, she clattered on high heels across the wooden floor to the kitchen, her ample breasts, augmented by two full packs of cotton wool and a few pairs of spare stockings, standing proud beneath her thankfully high-necked dress. Her long, slender hairless legs looked beautiful inside the sheer tights. It took her forever to unblock the sink afterwards, but the effect was well worth it.

Davinia lingered when she reached the mirror. She liked what she saw.

Her alter-ego, David, had heard that there was a square in the centre of Florence, by the Duomo, where artists drew caricatures of the tourists, thereby reputedly earning good, tax-free money. He was a keen caricaturist, and this was the only solution he could come up with to earn enough money to clothe and feed himself, other than stealing, which in his mind was not an option. Sitting in a crowded square in a foreign city was daunting enough, but he had enough youthful arrogance, cheek and talent to carry it off.

That said, having to do so in drag was, for him, a step too far. He shuddered at the prospect, but his rumbling stomach kept reminding him that he had little alternative. He filled his portfolio with pens, coloured pencils and the A3 cartridge pad he had purchased for practising his pencil techniques on, prior to doing his finished renaissance drawings on the tea stained paper.

This last-minute purchase had proved to be the most useful of all. It contained fifty sheets of paper, and at two pounds per drawing, minus a few false starts, he estimated that a busy day in the square could net him around eighty pounds, which would easily feed and clothe him. It was important that his caricaturing activity should only last a day, or maybe two at most. Otherwise, he would have little or no time to draw Lord Hickman's pictures. He grabbed his handbag, checked his make-up one more time in the mirror, and clattered out of the door. Ten seconds later, he was back, and changing into his comfy shoes, thanking the Lord above that their previous owner had large feet for a woman. He was about to go through hell and total humiliation before the day was over. He didn't need blisters as well.

David swaggered down Via Panzani with what he fondly imagined was a catwalk model's style, trying not to look anyone in the eye. In spite of it being a dull day, he wore a pair of Raybans, courtesy of his anonymous donor, which helped greatly in his attempt to block out the world. His progress was largely unnoticed, with the exception of a podgy man in a pink shirt who offered to do something indecent to him and was willing to pay good money. Had David understood a word he was saying, business might well have resulted. He was that hungry.

As he arrived in the Piazza Duomo, he could tell straightaway that he had not been lied to. Already there were several artists in a line along the pavement, and most of them had customers. It was then that he realized that he had a slight technical problem. The other artists had two fold-up chairs, one for themselves and one for the sitter, whereas he had none. Glancing around, he saw a café that had outdoor seating, and sidled over to it. To purloin two chairs was, for him, the work of an instant.

He quickly tottered over to the line of artists and set himself up on the end. The man immediately to his left stared at him in a strange way, but carried on drawing. It was then that David realized that he'd forgotten another aspect of the caricaturist's essential paraphernalia, the sample picture.

This was usually pinned up at the artist's pitch, so that punters could assess which artist's style they most favoured before committing themselves. Usually, the drawing was of a far higher quality than the mediocre scribble offered on the day, but by that time the deal was done, money had changed hands and it was too late. To get the ball rolling, he would have to offer his first picture for free. A German tourist and his wife were passing, and paused to look at the Duomo by where David had set up shop. Desperately trying to remember his O Level German, he introduced himself.

"Guten Tag!" he began, in a strangulated voice, remembering just in time to adopt a female register. The German said "Guten Tag" back, and then did a double-take that Stan Laurel would have been proud of.

"Möchten Sie ein Karicature?" he continued, flitting from octave to octave like a thirteen-year-old whose voice was about to break. "Es ist kostenlos fur Sie! Mein Special Offer von der Tag."

"Nein, danke," said the German, beginning to walk away, and who, in fairness, could blame him?

"Ja Ja Ja! Ich *liebe* Karicaturen!" insisted his wife, who shoved him forcibly into the seat. After around five minutes of protestation, he finally gave in to her demands, and asked what he had to do, all the time staring at David suspiciously.

"Setzen Sie still," David ordered, "fur funf minuten, bitte."

He began drawing, a little nervously at first, but soon finding his rhythm. The *Hausfrau* stood behind him, and began to laugh. Ordinarily this would not be a good sign, but as the drawing was a caricature it was excusable. Five minutes later, the drawing was completed, and David handed it over. The German seemed genuinely thrilled with the results, especially as the artist had gone very easy on his huge double chin. He began pushing his wife into the chair. She protested a little too much, as is the female way, but eventually sat down.

"You don't vant to draw *me*," she said, presuming correctly that David was English. "I'm not pretty enough."

He smiled, ignoring the bait completely, and assured her that he very much wanted to draw her. He needed the bloody money. His second picture mercifully received an equally enthusiastic reaction, and the German reached into his wallet for the reward. Despite David's rather weak protestations that the first drawing was free, he paid for two, and even let David keep the change. By his calculations, it amounted to around a fiver in sterling. Not bad for ten minute's work. The German leaned over to whisper in David's ear.

"I don't know wezzer to kiss you or shake hants. Aufwiedersehen!"

The artist next to David seemed a little miffed by this newcomer of dubious sexual origin mopping up the new customers, but the arrival of a family of six restored his spirits. Meanwhile, a group of Japanese tourists who had been observing as David drew the Germans, plucked up the courage and walked over to him. In broken English they asked if he could draw all of them.

An hour later and with twenty-five pounds now nestling nicely in his handbag, he was motoring. Quite soon friends were telling other friends, and he had an impressive queue forming. One unkind Englishman asked his wife rather too loudly if she wanted her 'photo' drawn by Danny la Rue, so David invited the pair of them over and gave him a huge nose, by way of revenge.

By lunch, he had amassed the grand total of fifty pounds. Not bad for a transvestite caricaturist in a strange city. His hunger pains were now so powerful that he had to stop. He scribbled a quick notice which he folded over his stolen chair.

Mangiare. Essen. Déjeuner. Dinner.

Back at 1.30.

His Grammar school education hadn't been entirely wasted. Gathering up his portfolio, he wandered over to the café whose chairs he had borrowed and ordered a falsetto ham and cheese panini. The waiter gave him a quizzical look, and David suddenly became acutely aware that he was dressed as a female. He'd been so busy that he'd momentarily forgotten. He blushed bright red, covered his eyes once more with the Ray-Bans and stared at a fixed spot across the street. He vowed to stick it out for the rest of the afternoon, and that evening go shopping for cheap clothing in the nearby street market.

To add to his woes, he was suddenly also aware of the call of nature. Indeed, it was calling rather urgently through several impenetrable layers of alien female undergarments.

He dashed through the busy café and followed the toilet signs, until he was finally locked in a very small and claustrophobic tiled cubby hole that just about had room for a smelly, hole-in-the-ground lavatory and a minute washbasin with a cracked mirror on top. He fumbled desperately with what seemed like twenty-six layers of elasticated nylon until he located what he was searching for, and with no time at all to spare, he sent gallons of urine cascading into the pit, groaning in ecstasy as he did so.

Feeling much better now, he paused to study his reflection in the mirror. No oil painting when he had left the apartment, his visage now was quite hideous. His eye make-up was smudged and his lipstick looked as if it had been applied by an inebriated chimpanzee.

David reached into his handbag and took out his lipstick. He desperately needed to freshen up his appearance. There were hideous mascara smudges down his cheeks and a five o'clock shadow was beginning to show through his foundation. He took a good long look at himself, and wondered how on earth he'd ended up this way. Less than a year ago, he'd been a perfectly normal grammar school boy, and now here he was, not only a forger of Monets and Botticellis, but also a woman.

"Ah well," he smiled, "something to tell the grandkids!"

He opened the toilet door and walked back through the café. A little Italian boy pointed at him and said something in Italian to his father. The meaning was lost on David, but it was probably something along the lines of, "Look Papa! That lady has just been for a pee in the men's toilets!"

After his lunch break he returned to his pitch, and had the difficult task of drumming up new business to worry about, now that his captive audience had dissipated. Just as he was thinking of reintroducing his 'free cartoon' ploy, an English lady sat down and asked him to draw her.

He began to mark out her face in coloured pencil, half hiding behind his tatty old portfolio, which doubled as a drawing board.

"I have a dress just like that," she said.

"Oh really?" squeaked David.

"In fact, I also have a pair of shoes just like yours too. Or at least I did. My bag got mixed up with someone else's at the airport in Pisa, and I ended up with a bloke's luggage. There was no address inside, so I couldn't contact him. I've lost the bloody lot. I've had to go shopping over here and get a whole new set of outfits."

"You're not going to believe this."

The manly voice emanating from behind the makeshift drawing board gave the lady quite a start.

"Of all the caricature joints in all the world, you have to walk into mine."

"You're a man!" said the lady, beginning to get out of her seat.

"No, no, sit down. I can explain," urged David. "This is the most incredible coincidence, you see. I was the one whose luggage you took off with. These *are* your clothes. I didn't have any money, and this was all I had to wear. I'm drawing cartoons to try and earn a few quid to buy new clothing."

"I took off with *your* stuff? That's rich! It was you that took off with mine."

234

"Well, whatever," conceded David. "At least we're here now, and we can sort it out. That's fantastic!"

The lady just goggled at him with her mouth open, and suddenly began to laugh out loud.

"I'm afraid I had to butcher your case a bit to get the stuff out. I was desperate," he said, trying to shush her laughter by holding his finger to his lips.

"Ditto!" she grinned. "Never mind eh? We can claim on the insurance. The main thing is that our stuff is safe. I'm sorry, can I turn away? Whenever I look at you I start to laugh."

"Yeah yeah!" he said, flushing scarlet. "Listen, it's been bloody hell for me, I can tell you. I feel like one of those men trapped in a woman's body that you see in documentaries."

The lady began snorting with laughter once more. "It's not that you don't make a rather attractive lady," she said. "From a distance you'd pass for the real thing. It's just that you haven't shaved since breakfast, and the stubble is coming through your foundation. It looks bloody awful, and your hair's gone all limp and sweaty."

David asked her if he could pop round to her hotel as soon as possible and swap bags. He desperately needed to get out of her clothing, as it was now getting past a joke. She gave him a card, telling him she was staying at the Hotel Gioconda in Via Panzani, just down the road. She was called Lisa Robinson, and she worked as a representative for an Italian clothing company. She had a few calls to make in the city, and would be there around five, in room number fifty. He thanked her profusely, and asked if she still wanted her caricature drawn. She laughed, and said that he could do it some other time, as she really couldn't sit and face him for ten minutes without cracking up. She stood up and walked away, still giggling, whereupon the next victim in the queue darted into the empty seat and asked how much.

Quickly remembering the falsetto, David looked up and, to his abject horror, saw Nicole.

"Ha!" she said, and she meant it to sting. "Here we go again, eh, madman?"

She got to her feet quickly and turned on her heels. As she passed the person behind her in the queue, she gave her best Gallic shrug.

"That woman is a man!" she hissed, to a nonplussed American lady. "Twice I have seen him naked and frothing at the mouth. Every time he drives 'is car it explodes. He is crazy. Believe me." She strode off purposefully into the crowds, tossing her head haughtily and mumbling to herself in French. The large American housewife sat down heavily on the borrowed chair.

"Hell Honey, *you* crazy? She's a fine one to talk. Draw me and leave off the double chin. I'll pay you double."

CHAPTER 26

The Mona Lisa

The Hotel Gioconda was not far from David's apartment. He reluctantly shut up shop at four o'clock, apologizing profusely to the three-hundred-and-seventy-six Japanese tourists that he'd had to disappoint, and returned the chairs to the café next door. He donned the protective Ray-Bans, gathered up his portfolio and hurried back to the apartment, where he picked up the English lady's case. Holding it together as best he could, he struggled over to the hotel, looking every bit the transsexual whore who had just been ejected from her pimp's flat after an argument about wages.

He breezed into the hotel and tried to waltz straight up the stairs, but the concierge stopped him and demanded to know what he was doing: he'd seen girls like her before. David explained that he had an appointment with a Mrs Lisa Robinson in room fifty, but the man remained unconvinced.

"Look," said David, abandoning his falsetto completely. "I'm a well-known comedy actor from England. The lady upstairs is a casting director for a film company, and they are filming a remake of 'Some Like it Hot' here in Florence later next year. Do you know the film?"

The concierge nodded.

"My agent has sent me to audition for the Jack Lemmon role, and I've decided to do it in drag, just like the film, so she'll get a better feel for it, do you see what I mean? Capito?"

The concierge nodded.

"So can I see her?"

The concierge nodded. David shot up the steps like a whippet. The concierge continued with his duties.

"She's a clothing rep," he said to no one in particular. "But what do I care?"

David knocked on the door of room fifty and a few seconds later, Lisa opened it and immediately burst into hysterical laughter, holding her right hand stiffly in front of her mouth in the way that certain ladies do, as if they believe that showing their teeth is socially unacceptable. She was around thirty-eight years old and pretty, in a secretarial kind of way. She wore thin, black-framed glasses, which matched her straight black, bobbed hair, and she was dressed in an elegant business suit that David liked very much. It must have been a recent acquisition, as he had all her clothes either in her case or on his person. She would certainly have looked better in them than he did.

Lisa invited him in, and offered him a cup of tea. She went over to the complimentary tea-making equipment next to her bed, and took the kettle off into the bathroom to fill it. She shouted through to him that his bag was over by the wardrobes if he'd like to check it, and make sure everything was in order. It was in decent condition, except for the locks, which she had presumably gelignited, judging by the state of them. David was looking forward to explaining it to his mother. She'd only ordered the luggage from Grattan's catalogue a few weeks before, for a promised trip to the Isle of Wight.

Lisa emerged with her kettle and went over to make a pot of tea. Every time she took a look at him, her face began to crumple.

"I could do with you swapping your clothes over," she said, stirring the pot. "You can use the bathroom. Take what you need from your luggage and get changed will you? I can't take you seriously in that dress. Oh yes, and if I were you, I'd take a shower while I finish the tea. You're plastered in make up."

David collected his shirt, his jeans and a welcome fresh pair of Y Fronts, and shuffled past her, thanking her profusely. It was great to be reunited with his clothes. If that was what women felt like all day, he was glad that he was a man. In his informed opinion, the worst aspect of wearing feminine attire, discounting the ridiculous shoes, was the make up. David had a habit of fiddling and messing with his face all day long, and couldn't get used to leaving well alone. When he was tired from drawing for hours, he liked to rub his eyes, and this had played havoc with his mascara. He looked like an extra from 'Night of the Undead.'

He shut the door behind him and took his dress, bra and panties off, hanging them on the peg. It felt good to get under the luxurious hot shower and wash away the make-up and dried-on perspiration. As he soaped himself, he warbled 'O Sole Mio' cheerfully. It had been a terrible day, but now all was well. He had his own clothes once again, and a few quid in his pocket. That night he could dine out, safe in the knowledge that he could always fleece a few tourists again if the money ran out. He had been humiliated time and time again by Nicole, each time more painful than the last, but now she was thirty-five-thousand feet high and out of the way for the time being. Yes, life was getting back to some semblance of order. It was time to enjoy the city, and also get cracking on his renaissance drawings.

Lisa tapped the door and shouted something about sugar, which interrupted his operatics. He shouted back, "Just one sugar please!" and pulled across the shower curtain to get out. The room was steamy and hot, and he smiled wryly as he remembered his last shower, which had resulted in Lord Hickman's sitting room being turned into a scale model of Lake Garda. Just at that moment, the bathroom door opened, and Lisa stood holding his tea cup, drinking in his naked, ringing-wet body.

"Have you got anything you can stir this tea with?" she asked, as she removed her steamed-up glasses and placed them on the shelf. "Oh my! I see that you have!"

David just stood there, dumbstruck and dripping, as she began to undo the buttons on her business blouse. Finally, after a few abortive attempts, the power of speech returned to him.

"Oh my God! Mrs Robinson!"

* * * * *

It was ten-thirty before David crawled back up the bleak stone steps to his apartment. A thousand thoughts were jockeying for pole position in his head, and he had a look on his face that was an equal mix of exhilaration and exhaustion. He turned the key and walked in, flicking the light switch as he did so. The magnificent chandelier burst into life, revealed to him that there had been no major floods, earthquakes, burglaries or fires while he'd been away. He threw his battered suitcase onto one chesterfield and himself onto the other. He was so tired that he couldn't raise the energy to get himself into bed. Instead, he stared at the wall for twenty minutes with a dopey grin on his face. He pondered on the day's crazy happenings, which were remarkable, even by his standards, and mused that the best way to find adventure or romance was not to look for them. Gradually his eyes began to close more and more frequently, and for ever-longer periods of time. He knew that, unchecked, he would soon be asleep, and so, with an almighty effort, he dragged himself off to bed, where he awoke the following day, still clad in the previous night's attire.

It was a lovely sunny day, so he decided to go down into the street and get some breakfast at the small café just a few yards away from his front door. After several cups of absolutely disgusting tea, which looked and tasted like lukewarm dishwater, he returned to his apartment and set about the task that he had been set. Finding the Botticelli was a challenge in itself, and David had to read and re-read his patron's notes before they made sense. Presumably for security reasons, Lord Hickman had devised a cunning ruse to hide his picture from prying eyes. One framed drawing in the room did not appear to be of the same high quality as its neighbours. It was a rather wooden and pedestrian looking effort portraying a young girl with a dog, obviously the work of a third division artist from around the late Victorian era. When the frame was removed from the wall, David discovered that it was in fact two-sided, and the picture facing the wall was the real treasure. Cunning and ingenious! He took the picture frame down and began carefully to dismantle it, along with the two others that had to be copied. He then retired to the kitchen to make one last cup of Earl Grey before commencing, just to steady his hands.

Lord Hickman was tremendously proud of his art collection, and it had taken him a long time to amass such wonderful pictures. Undoubtedly, the jewels in the crown were the Monet and the Botticelli, but many of the others were quite exquisite too, not to mention expensive. He had acquired them all by various means, usually dubious, and sometimes downright criminal.

Whilst scouting around for a holiday apartment in Florence, some five years earlier, he had been introduced to a gentleman named Marco Bonini in a very swanky restaurant on the Lungarno Amerigi Vespucci, overlooking the river. Mr Bonini was a multi-millionaire who lived in a town called Arona, on the shores of Lago Maggiore in the north of Italy. He was a forty-year-old with round glasses, curly hair and very English looks, who had made his fortune in the plumbing business, as had many people from that area. Marco owned several huge factories that produced fancy bathroom taps, boilers and central heating valves. He was a charming, friendly man who loved the staff on his factory floor just as much as he loved his wealthy friends. Unlike his counterpart, the English multi-millionaire, he would often socialize with the humblest floor sweeper, and could frequently be seen wining and dining with such characters at weekends, always at his expense. His staff, eager to pick up the tab for the odd dinner here and there in order to preserve their own self-respect, were always told that they had provided his wealth, and this was his way of paying them back. In short, the thirty-five-million pounds that lived in his bank account couldn't have found a nicer owner if they'd tried.

He had begun to chat to Lord Hickman whilst waiting for his bill, and the Englishman had told him about his desire to buy a small place in the town centre that would be handy for the museums and galleries. Mr Bonini suggested that he looked at his own apartment, and invited him around for tea the following day. He was not a snobbish man, but it was very flattering to have a real English Lord as a friend, and he wanted to hear all about his stately home, his visits to Parliament and the machinations of the British hereditary system. Lord Hickman duly turned up at the appointed hour and charmed his new acquaintance out of his socks with tales of how he'd met the Queen and dined at the palace. He waxed lyrical about his ancient home and his art collection, and this made the Italian's ears prick up. He told Lord Hickman that he too was a keen collector, and he showed him a room in the Florence apartment where he kept his Monet and Botticelli, amongst many others. For security reasons he didn't let it be known that the pictures were in the apartment, but, because his guest was not only an art collector but also a real English aristocrat, he made an exception.

The two were then seen dining together in Florence, at all the best places, and Mr Bonini even offered to help his new friend find a place of his own. Lord Hickman explained that he had limited funds, and didn't want to splash out on anything as grand as the palatial building that Mr Bonini owned, so the Italian phoned a few colleagues, and came up with the Via de' Canacci property.

The street was not the most salubrious. In fact, it had the look of a graffiti-strewn back alley, but Mr Bonini had advised his friend that often the outside belied the charm of the inside, and one had to make a choice when working to a budget, of having a lovely apartment in an average street, or a seedy apartment in a good street. The Lord chose the former, and once up the dingy stone stairs, the place was indeed quite splendid. He was, after all, buying the apartment with his wife's money, and she was tightening her grip on His Lordship's expenses.

The new apartment needed to be renovated and rewired before Lord Hickman could move in, so Mr Bonini, over dinner one evening, came up with a plan. He was going back to Lago Maggiore for a few months, and would not be visiting his own apartment at all in that time. Lord Hickman was cordially invited to take a holiday there whenever he wished, in order to keep an eye on the builders and electricians. The Canacci apartment was a five-minute walk from his own, so it was an ideal base, which would save him from camping out at some expensive hotel for weeks. Also, Mr Bonini had an ulterior motive in asking his new friend to stay at his house. There would be someone at home to keep an eye on the paintings. In the last few years, there had been a spate of robberies from up-market apartments, and it was making him a little nervous. The rooms were alarmed, and the doors had security locks, but a presence at the property, keeping an eye on things, was always more comforting.

Lord Hickman thanked his newfound friend profusely for such hospitality, and arranged for an old acquaintance to stay at the Florentine apartment with him, just to keep him company. His name was Bertie Jolliffe. Charles wasn't a particular friend of Bertie's, but he did admire him greatly, and considered him to be one of the world's greatest craftsmen. Mr Jolliffe was at least seventy years old, bald as a coot and prone to wearing hideous suits and bow-ties. He came from London, but didn't have the upper crust accent of

His Lordship. His was more akin to the sound of those who frequented the area known as Bow Bells. Bertie was not big on conversation, or dining out, but Charles had not sought out this companion for his social skills.

This particular cockney sparrow was chosen to be his flat mate for one reason only. He was probably the best art forger in Britain.

While Mr Bonini was back on Lago Maggiore, knocking out his gold-plated bath taps for those with more money than sense, Lord Hickman and Bertie were busy defrauding their benevolent and trusting host to the tune of one Monet and one Botticelli, safe in the knowledge that they had a leisurely month to complete their despicable task. This beautifully thought-out plan didn't come cheap, however. Bertie was a master, respected by the underworld throughout the land for his superbly crafted forgeries, and Lord Hickman had to pay through the nose to gain his services. At least, he would have done, had Bertie not keeled over and died of a heart attack two days after completing the Monet.

It was a great shame for Bertie, his family and the criminal under-classes, in the order named, but a stroke of good fortune for His Lordship, who was instantly absolved of any obligation to cough up. The only minor inconvenience was that he would need to find another forger for any future ventures, but he cheerfully resolved to cross that Ponte Vecchio when he came to it.

Lord Charles had even felt a pang of conscience for his wealthy Italian victim, which was an unusual, not to say novel experience for him. The man had after all stood him some excellent dinners and lent him his luxury apartment for the best part of a month. Marco had called in the press and been proudly photographed with his aristocratic English friend, for a frothy socialite magazine that featured homes of the rich and famous. This really wasn't the way one repaid such a friendship. It wasn't befitting an old Etonian, a Lord and a gentleman, but he had to override such sickly sentimental feelings and be strong. After all, this was business, pure and simple. He needed the money more than his friend needed the Monet, and that was the end of it. As for poor old Bertie, Charles gave him about as much consideration as he would expend on a fly hitting the windscreen of his Bentley. Thank God the boring old swine had managed to finish his task before he shuffled off his mortal coil. Lord Hickman would have found it hard to forgive him if he hadn't.

David returned from Italy late on Saturday evening, exhausted but happy, having accomplished all he went there to do, and a bit besides. Len picked him up from the airport at nine o'clock, and as soon as they reached home, David went straight to bed and slept until lunchtime the following day. He spent most of the afternoon telling his family about his visit, carefully omitting all references to floods, sexual encounters with older women and earning his living as a transvestite. Mothers didn't like to hear that kind of thing, and neither, for that matter, did fathers. He did, however, come clean about losing his wallet, and apologized for the lack of presents. The only thing he could afford was a plastic model of Michelangelo's David, which he expected them to share. Paul was suitably unimpressed, and begged their leave to continue doing his jigsaw. Len examined his jointly-owned statuette and asked if everyone in Florence wandered around stark naked.

"Only if your name is David," said his son, quickly changing the subject. He showed them the three original drawings that he had brought back, wrapped carefully in tissue and kept flat in his portfolio. Ruby, on learning their value, edged away from the table with her teacup, and begged him to return them safely to their owner. Having them around was beginning to make her nervous, especially with young Paul about the place. David reassured her that first thing Monday he was going to call at the castle with them, and then take the day off to visit his college. He had estimated that he would need another week at Lord Hickman's place to complete his tasks, but he desperately wanted to visit his friends and tell them all about his adventures in the city of culture.

After lunch he phoned Lazlo to ask if anything of interest had been happening while he was away. Lazlo replied that the band had had a few rehearsals, now that his hand was a little better, and all they really needed was a gig somewhere. Other than that, nothing to report, except that he had returned the easel to Katie as promised, for which he thanked David profusely.

"Surely," argued David, "I should be thanking you."

"The pleasure was all mine!" said Lazlo. "She's got this fantastic pair of bra-less breasts with a mind of their own. Have you got anything else I could return to her next week?"

CHAPTER 27

A New Contender in the Frame

David parked the Mini in the castle grounds and headed for the front door, clutching his portfolio under his arm. His Lordship had seen him approach from his study, and opened the door himself.

"Ah, the very fellow! How was Italy?" he asked, slapping him heartily on the back.

"*Molto bene!*" replied David, employing the only Italian phrase that he knew. "Mission accomplished, sir."

"Excellent! Come in, and we'll have a cup of tea and catch up," said Lord Hickman, beaming.

They proceeded to David's studio room, where he laid out the drawings on the trestle table. Lord Hickman looked briefly at them and then replaced their protective tissue paper.

"And how do the replacements look?" he enquired. "Up to your usual standard?"

David assured him that they were.

"Excellent. Any problems? Manage to do any sight-seeing?"

"No problems at all. It all went like clockwork," said David, who obviously believed that the odd white lie didn't count as a sin. "And yes, thank you, I managed to see a few interesting sights too. Did you know, for instance, that the Gioconda Hotel in the Via Panzani was where the Mona Lisa was found, after it was stolen in nineteen-thirteen?"

"Well I never," said Lord Hickman. "How did you discover that?"

"I probed a lady that was staying there, as I was removing her dress," said David, grinning.

"You old dog!" grinned His Lordship, impressed with his young employee's rakish behaviour. "Now, I'm afraid I'll have to leave you to your own devices today. Jean Jacques, Brigitte and I have to go to the bottle manufacturers on business. I just have to make an important call and we'll be off. Do you need anything before we go?"

"I'm only here for an hour. I have to pop into college," said David, "but just a couple of things while I've got you - firstly, do you have an old canvas of the right size that I can over-paint for my last oil painting?"

"Ah! Let me see. It's quite large isn't it?" Lord Hickman scratched his chin and pondered. "There's an awful old portrait hanging up in Jean Jacques's reception area that's about the right size, but you'd have to go and measure it. You may just be lucky, if my memory is accurate. If it's any use, just paint over it. It's a piece of tat we got from the attic to liven up the walls when we converted the old stables into the Vineyard offices - worth about a fiver at auction. If that's no use, you'll have to do your best and antique one yourself. What was the other point?"

"Oh, er, any chance of getting paid a few quid to keep me going," asked David, blushing, "That's if, you know, it's not...."

"No problem, dear boy. Finish off this last picture, and we'll settle up then, at the end of the week eh?" Lord Hickman glanced at his watch. "Look old chap, I must fly, I have a call to make before I dash off." He hastily made for the door, but turned before he left the room.

"Oh, just one other thing. I'm having a birthday party at the castle next Saturday for my fifty-first birthday. Largish affair, marquee and whatnot. I've hired a big band for the older inmates, but I wondered if your rock band would like to play for half an hour or so - you know - for the younger folks. You can bring a few guests too, if you like, and you'll get dinner thrown in."

David was thrilled. "That would be fantastic! I'm sure they would love to play. Thank you very much!"

"Well we'll say it's a deal then. I can afford a hundred quid. Will that cover it?"

David said that it certainly would, and he could consider it organized. Lord Hickman shot off to make his call, leaving David reeling. A gig at a real-life castle, for a real-life Lord. He couldn't wait to tell the lads that evening. It was a hell of a move in the right direction, after the Belton Court debacle.

He stood for what must have been ten minutes, lost in thought, before he finally snapped out of his daydream and got down to the task in hand. His Monet forgery was still under wraps where he had left it, and the original still on the wall, but something about it looked odd. He walked over to get a closer look. It was definitely not the picture that he had spent ages copying. He should know, after all. He had stared at it intensely for a whole week, and this wasn't it. It was too bright, for a start, and there were only nine large poppies on the left-hand side. The original had ten, he was sure of it, because he had deliberately put eleven on his forgery. Maybe this latest mystery forger had decided to buck the trend and paint one *less* than the original for reasons of identification, which was quite sensible. After all, the way these faked pictures were breeding unchecked, it would only have been a matter of time before the cornfields were just a solid block of cadmium red.

He ran a finger lightly across the female figure in the picture's white sun hat, causing the paint to smear. White was always the last to dry.

"Curiouser and curiouser thought Alice!" he mused.

What was also curious was the sound he could hear in the room. All the time he had been studying the picture, he was conscious of a strange noise, like garbled pixie voices in conversation. He looked around, but could see no one. He glanced out of the French windows, to see if it was Jethro talking to his barrow of manure, but the gardener was nowhere to be seen. No, the voices were definitely coming from within the room. Slowly, he paced around, trying to locate the epicentre of this poltergeist activity, until he came to the old telephone on the desk by the window. Someone had failed to replace the receiver properly, which meant that David could clearly hear the conversation, if he held his head very close to the phone.

One voice was almost certainly that of Lord Hickman, whilst the other had a distinct German accent. Having solved the mystery of the pixie voices, David was happy to leave the two gentlemen to their private chat, until he heard the word 'Monet' mentioned, and curiosity understandably got the better of him. He held his breath and listened in.

"Yes, Herr Grunstrasse. I'm sorry for the delay, but I now have the Monet and the Botticelli here at the castle."

"Good. When do you want me to arrive?"

"I am having a birthday party next Saturday evening. There is a dinner, followed by a rock band until nine, after which there will be a disco. Then we have a big dance band until late. I will quietly disappear and meet you at the aerodrome at nine-fifteen, if you can make it for then. That way I can kill two birds with one stone, and avoid the blessed disco. You must have the money ready in the obligatory black attaché case, like in the movies, ja?"

"Ja, very funny. My pilot, Pierre is here with me. Is nine-fifteen possible Pierre? Ja, he says that is okay. One last thing, Lord Hickman. I have learnt of your reputation from various colleagues of mine in the art world. I am an expert, and I know what's real and what isn't. Do you get my drift?"

"Certainly, though I resent the slight, old boy. Be assured that these are the real McCoy. I would not waste your time with anything less, Herr Grunstrasse."

"Okay, until Saturday at nine-fifteen, Auf Wiederhören."

David lifted his head from the desk and rubbed his stiff neck. He was in a state of shock. He had absolutely no idea what Lord Hickman was up to, but it was obvious from the tone of the conversation that all was not as it seemed. Charles Hickman had fed him some cock and bull story about insurance, and all the time he was selling off the real pictures to a foreign collector. Then again, they *were* his own pictures, and he could do what he liked with them.

Perhaps he was strapped for cash and selling off the family silver, whilst trying to save face by substituting the copies.

Well, whatever His Lordship did, it was none of David's business, as long as he paid up at the end of the week. The good news was, once the mysterious German had arrived with his attaché case full of cash, he'd be in better shape for paying David's bill. Maybe, he reasoned, that was why he'd deferred with the payment until the following week. He was waiting for his own payday first. This, however, didn't solve the mystery of the new Monet on the wall. There were two of the bloody things in his room already, and another floating around in the ether somewhere. It struck David that they were at risk of becoming common.

He took a walk over to the Vineyard offices, partly to clear his confused mind and partly to size up the old oil painting. By now, everyone had obviously left for the meeting at the bottle plant, as no cars were in evidence. He wandered into reception and found the old painting above Jean Jacques's desk. It was as Lord Hickman had described it, a stodgy old painting of a country gentleman in a dark coat, looking pompous and arrogant. It was so darkened with age and thick, cracked varnish that David could just see a head, looming out of a filthy brown background. He couldn't be sure of the size, so he lifted it off its hook and placed it down on the desk, turning it over to examine the state of the stretcher. To his surprise, it was covered over with a plywood panel, which had been tacked onto the back of the frame.

David could see no good reason for this to be done, as it was important to have access to the stretchers now and again if the picture ever went slack. He measured the frame, and it was exactly the right size, which pleased him no end. Grabbing a screwdriver from the cupboard nearby, he began to prise the plywood backing sheet away from the frame so that he could look at the condition of the canvasback. It was while doing this that he became aware of something rattling around within the cavity. It appeared to be the back of another, smaller unframed canvas and what looked like a yellowing magazine.

As the plywood came away, he was able to remove the stretched canvas within. It was a picture he knew very well indeed, but it wasn't a version he had ever seen before.

Staring him in the face was the real Monet.

He knew, instinctively, that *this* one was the authentic article. He also knew that it *wasn't* the one he had laboriously copied on Lord Hickman's wall, and it certainly wasn't the wet one that was hanging there now. He ran the gamut of emotions from A to Z in a new world record time, shaving tenths of a second off his previous A to Z emotional gamut. If Lord Hickman had wanted a Monet copied, why hadn't he supplied David with the real thing to copy? Why would he choose to hide it away, only to let David waste time forging another copy? It made no sense whatsoever. Whoever had hidden this picture, it certainly wasn't Lord Hickman. That much, at least, was obvious.

David picked up the old magazine and flicked through it. Maybe there was a clue within as to what this was all about. Eventually, he found what he was looking for. A full-page picture of Lord Hickman with another gentleman, and behind them, in pin-sharp detail and focus, the Monet painting.

Feverishly, he read the article. The gentleman was a Mr Bonini, pictured with his new friend Lord Hickman at Mr Bonini's luxurious apartment in Florence. Behind them, his Monet, which Lord Hickman had greatly admired, a new acquisition from a major sale in New York. A chance meeting in Florence turns into a firm friendship between English aristocrat and Italian millionaire.

David studied the painting in the magazine picture, and compared it to the picture on the desk in front of him. They were the same in every minute detail. His instinct was right. This was indeed the real thing. Just for devilment, he counted the poppies - there were nine. The artist who painted the latest, still-wet incarnation had at least got one thing right, probably by accident! David read hurriedly through the rest of the article, which was mainly lightweight pap, until a word near the end caught his eye.

Botticelli.

He backtracked and read the sentence again, this time letting the words sink in.

Lord Hickman was full of praise for his host's good taste in pictures, singling out a rather wonderful little Botticelli drawing as 'quite exquisite', adding that he was deeply jealous and longed for it to be in his own collection. Mr Bonini laughed, and assured his friend that he had no intention of parting with either his Monet or Botticelli, but was interested in buying Lord Hickman's Gozzoli drawing.

David was in turmoil; he felt as if his brain was full to the brim with writhing maggots. As all the pieces of an incredibly complex jigsaw were beginning to fit together, it was becoming obvious that serious treachery was afoot.

What he still couldn't ascertain was who was doing what to whom and why. On the surface, it seemed that Lord

Hickman had somehow swindled his Italian friend out of at least two valuable works of art. It didn't take a genius to work out how that could be done, given that David had been doing something similar for the last few weeks. There were clearly two avenues for a thief to take. One was just to steal the pictures, but then surely Mr Bonini would have raised the hue and cry, and a list of suspects would be drawn up. No matter how unpleasant the task, Mr Bonini would have to inform the police of any possible candidates from his personal acquaintances, and inevitably he would have to mention Lord Hickman. The second avenue was to copy the pictures and leave the forgeries on Mr Bonini's wall. This way, they might never be spotted, but if they were, the trail would hopefully have gone cold by then.

David realized that he had a very important call to make. He sat down at Jean Jacques's desk and phoned the international directory enquiries number. As he waited for a response, he idly flicked through the Frenchman's diary, and saw an appointment for the following Saturday, scribbled in biro. It read;

Herr Grunstrasse. Twopenny Green. 9.15pm.

The operator asked David for a name and address. He requested the number of Bonini Spa. Fontaneto d'Agogna, Italy. The lady found the number, and David wrote it down. He dialled and asked to be put through to Mr Bonini as a matter of some urgency. A receptionist with the strongest Italian accent he had ever heard asked him why he needed to speak to the chairman, but David insisted that the matter was extremely private and a matter of life and death. Such was the quality of his performance that the young lady asked him to hold for a moment, and seconds later, a male voice answered the phone, introducing himself as Marco Bonini.

"Excuse me, Mr Bonini," said David breathlessly, "this may sound very peculiar to you, but can I ask you one question? Do you still own the Monet and the Botticelli?"

"Yes I do," replied the Italian. "Who is this please?"

"My name is David Day. Do you have a moment to speak?"

David put down the telephone after what seemed like half an hour and took a series of deep breaths. His head was swimming, and he didn't yet feel capable of rising from Jean Jacques's chair. He looked at the diary entry once more. He knew that name. Herr Grunstrasse. He'd heard it somewhere before very recently. The time and location written next to it rang a bell too.

Eureka! It was the man who had been talking to Lord Hickman on the telephone. He was an unscrupulous art dealer - another piece in the jigsaw. It was plain from reading Jean Jacques's diary that he and Lord Hickman were in it together. Why else would they both be going to this clandestine liaison with the mysterious German on a lonely airfield? But if this were true, why then would His Lordship employ David to copy a *copy* of a Monet, and why did Jean Jacques have what appeared to be the original stashed away in his office? Perhaps the Frenchman had stolen the original from Hickman, and substituted the one that David had been copying.

That made sense, but why then agree to meet the same dealer at the same time at the same aerodrome? Added to that, who on earth had painted the still-wet Monet, and why?

There were more questions than answers, as usual. David had to think on his feet now. Lord Hickman and his cronies might be back soon, so time was tight. He grabbed the real Monet, the old portrait and the magazine, ran over to the castle and headed for his studio. Once inside he locked the door and laid the old portrait face down on the trestle table. He placed the still-wet Monet copy inside the frame's cavity with the magazine and sealed it up with the plywood sheet. He placed the real Monet under his dustsheet on the easel, and put his own Monet back on the wall where Dylan's had been, (and Nicole's before that) after hastily removing the surplus poppy with a cotton bud soaked in white spirit. He then unlocked the door and ran back across the courtyard with the old portrait which he slipped back onto the hanger above Jean Jacques's desk - mission accomplished. David walked back to the castle and paused outside Lord Hickman's study. He had one more important task to complete before they returned.

Lord Hickman, on receiving the original renaissance drawings that David had copied at the castle, had taken them away to his study for safe keeping. This was presumably where the Botticelli and the other Florentine ones were too, and David needed to borrow them back for a short while. He tried the door, and miraculously, it was open. His patron obviously trusted him more than David trusted his patron.

Once inside, there seemed only one logical place where such pictures could be stored, and that was in the old oak plan chest. He opened the top drawer, but it was full of etchings and small prints. The second drawer contained sellotape, envelopes, two dead woodlice and a stapler, and the third, fourth and fifth were almost empty. David was beginning to panic. An awful feeling engulfed him. It was very similar to how he'd felt when he realized he didn't know the answer to a single question on his maths O level paper. Suddenly he felt an overwhelming urge to use the toilet. He opened the bottom drawer, and it too was empty. He was about to close it when he realized that this drawer looked different from the others.

Bingo! It was too shallow inside, when compared to the outside. The plywood bottom was false! The fit was so tight; it looked for all the world like the base of the drawer. Very clever! The only problem was, how did it come out? He pulled the entire drawer out of the chest, tipped it upside down, and *voila*! The false base fell out, and with it fell all of the original drawings, wrapped in tissue. He picked them up carefully and dashed round to his studio, locking the door behind him. Then, one by one, he added a small, insignificant black dot to the bottom right-hand corners of the drawings in soft pencil. He took down his own copies from the walls of the two rooms where they hung, and began to remove the backs from the frames.

An hour later, the originals were once more in their frames, with their new black dots, and the copies were wrapped in tissue with their dots removed. David's hands were trembling like an alcoholic's at breakfast time as he dashed down the corridor and placed the pictures back into the false bottom of the plan chest.

All but the Botticelli, that was. He needed that for the rest of the week, so that yet another copy could be made, and he hoped to God that His Lordship didn't pop back to the plan chest to take a quick peek before this last task was completed. As he pushed the drawer back in, he heard the crunch of expensive tyres on gravel. Lord Hickman and his friends were back. David exited the study slightly faster than a peckish cheetah and tried his best to look nonchalant as he headed for his studio. As he strolled breathlessly down the corridor with his heart pumping violently against his ribs, a voice called out behind him.

"Good morning, how's the restoration coming on?"

Lady Hickman was on her way to the car park.

"Goop!" he spluttered. "Oh, you know, slow but sure. Can't rush these things!"

The unexpected voice had spooked him completely. He rushed to the sanctity of his studio and locked the door.

"Jesus Christ!" he panted. "I forgot she bloody lived here!"

CHAPTER 28

A Thin Chapter about a Fat Man

Herr Grunstrasse was a fat, sweaty, middle-aged German with a penchant for cream-coloured linen suits. He sat in the dowdy office of his diminutive swivel-eyed Dutch pilot, Pierre van der Truck, idly watching the ceiling fan rotating as he sipped his espresso.

"It is a farcical situation. Something is going on and I can't fathom it."

"No, my friend," said Pierre, lighting a Gauloise and puffing smoke at the ceiling fan. "It does seem strange. Why would this Frenchman try to sell you the same pictures that his boss has already arranged to sell you? Obviously he plans to steal them from him."

"Obviously. That's why I asked him to meet us at the aerodrome at precisely the same time as Lord Hickman. I like a little sport, don't you?"

"Absolutely, but we must be careful," warned Pierre. "I will take my little friend here, just to be safe."

Pierre pulled aside his coat, to reveal a small automatic pistol.

"Good God! I had no idea that you carried such a thing -
I'm impressed!" said Herr Grunstrasse, wiping his brow
with a handkerchief.

The seedy little man smiled a nasty smile.

"Ah! You respect me more now, don't you Richie?"

CHAPTER 29

The prodigal returns

David arrived at the art college much later in the afternoon than he would have liked. He hadn't foreseen the goings-on at the castle, where his mad flurry of activity had set him back several hours. On his way out, he had seen Lord Hickman and assured him that he'd be back at work on Tuesday at nine sharp. Lord Hickman had asked whether the old picture in the stable block had proved satisfactory, but David bluffed his way out of it by explaining that it was so encrusted with cracked varnish that it was useless for over-painting. They arranged to go hunting for replacements together the following day.

As he bounded up the staircase, David was met by John Auberton, who was leaning on the balustrade at the top, watching his students return from their coffee break half an hour late, as usual.

"Aha! The prodigal son returns a week early!" he grinned.

"Not quite," frowned David, shaking his hand. "I just thought I'd pop in because I know you miss me if I'm away too long."

"I'm just grateful to see the odd student, Dave," said John. "They're deserting me in droves."

"Like who?" asked David. He hated missing out on the gossip.

"Well, first you went to Italy, which was fine. Then Nicole went on a mercy mission to see her grandmother on her deathbed. I got rid of our hippy friend Nigel because he hadn't done a tap since he arrived. Then Dyl vanished for a week with a mystery virus. I hope you've bought me a stick of rock back. I need cheering up!"

David pondered John's comments. He was intrigued by the Nicole story in particular.

"Better than that, boss," he chirped. "Here. I've done you a nice terracotta chalk drawing of Michelangelo's David, drawn from life no less. You can stick it in your office and think of your favourite David, every time you glance at it, which'll be often 'cause it's so good."

"Why thank you!" said John, genuinely touched at the thought. "I'll treasure it - or I may sell it to Alf for a fiver."

"Don't," snapped David, wincing at the memory. "That still stings."

"I'll change the subject. Did I tell you that we had a new student?"

"No, is he or she any good?"

"It's a he. He's been coming here every day while you've been away. Loves the college lifestyle, holds court in the refectory with his amusing anecdotes. He's settled in nicely, so it was a shame I had to ask him to leave, especially as we're down on numbers. The problem being, I didn't know who he was. He just *appeared*, and every time I wandered into the studio there he'd be, chatting to the others. It's a wonder he didn't apply for a grant, the cheeky bleeder.

Turns out he's your car mechanic mate - the one who you asked to return Katie's easel. He liked the place so much; he's been back every day since. I wish he could draw; I'd have taken him on. Sorry if I was a bit official with a friend of yours, but obviously we can't have strangers floating about. The Dean would have a fit!"

"Christ! Lazlo. He had an accident at work and he's been at a loose end. Perhaps he just likes the atmosphere here."

"I'm flattered that I've created such a welcoming place for all the waifs and strays of Wolverhampton and its surrounding districts. When I confronted him, half the students in the studio shouted, "Can we keep him John, can we? can we?" like he was a bloody guinea pig.

"Well I'm sorry. I've got to ring him tonight. I'll give him a bollocking for embarrassing me in front of my esteemed leader."

"No problem David, not your fault," John assured him, massaging David's shoulder.

They wandered into the main studio, John peeling off to the sanctity of his cramped little office and David making a beeline for Dylan, who didn't look remotely as if he'd suffered a recent virus-infestation.

"Howdy doody!" bellowed David cheerfully, slapping him on the back and sending Dylan's pencil flying.

"If you'd ruined that drawing I'd have had your knackers off with a blunt scalpel," he snarled. "Anyway, how are you, my son? Or should I say *come stai*?"

"You can, but I wouldn't have the foggiest what you were talking about. Listen, have you got time for a wee tea break? I need some advice."

Dylan always had time for tea breaks. He placed his pencil back on the board and followed his friend down the stairs. They grabbed their usual table in the top corner and David broached what for him was a difficult subject.

"Listen. This is a bit awkward. You know when we saw the ad for the artist, and we both told a little white lie about not ringing for an interview?"

"Yep."

"Well, I told you another one. Lord Hickman *did* actually offer me the job, and I took it."

"Oh yeah?"

"Yeah. I'm sorry. What it was, he made me promise that I wouldn't tell anyone, not even you, that I was doing the work."

"So why tell me now then, you sneak thief?" asked Dylan, grinning a sarcastic grin.

"Don't be like that, ratbag. Listen. I was sworn to secrecy because I was asked to copy some famous pictures. He wanted to have the fakes on display, and keep the originals under lock and key, and he didn't want anybody to know, because that kind of gossip travels fast. Right?"

"Er, right," said Dylan with uncertainty, as if he were trying to get the three plastic cogs that made up his brain to intermesh and produce a result. "So I repeat, why tell me now?"

"Well, something isn't quite right about all this, and I need an accomplice with a sharp mind and nerves of steel. I can't find one, so you'll have to do."

He unravelled the complexities of the tale over a Wagon Wheel and two Penguin bars. Dylan weighed the evidence carefully, as he chomped on a meditative biscuit.

"You've been very straightforward with me," he said, "So I have to be the same with you. You know when I said I didn't get the job, at that same interview? Well, I lied. Well, I sort of told the truth, but I lied really, do you know what I mean?"

"No."

"Lord Hickman didn't give me a job. I told the truth there, but his *wife* did. She asked me to paint her a Monet."

"Bloody hell!" said David. "That explains the mystery virus."

"How did you know about that?" asked Dylan, amazed.

"Nothing gets past me, mate. You cheeky bugger! Coming on all sanctimonious with me when I admitted to lying just now. I think I've seen your Monet, by the way. It's still wet for God's sake, man. Didn't you use an accelerant?"

"A what-erant?"

"Never mind, *dummkopf*. Anyway, I've seen it. It's a bit bright, even allowing for the cleaning job I'm supposed to have done on it. It didn't fool me."

"Look," said Dylan indignantly, "I was working under difficult conditions. All I had to work from was a few photos, which weren't very good. I bet you had the real thing in front of you."

"I *thought* I did," said David. "But it appears that I was copying a bloody copy. Anyway, why on earth did she need a copy done? I'm getting bloody confused now."

"Oh, she suspects the old man of subterfuge, so she's getting her retaliation in first," said Dylan.

"Well, she was right about that," said David. "He's up to no good, that's for certain. I've spoken to the rightful owner in Italy, and he assured me that he still had the originals on his wall in Florence. I had to break it to him that they probably weren't, and he's gone away to check it out with the so-called art experts. He sounded ever so nice, but completely distraught, because Lord Hickman seemed so plausible and respectable - I told him that I'd been suckered in the same way. If con artists looked like con artists, no one would be conned would they? They *have* to seem plausible. Now I've done a month's work, and I probably won't get paid a penny. This makes even Alf's wages seem good. What a pisser!"

"I see what you mean," said Dylan sympathetically. "At least I got paid well. That mystery virus earned me a packet!"

"Rub it in why don't you?" moaned David moodily. "Look, I've got a plan, and I could do with your help. Do you fancy a good night out on Saturday? Lord Hickman's having a posh marquee do for his birthday, and my band's playing there - for free now, by the looks of it. I've been told I can invite a few friends. There's a dinner too. At least we can try and drink him dry and take our money that way.

I was going to ask you and Katie. In fact, if I can pluck up the courage, I was going to ask her to go with me, if you know what I mean. You don't have designs on her do you? You haven't got a good track record with telling me the whole truth and nothing but the truth."

"You cheeky bloody monkey! No I don't. We're just good mates. Ask away, and yes, I'd love to go. I quite fancy old

Lord Lucan's missus actually. I wonder if she fancies a bit of rough?"

"Out of your league I'm afraid," sneered David. "Know your place, you plebeian. Now, leave the plan to me, and I'll keep you informed. No more secrecy, eh?"

Dylan shook David's hand, to seal the deal. "No more secrecy!"

David wandered back to the studio with his ally, who returned to his drawing. David then sidled nervously over to Katie's easel to say hello.

"Ooh! Look who's back," she squealed, pleased to see her close friend and confidante of a thousand tea breaks. "Have a nice time?"

"Interesting, though some of it was just a drag," he smiled. "Listen dear. I'm no good at this kind of thing, so don't laugh, or make me seem an inch tall, or totally embarrass me, or just laugh hysterically, because It takes lots of courage, this kind of thing, and…."

"Get on with it."

"My band is playing at Stanmore Castle on Saturday. Can I take you?"

He flushed bright red. He didn't exactly interlock his hands at groin height, look down and make circles in the dust with his foot, but it was a close-run thing.

"Oh David," said Katie. "Oh David, I would have loved to, but I promised someone else that I'd see him on Saturday. Any other time, you know that. Oh come on, give me a hug. That took lots of courage didn't it?"

David feigned broken-heartedness, sobbing onto her back.

"We're big friends aren't we?" she cooed into his ear.

David produced a convincing post-tearful shudder, as popularized by young toddlers, after their tantrum has subsided. Suzanne, erstwhile school friend of Nicole, passed Katie's work area just in time to see this open display of emotion.

"No sexual activity in the studio," she warned. "Auberton has been known to rush out with a bucket of water."

"He needs comforting," smiled Katie. "He has just been rejected by the woman he loves."

"Oh!" said Suzanne, who then, rather uncharacteristically, headed for the tearoom without further comment. David thought to himself that his old youth-hostelling adversary seemed unusually distant, and resolved to ask if she was feeling okay when the time was right.

At five o'clock, he stopped off at the pay phone in the reception area, prior to driving home with Dylan. He handed his friend the keys, and asked him to sit in the car for a while. He had two important calls to make that wouldn't wait. Firstly, he phoned Lazlo, and told him about the gig at the castle on Saturday. Lazlo, who was thrilled by the news, promised to phone the others and arrange a last-minute rehearsal on Friday night. Airing his rarely-seen authoritative streak, David made it clear that anyone who was otherwise engaged would have to cancel whatever it was they were engaged in, as this was a huge opportunity for them all. Lazlo agreed, and volunteered to organize the troops. David then rang The Sound Hole, to be answered by Bob Burns.

"Hello Bobby," said David. "Could I possibly have a word with Jack, or is he busy?"

"No Dave, he's in the back room, doing a 'paint by numbers' of a Spitfire. There's not a customer in sight."

"Paint by bloody numbers?" queried David. "It's not art - you know that, don't you? It's more like knitting. That crap is for little kids and old ladies. I would never have believed it!"

"Oh, he just likes world-war-two aircraft, the daft old git. I'll tell him to pick up the phone."

"Hello young Dave!" said Jack. "And before you say a word, less of your sarcasm, you upstart. You show me how to paint properly and I'll show you how to play the guitar. Till then I'm stuck with the paint by numbers."

"Ah! The other man's grass eh, Jack? We all want what someone else has, and we never realize what we possess ourselves. God, I'm philosophical today. Anyway, listen…"

David got down to business, and after more merciless ribbing about Jack's hobby, asked if he could do him a gigantic favour on Saturday night. After nearly half an hour on the phone, David returned to the car to find Dylan snoring peacefully.

"Poor little critter," he smiled, "he's plum tuckered out."

It was not until Sedgley that Dylan woke with a start, and asked the classic question, "Where am I?"

David had stopped rather abruptly to let the bus out of its stop, causing Dylan to be unceremoniously jerked back into consciousness, just as the Jamaican bus driver looked out of the window to acknowledge the kindly gesture.

"Hello there!" he shouted. "So you passed your test, passed your test, passed your test!"

David smiled. It was comforting in his complicated new world, to know that some things could be relied upon to remain the same.

CHAPTER 30

Monet Worries

It was Friday morning, the day before the castle gig, and Ruby had just answered the door to a courier man delivering a large parcel addressed to David.

"Are you expecting anything David?" she enquired. "I thought these were the brown slacks that your Aunty had ordered for Uncle Bill from the club book, but it's addressed to you."

"What an interesting and varied life you lead, mother," said David. "Let me see."

He began to cut away impatiently at the many layers of brown parcel tape, until he gave up and tore huge chunks out of the packing cardboard.

"For someone who has infinite patience for painting, you haven't got much left for anything else," observed his mater.

He finally pulled off the last layer of bubble wrap, and gasped with shock as the contents revealed themselves. Staring back up at him from the breakfast bar was yet another incarnation of the Monet.

David's eyes goggled as he inspected it. It looked as real as real could be. He lifted it carefully from its packaging, and discovered another package beneath, which he opened with a lot more care than before. Inside, wrapped in tissue, was a drawing by Botticelli, and a smaller renaissance sketch in red chalk, of a boy playing a lute. Beneath the drawings was a typewritten letter. It read;

Ciao David,

Please disregard my English. I learn eventually. I can thank you not enough for all the thing that you do. I have never meet you, but I will always owe for you the big debt.

Please find the two pictures, Monet e Botticelli.

I have done the digging. The auction house say it is almost certain the work of a brilliant English forgery named Bertie Jolliffe, who is now diseased.

Very strange they tell me his pictures sell now for much money because he was a famous forgery. I would like you to keep for the memento, or give to you mother.

Also, please accept a real Firenze drawing from Raffaello Sanzio (circa1503.) Please insure it as it is much money, and keep it away from aristocrats.

I hope it goes for you without the problem on Saturday.

Grazie Mille,

Your new friend.

Marco Bonini.

Bonini Spa. Fontaneto d'Agogna. ITALIA.

David showed his mother the pictures, and tried his best to convince her that the little sketch alone was worth a small fortune, discounting the two forgeries. All three at auction would probably net him a small house. She smiled indulgently at her dreamy offspring, as if to say, "There there now, my angel, if that's what you wish to believe." Then she returned to her ironing and added, "I'm a bit disappointed that it wasn't Bill's trousers though. They should have been here last Wednesday."

* * * * *

That evening the band met at Lazlo's dad's factory for a final run through. Everyone was very excited.

"We're only on for half an hour," said David, "so let's pick the very best material and storm the place, eh?"

The others agreed.

"We need to dress well too," added George. "Not the usual sacks of shit."

"Absolutely," agreed Lazlo. "Make an effort, lads. There's a big posh dinner as well."

"Shit!" said Nick. "I can never remember which bread roll's mine, or which bloody fork to use."

"Start from the outside," suggested Ken, "and your roll's on the left. Or is it the right? Look, we'll all be on the same table so it won't matter. As long as there's drink, I'll be okay."

"But not too much, eh Ken?" suggested Mo.

"I wonder if it'll be cod and chips?" said George hopefully. "That's all I like."

"I shouldn't think so!" laughed David. "It'll probably be a roulette of smoked ostrich, flummoxed on a bed of seared mangey trouts with a smoked paraffin dressing, served with a vintage *Chateau Chien-Pisse* 1948, chilled to room temperature."

George was beginning to look truly panicky. He tried to change the subject.

"Hey! How's my guitar coming on? You've had it for ages."

"Oh yeah!" said David. "I'm, er, hopefully bringing it tomorrow."

"Good," said George, "because I've started to collect Gretsch guitars. I got myself another one recently. Not in such good nick as my original one. The varnish looked a bit stained, like it had been left out in a thunderstorm, but the electrics worked and it sounds great. I might rub it down and get it re-varnished when I have time."

It was now David's turn to look truly panicky. He tried to change the subject.

"Okay lads. Once more with feeling. Let's begin with the two Beatles numbers. George, can you do me a little favour with the lyrics? A little change I want you to try. It's just a bit of a private joke."

CHAPTER 31

The Last Supper

Mo rolled the mighty tour bus into the castle grounds. The occupants let out a perfectly synchronized "Wow!" as they looked around at each other in stunned excitement. He parked the transit and everyone piled out to greet David, who had, with impeccable timing, had just arrived in his Mini and had taken the place next to Mo in the car park.

"And you've been working HERE for a month?" gasped Nick. "God, man. I had no idea you were friends with the ruling classes."

"After tonight, I probably won't be," said David, looking melodramatically to the heavens and sighing a world-weary sigh.

"Come on mate," reasoned George. "We ain't that bad a band!"

Brigitte showed them to the rear garden area, where a huge white marquee had been erected. A couple of female members of staff were busying themselves with the fresh flower displays, and a man in a donkey jacket was laying a red carpet that led from the house to the marquee's front entrance. Most of the band had never been to a dinner in a marquee, and it was proving daunting for some of them.

"We're out of our depth here," said George, showing classic symptoms of succumbing to a massive inferiority complex. "This is too posh for me. I can't speak proper. They'll never understand me."

"Nonsense," said David, rubbing his friend's shoulder. "You are no better or worse than anyone else in this world. Don't be put off by posh accents. There are some who have accents like ours who are the scum of the earth, and some who are saints. The same applies to this lot. Go on tonight and sing your heart out, old pal. They'll love you. If you're self-conscious, *I'll* introduce the songs. I'm one of those poncy, college-educated lads, so I think I can handle it. Besides, I've been working here for a month, so Lord Snooty has learnt to understand me by now."

This was just the medicine George needed. Preserving a dialect that went right back to Anglo Saxon times was of course admirable, but it was also debilitating sometimes. Many people in the Black Country found it nigh-on impossible to speak even one sentence from start to finish without adding dialectic words. George, for example, had once informed David that his 'Spakers was bost,' meaning that his speakers were broken. He could only ever hope to communicate fully within a ten-mile radius of home, which was almost medieval. The whole of England must have once been similarly afflicted, before the advent of affordable travel and the radio. The thought of getting his message over to a bunch of toffs was clearly getting to him, which prompted David to launch into his favourite 'party bore' diatribe. He was about to explain to his friend that the toffs mangled the language better, or for that matter, worse than he ever could, but George quickly changed the subject.

"Did you bring my guitar? I was thinking of playing a bit of rhythm tonight, in the Beatles medley."

"Er, well, you see…" spluttered David.

"Make way folks - Mr Universe coming through." Mo followed up the rear with what looked like twelve amplifiers in his arms, this time giving David the perfect excuse to change the subject yet again. He quickly took one of Mo's cabinets from him and gestured airily to George that he'd fill him in later. Behind them, the other band members were snaking across the manicured lawns with mike stands, guitar cases and drum boxes, stopping every now and then to stare at the venue in awe. Brigitte showed them where to set up, and told them they could sound-check until six, after which the first of the guests would be arriving. On a much larger stage at the opposite end of the marquee, around fifteen middle-aged men in matching tuxedos were setting up their large white boxed music stands with corny treble-clef motifs and the initials 'TC' painted on the fronts. The Tony Catalano Big Band had arrived.

A small army of waitresses was busying itself laying out knives, forks and spoons, and an effete young man with a floppy hairdo was tying gold helium-filled balloons to the centre pieces of each table. Meanwhile, a sleazy-looking gentleman with the merest hint of moustache and a black nylon shirt that was open just a tad too far, was mumbling incoherently into a microphone.

Though no actual words could be deciphered, partly due to appalling diction but mainly due to the microphone being half way down his throat, David could tell immediately that this reptile was the disc jockey. These loathsome creatures had distinctive vocal patterns, inherited from their empty-headed idols on Radio One, and were never happier than when listening to their own voices blurting out inanities. This particular specimen seemed to be trying to reposition his mouth halfway up his left cheek, and though he was

279

plainly local, the thick audio treacle oozing from his mouth was desperately yearning to sound mid-Atlantic.

David was not a particularly vindictive young man, but if he had any vitriol within him, he chose to expend it on disc jockeys. To his way of thinking, they just basked in the reflected glory of the music they played, as if they had in fact written it, rather than merely placed a record onto a turntable. To add insult to injury, most of them then talked all over the record, perhaps because they couldn't face not hearing their own voices for two and a half minutes, or maybe because by marrying their own sound to that of the musical artist, they were somehow, in their tiny minds, becoming part of the music they so admired but were incapable of creating.

The microphone man was now repeating the words "mighty fine sound" over and over again, and adjusting his amplifier each time to make sure that each successive attempt sounded even worse than its predecessor.

Lazlo took on the unofficial role as site manager, and was chivvying the boys along to make sure that the equipment was set up well in advance. Like David, he liked to be organized and in control, and after the debacle that was Belton Court, they were desperate for a good, professional performance at their first stately home. David gave a good impression of someone being busy which would have fooled the casual observer, but in reality he was just whizzing around trying to do a hundred things at once and not actually achieving anything, other than making the others even more nervous.

He would punctuate his bouts of frenetic activity with sudden dashes to the mobile lavatories behind the marquee. His nervousness had always manifested itself as either

280

indigestion or diarrhoea, depending on its whim, and this had caused him to spend a good deal of his leisure time in the toilets of England, which, in turn, had led to him appreciating them in the same way that normal people adjudge hotels and restaurants. His interest in all things scatological had often prompted Lazlo to recommend that his friend publish a 'Good Toilets of Britain' book - a sort of Michelin Guide, but for lavvies.

This had become such a standing joke over the years that on his colleague's return from whichever public convenience he'd been visiting, Lazlo would always enquire as to the precise nature of David's bowel movement, including colour, quantity and consistency. He would also ask for a mark out of ten for interior décor, softness of paper and cleanliness of the pan. On this occasion, David had returned with much excitement after his initial visit to the 'Stanmore Mobile Conveniences', enthusing wildly about the perfumed atmosphere and the fresh lilies. His description was so vivid that Mo temporarily abandoned his duties to investigate for himself, much to the annoyance of Lazlo, who was desperate to see the amplifiers lit up so that he could go through a few songs to settle his nerves.

The DJ, who had been studying this scruffily-dressed and unshaven rabble from behind his decks, plucked up the courage to present himself.

"'scuse me lads, I'm Mark Duvall, the disc jockey," he began, the mid-Atlantic accent mysteriously absent from his voice, and replaced by a thick local one. He proffered a stubby hand in George's direction. It was a hand that had obviously loaded millions of bricks into wheel barrows in its time.

"Yeah!" whispered David to Lazlo. "And my name's Johnny Cougar."

"I'll be introducing you when you go on stage," he continued. "What shall I call you?"

"We're The Stubbles," said Lazlo proudly.

"I can see that!" laughed Mark Duvall, a.k.a. Brett Whittle, weekend superstar and weekday hod carrier from the Wrens Nest, a rough council estate near Dudley.

"Oh, we haven't shaved yet, and we came in our work clothes to hump the gear," said Nick. "We're gonna clean ourselves up later. I suppose you will too."

If the comment hurt, the DJ made a good job of not showing it.

"How did *you* get the gig?" asked Nick, as if he was actually interested.

"Oh, I'm a close personal friend of Lord Hickman," said the disc-spinner, puffing up his sizeable chest.

"As opposed to a distant impersonal friend?" asked David, who had been known to be pedantic at times.

"You what?" asked the DJ.

"Oh, nothing," said David. "How did you meet?"

"I helped convert his stable block into the French bloke's offices," said the DJ. "I only do discos at weekends. I work for a building company as well, just till I can get some radio work. How did you get the job anyway?"

"I'm a friend of Lord Hickman too," bragged David, stopping just short of saying "Nar-nar-nee-nar-nar", because he feared that it might come across as a little childish. "I'm

282

an artist, and I've been working at the house for a month, cleaning the oil paintings."

"Ah!" said the DJ, putting two and two together and making four for a change. "You're the picture restorer. My mate Jethro told me about you."

"Yes, that's me," said David. "The picture restorer. I'm going to try and restore a few pictures tonight, hopefully to their rightful owner." He gave a self-satisfied smirk, pleased with his little witticism.

The DJ could make nothing of this. He cocked his thumb up to David and the others, made his excuses and returned to his decks to twiddle a few knobs, in an attempt to banish any semblance of clarity from his tinny mike.

After the usual panic about insufficient power supplies and missing plug boards, which resulted in Mo's mad dash to the nearest hardware store and David's mad dash to the portaloo, the amplifiers were up and running. There then followed a cacophony of noise, as each guitarist became enthralled by the sound of his own amplified instrument, unaware of and uninterested in what the others were playing alongside him. The net result was ear-shattering and unpleasant to anyone other than the musicians themselves, a fact that was pointed out by not just one member of the Tony Catalano Big Band, but all of them.

David, ever the peacemaker, shouted for the band to cease their self-indulgent waffling and begin the tuning up process. He shouted over an apology to the big band, who took it gracefully, muttering to themselves about how they were young once. Just at that point, a middle-aged man in wire-rimmed specs and a mustard-coloured cashmere coat walked into the marquee carrying a large guitar case, and made his way towards David.

283

Tony Catalano, a sixty-plus Italian crooner with hair that was blacker than even Ronald Reagan's, shouted across the dance floor to the new arrival.

"Hey, ciao, big boy! What are you doing here?" The rest of the band began to recognize the newcomer, one by one.

"Jeez!" said a sax player. "As I live and breathe! A legend. We are not worthy!"

Jack McCartney spun round to see who was heckling him, and a huge smile spread across his face. "Tony Catalano. Goodness me! Well I never, and you brought the entire loony bin with you."

The two men met each other half way and hugged, Italian-style, with much manly kissing on both cheeks. David and Lazlo wandered over to see what the fuss was about.

"Hi Dave," said Jack, breaking loose from the big man's clutches. "This is Tony. We go way back. I used to play guitar with his band years ago."

"That was when we could afford the son of a bitch," laughed Tony. "This man was a pioneer. He was the very first electric jazz guitarist in Britain. Did you know that, son? He's a legend. He's played for all the greats, haven't you Jacko? Sinatra, Dean Martin, you name it!"

David and Lazlo were impressed.

"What, the bloke who robs us of our hard-earned pocket money in that poky little shop in Dudley was a star?" asked Lazlo, grinning.

"*Was* a star? *Is* a star! It's always Jack they call when they tour the UK, eh Jack?"

284

Jack nodded modestly. "Anyway, enough already," he said, genuinely embarrassed by the adulation. "Great to see you all. We'll catch up later. Listen to these guys, Dave - you too Laz. They may never see sixty again, but they can rock."

He picked up the guitar case and handed it to David.

"I think this is what you've been waiting for," he said. "I should have kicked two hundred quid's worth of value out of Dave Lowe's arse for selling George's guitar, especially after old Bob spent days repairing the bugger. Anyway, we invested the proceeds, plus a considerable amount more, I'll have you know, and located this little beauty for him."

He opened the case to reveal a pristine black Gretsch guitar.

"Wow!" said David. "That's a beauty. Just one small, insignificant point. I hardly feel it's worthy of bringing up…"

"But you will," added Lazlo.

"George's guitar was orange."

"The fact did not escape me," admitted Jack. "That's where you come into play, with your golden tongue. I'm sure you'll concoct some totally plausible reason why you took an average orange guitar off him to repair the electrics and returned with a better quality, top of the bloody range black one in a fitted hard case and not a soggy cardboard box."

David was quick. He grasped the essence of Jack's barbed comment and felt duly ashamed for being so churlish. To create a convincing scenario for the introduction of a superior black guitar into George's life would be for him the work of a few seconds of deep thought, and no more. He thanked Jack profusely.

"Now, if no one minds," said the music shop proprietor, "I'll go and catch up with my old sparring partners over there, and mingle, chameleon-like, with the guests. I hate freeloaders and gate-crashers, but I'm damned if I'm going home just yet. The wife is watching some dire shite on TV and I want to catch some jazz. I may even listen to you lot too, if my old ears can stand it."

He winked knowingly at David and wandered over to catch up with Tony Catalano.

George, who, in sharp contrast to the DJ, had been preoccupied with getting his vocal sound perfect and had at last succeeded, breezed over to David to see what Jazzy Jack had delivered. David handed the instrument to the delighted, if perplexed singer with a flourish, promising to explain all when the night was over. By now, and with absolutely no thanks to David, the equipment was in place, the amps turned on and the drums and guitars tuned to perfection. It was time to run through a few songs so that Mo, who was standing at the back of the room, could help them to balance the sound by yelling for Ken to turn up and add treble, or Lazlo to turn down and add bass. This was done in accordance with Mo's wishes, and as soon as he had given the thumbs up and returned to the stage, the two guitarists secretly turned secretly themselves back up again. George, by day a poorly-paid light bulb tester in a Tipperton factory, had long dreamt of owning a proper mixing desk, so that Mo could sit behind it at the back of the hall and control the sound independently of the people on stage. That way he would fulfil his lifelong dream of being heard above the noisy guitarists.

The band took to the stage and plugged in their guitars, carefully and professionally avoiding a repeat of the free-for-all din they had created earlier. This time, in a deliberate attempt to impress their elders and betters, not to mention one of England's best jazz guitarists, George began with a discreet count in, and the magical opening chords of 'She's a Woman' by the Beatles cut through the empty marquee like a scalpel. Jack interrupted his chat with Tony to look at the stage. The waitresses paused to listen, only to be chivvied along by the effeminate balloon-tying fop. The sound was perfect, the band sounded tight, and all was right with the world. It would have taken a skilled surgeon to remove the broad, fixed grins from their faces. After several dodgy gigs and some sloppy performances they had raised their game, and a spark of sheer magic had resulted. They sounded bloody marvellous!

A few early guests began to find their way into the marquee and were heading for the bar in twos and threes. The men were immaculate in their dinner suits, and their ladies nothing short of stunning in low-backed ball gowns and pearls. David had always said to Lazlo that, should he become Prime Minister, formal dress would be made compulsory. He loved the old black and white films of the forties, with satin-draped beauties sharing a cocktail with rugged wisecracking Phillip Marlowe-types in snap brimmed fedoras. He liked the fast, witty dialogue, and the way that the camera suddenly switched to soft focus whenever the lady had a close up. It was a golden age, and here, in front of his very eyes, it was coming to life again. The band laid down their instruments and headed for the bar, chatting amongst themselves about how good they sounded and how keen they were to give the audience the show of their lives.

George took Ken to one side, and asked him as tactfully as he could to resist the temptation to drink until the gig was over. He was dreading a tongue-lashing, but to his relief, Ken had already decided to abstain that evening.

"I couldn't let the lads down tonight of all nights," he said, whereupon George threw his arms around him, planting a wet kiss on his stubbly cheek.

"Lay off!" shrieked Ken, horrified. "That's enough to send me back on the bottle again!"

David was talking to Lazlo by the bar when a lovely-looking creature in a purple dress shimmered towards him. She had her hair up, which made her neck look about two feet long, and her beautiful bare back and shoulders were just asking to be caressed. Such was this lady's impact that David stood and gawped, totally ignoring Lazlo's request to lower the volume of his guitar just a tad.

"Hello David!" said the vision.

"My God! S-S-Suzanne!" he stammered. "You look fantastic. What on earth are you doing here?"

"Nicole invited me," she replied, smiling a smile that made David feel weak. "Her mother works for Lord Hickman apparently. She didn't want to come on her own, so she asked me to come with her. I must admit I was a bit surprised, because since we've been at college we haven't been as close, to be honest."

"Would you like a drink?" asked David, still visibly stunned. "This is my best mate, Laz, he was just about to get the drinks in, weren't you old pal?"

"Apparently, yes," said Lazlo. "What would you both like?"

David distractedly gave him their order, without once breaking eye contact with her. He had seen her a million times at college in an old pair of jeans, and never really noticed how lovely she was. Tonight she had opened his eyes, and he couldn't believe that he'd been so blind. She was truly beautiful, in an Ingrid Bergman kind of way - not flashy or not overly made-up. Just achingly gorgeous.

He'd always imagined she would be self-assured and bitchy, like her friend, but tonight she seemed vulnerable and eager for company. Best of all, she seemed completely unaware of how lovely she was - a quality that appealed greatly to David, who intensely disliked women who *knew* they were stunning. Even worse was the girl who knew damned well that she was beautiful, but coyly informed her fawning entourage that she considered herself ugly, in the hope that at least one salivating man would take the bait, and tell her what she already knew.

"I heard you sound checking when I arrived," said Suzanne. "I knew you were in a band because Katie told me, but it was a complete shock to see you here. You were fantastic! I can't wait to hear you later."

"Thank you," said David, his embarrassingly autonomous cheeks burning red at the compliment. "Yes, we got the gig because I've done a bit of work here at the castle, and Lord Snooty invited us to play. We're all petrified."

"You'll be great," she said, rubbing his arm, and causing the hairs on the back of his neck to stand up. If that was what rubbing his arm did to him, he couldn't begin to imagine what penetrative sex would be like.

Lazlo arrived with the drinks, and reminded David that they needed to get changed, as they were on straight after dinner.

"Look," said David. "Are you okay on your own, because I have to get ready? I suppose you've, erm, come with some hunky bloke who…"

"No." said Suzanne, looking at her shoes. I only came at all because…"

"Dave!" said Lazlo. "We have to go, mate."

"I'll be fine," said Suzanne. "Katie from college is coming soon, so I can talk to her. I don't know where Nicole is, but between you and me, we're not really that pally nowadays. I'll hang around for Katie."

"Katie is coming here?" asked David. "How come half of the Art College is here anyway?"

"Oh, she's been invited by one of the band, didn't you know?" asked Suzanne.

"Oh, erm, Dave," interrupted Lazlo. "I forgot to mention it. I invited her. I'll explain all in the changing rooms."

David promised to see Suzanne later, and hurried off with Lazlo to round up the others so they could change into their stage clothes.

"Let me guess," said David, as they meandered over to collect the others. "Katie is here to see you, right?"

"Er, well, the thing is," began Lazlo, eyes fixed on the floor, "When I took that easel back, I began chatting to her, and you know how it is, we sort of started seeing a lot of each other, kind of thing."

"How much of each other?"

"Well, you know, a lot, only what makes this deeply embarrassing is, I know you asked her to come with you, didn't you?"

"Yep!"

"And you're no good at chatting up girls are you? It must have taken lots of courage."

"Yep!"

"But if I'd have realized you fancied her, I'd never have been so forward, honest! Anyway, that girl you just spoke to was all over you like a cheap suit. She's blooming gorgeous."

"Yes she is. I've only just realized it as well. She just didn't register before, for some reason. I was too busy drooling over her French mate, who, incidentally, is a bloody nasty piece of work in my humble opinion. Then my attentions turned to Katie, who is obviously much more my cup of tea, so I pluck up the courage to ask, and old mega-dick's already been there."

"It's not *that* big," insisted Lazlo, coyly.

"It isn't half! You and your knob are in two different postal districts. It's bound to turn a girl's head. What chance have I got, with a todger that looks like a sparrow's nest with one egg in it? The only person who'd even consider swapping with me is Hank Frill."

"Who?" asked Lazlo, confused. "Listen, forget the size of our bloody todgers. That girl back there fancies you, and she's on her own. You wouldn't recognize a come-on if she tore off that dress and snogged you naked, that's your trouble. Have a talk to her over din-dins and just be yourself. If you get within a mile of a fanciable girl you either clam up completely or make a complete turd of yourself by showing off. Why not be the David that *I* know? The one who talks about stuff till the early hours in my car and makes me laugh?"

David smiled weakly and said he'd give it a go, but meanwhile it was time to get changed, as dinner was being served in ten minutes. Mo's dad owned a market stall in Wednesbury, and he'd kindly donated six garish Hawaiian shirts which even the people of Wednesbury had turned their noses up at. Some people obviously preferred to look drab. The band's general consensus was that the shirts were so awful - they were good. David's was predominantly blue, featuring naked women with breasts that were strategically covered up with garlands of flowers, whilst Lazlo favoured the green palm-tree/camel combination. When seen *en masse*, the effect, like it or hate it, couldn't be ignored.

Mo sported one too, more as an act of solidarity than anything else. Even the Beach boys wouldn't have been seen dead in them.

There was no designated changing room, so the five grubby and unshaven lads used the fancy portaloo. Minutes later, they emerged like garish butterflies, chattering nervously and comparing shirt designs, with Nick complaining bitterly that he'd had his eyes on the naked women. Apparently, he didn't think much of his bright pink fuchsias on the emerald background, which he argued made him look like Quentin Crisp.

They made their way back into the marquee, which was by now buzzing with activity. It was full of elegant people, chatting and laughing loudly, as waitresses weaved between them offering *hors d'oeuvres* from large silver trays. Dylan, who had just arrived, raised his arms to greet David and gave him a bear hug that fractured at least three ribs. Introductions over, he excused himself to go in search of Guinness. Lazlo spotted Katie and called her over. She had been talking to Suzanne, who came over with her. Katie smiled at David and kissed him.

"Hello you!" she grinned. "Can't wait to hear this band of yours. You'd better be good, and I hope you're not too loud."

"No, we're not," said David, "but our shirts are. What do you think?"

"They're certainly shirts!" said Suzanne, diplomatically.

Nicole emerged from the now-heaving crowd and said a frosty hello to the two Hawaiians and their lady friends.

"So, David," she sneered, "what do you 'ave in the store for us tonight? I would 'ave thought you 'ad 'ad enough of the public humiliation for a lifetime, and still you come back for more, eh? Let me guess, tonight you are a drag act stripper? Or perhaps you are trying to win ze worst-dressed man competition? What is it? Maybe you've come to flood ze place!"

She turned and disappeared into the crowd.

"She wants me," said David, with a wry smile.

"What was that all about?" asked Lazlo angrily. "What's her problem, Dave?"

"Oh, it's a long story," replied David, who couldn't cope with more public humiliation, especially in front of the two women he fancied. "She just doesn't like me. We got off on the wrong foot."

"Ignore her," advised Suzanne. "She's a cow sometimes. *I* like you - you make me laugh. Especially wearing that shirt."

"Thank you," said David, his cheeks getting hot again. "Shall we sit down? Everyone else is."

The band members were all seated together, along with Katie, Suzanne and Dylan. Nicole was not far away with her mother, and Lord Hickman was on the top table with his wife and a load of braying, ruddy-faced country types from the local hunt. He called over to David and said hello, adding that he was looking forward to the music later on. Ken nudged him in the ribs and said something cutting about David having his nose up the backsides of the aristocracy. George, meanwhile, had a look of abject terror on his face, not from the thought of having to sing, but from having to eat rich, unidentifiable food that patently wasn't cod and chips.

The girls were formally introduced to the other band members and Mo, who proposed an early toast to a good evening. David emptied his glass, and shuddered at the prospect. Not only did he have to play in an hour's time, but he also had other, infinitely more nerve-wracking duties to perform later, while the others were letting their hair down.

The dinner went without incident, with the exception of Ken's dramatic refusal of wine when offered a glass by the waiter. Nick, sarcastic as ever, pretended to faint with shock, but Lazlo, who could himself drink for the national team, congratulated him on his will power.

"Just half an hour on stage, old pal," he added, "and then we can get bladdered."

Jack McCartney had found his way onto the big band's table and was having the time of his life. Tony Catalano had employed his considerable charm on the young waitress to secure a spare dinner for his old friend, whom he had introduced as his secret guest star - so secret in fact, that he'd inadvertently forgotten to add his name to the dinner list. Lazlo noticed that Jack too was conspicuously abstaining from alcohol. Could he be planning to perform too, he wondered.

"I hope not," said David. "He'd wipe the floor with us."

Coffees were now arriving and plates being taken away, and six young men were getting increasingly nervous with every passing minute.

"I just want to get on there now and do it," said Ken, sucking shakily on a Park Drive. "It's the waiting that kills me. I'd kill my granny for a pint of lager."

"Relax and enjoy it lads," advised Mo. Easy for him to say of course. He could hide in the portaloo if they went down like the Titanic.

After what seemed like an eternity, when the guests were advised to take what is euphemistically called a 'comfort break', the DJ turned on his cut-price mike and treated the assembled multitude to an ear-shattering display of feedback that had the elderly contingent rushing for the wide open spaces. Finally, after George had rushed to help bring it under control, 'Mark Duvall' announced in his phoney mid-Atlantic accent that the band were about to grace the stage, and could everyone put their hands together for 'The Struggles.'

"Twat!" whispered David, to no one in particular.

CHAPTER 32

Play it again

The boys were now on stage; guitars strapped on and ready to go. Nick counted them in on his sticks, and the band launched into the powerful opening riff of the Beatles song, 'Money'. George stepped up to the microphone and sang:

The best things in life are free,

But you can keep them for the birds and bees,

I want Monet,

That's what I want,

I want Monet.

The majority of the audience, who were by now well oiled, courtesy of Lady Hickman's free bar and the never-ending supply of wine at the table, immediately rose to their well-heeled feet and headed for the dance floor. This pleased the band no end, and any semblance of nerves evaporated. Right at the front, near the stage, Katie and Suzanne were dancing together and looking up admiringly at Lazlo and David, who reciprocated by affecting corny rock star poses and grinning their heads off. The first song drew to a close, but instead of waiting for applause, they neatly segued into another Beatles classic, 'Can't Buy Me Love' which drove the inebriated crowd wild, mainly due to George's vocals. His voice sounded so uncannily like McCartney's that guests who had previously been chatting at their tables instantly ceased all conversation and glanced towards the stage. Once more, he had adapted the words, as David had instructed him to.

I don't care too much for Monet,

Monet can't buy me love.

David scanned the floor for a glimpse of Lord Hickman, trying to see if the subtle changes to the wording had had an impact, just as Hamlet had observed his wicked uncle as he watched the travelling players perform. If Hickman *had* understood the reference, his face didn't betray it. More likely, he was probably just thinking to himself that the singer had a strange accent, which, after all, was true.

Dylan, who had spent most of his time at the bar trying to make Guinness extinct, suddenly put his glass down and pushed his way to the front where he began throwing Suzanne around like a rag doll, as he performed what he fondly imagined was a rock and roll dance, but was actually closer to all-in wrestling. As the song ended, virtually everyone in the marquee was applauding, and the band looked around at each other as if to say, "Life doesn't get any better than this."

David was just about to don the mantle of spokesman and compère, in light of his friend's earlier reticence, when George unexpectedly addressed the crowd.

"Yer woe understond me, but yo'le understond this!" he said, pointing to David, who let rip with the mighty opening chords of 'All Right Now', which nearly took the roof off the marquee.

The lads had originally feared that the upper-crust audience of Henry's and Camillas would hate their brand of earthy rock and roll, but they were wrong. It was the best crowd they'd ever played to - which admittedly didn't mean too much, with only Belton Court and a Butter Factory's social club to choose from. Even Lady Caroline was on her feet now and dancing a tad too closely with Dylan, a sight which caused David much amusement as he screamed his way through Paul Kossoff's classic guitar solo.

Katie and Suzanne were having a good time too, and were blowing kisses at the two guitarists whenever they thought they were watching, like a pair of groupies hoping for some action after the show. Birthday boy, Lord Hickman was having the time of his life, cavorting around with several of his friends and groping Brigitte's bottom whenever he thought that no one was looking. Meanwhile, Jean Jacques stood at the bar smoking and looking nervous.

David glanced across the dance floor at his prancing patron, and swallowed hard as he realized what lay ahead. He had grown almost fond of the man in a strange kind of way, but he also knew exactly what he was. He understood that the Hickman's of this world caused heartbreak and financial ruin for others, and it couldn't be allowed to continue. He was friendly and plausible, but these qualities were merely the tools of the con artist, and people like

Marco Bonini would continue to suffer if Lord Hickman was allowed to get away with it. No, it had to be done, and if t'were done at all, it was best t'were done quickly, as another one of life's castle-dwelling chancers once put it.

The most galling thing was that David had to kiss goodbye to his fee. He couldn't see His Lordship coughing up somehow, after what lay ahead. David resolved to put such thoughts out of his mind until he'd finished playing - otherwise his concentration would begin to slip.

With only half an hour to play, the band had selected their favourite songs, and played them in an order that was guaranteed to constantly raise the temperature. They rattled through classics by the Kinks, The Faces and Eric Clapton, ending with a medley of rock and roll songs.

"That's all we have time for," shouted Lazlo hoarsely, waving at the crowd and lifting his guitar above his head, like all the best rock stars do.

"Tara a bit!" added George. "Yo'm the best we've ever played to. Yo'm bostin'!"

The audience began to applaud even more loudly, and Suzanne was wolf-whistling with gay abandon. Katie and Dylan started stamping their feet on the wooden panels that made up the dance floor area, kicking up a terrible din. This, in turn, was the signal for the entire audience to join in, and soon the marquee was struggling to contain a cacophony of sound that seemed intent on waking half of Staffordshire.

George walked up to the mike, clearly touched and close to tears, to thank them profusely. The Black Country gent strapped on his black Country Gent and strummed a few quiet chords, which caused the crowd to cease their noisy acts of appreciation and listen. The rest of the band listened too. They hadn't got the foggiest idea what was coming next either, as they had foolishly forgotten to rehearse an encore.

He walked up to the mike and sang;

Hey Jude, don't make it bad,

Sing a sad song, and make it better.

Remember, to let it into your heart,

 Then you can start, to make it better.

Nick let him sing the first verse on his own, and augmented the second with drums, nodding to Ken to add a bass line. This was no problem for him, as he virtually idolized the Beatles and knew their songs note for note. (Unlike the Led Zeppelin ones) The effect on the crowd was magical. All night, the songs had been raucous and loud, and now this lovely ballad had completely and cleverly changed the mood. Dancers smooched together, women with their arms around their men's shoulders and men with their hands on their women's behinds. The unattached, dewy-eyed and sentimental, swayed gently from side to side, helped no doubt by the continuing generosity of the free bar. Only two people in the marquee seemed uninterested in George's singing, and coincidentally they were both French. Nicole, trying to make herself heard above the music, was cupping her hands and shouting into her mother's ear.

"Where is Father? 'as he gone yet?"

"Yes. A moment ago. I'm very nervous, for some reason. I told him that I'd stay here and talk to Lord Hickman. Otherwise it would look a little suspicious."

"Of course!" shouted Nicole. "Where is he anyway? I can't see him."

Brigitte scanned the Marquee, but he was nowhere to be seen. "Maybe he's gone to the toilets. Maybe he's around the back of the tent with a young debutante. Who can say?" she shrugged, nonchalantly sucking on a long French cigarette.

"I'll go see," said Nicole. "I have to visit the toilets myself. I 'ave some awful English rosbif I need to dispose of, and I need a rest from zis terrible row! I bloody 'ate the Beatles."

Unaware of the effect he was having on Nicole, George continued to enchant the rest of his flock with McCartney's magical anthem. Suzanne swayed with Katie at the front, arm in arm, and looked up proudly at their college friend, happy for him on his big night. The song began to gather its momentum, and by now at least half of those present were singing along. By the time George had reached the wonderful 'Nar,nar-nar,nanana-nar' section of the song, they were all standing on the chairs and swaying, arms aloft, like a football crowd at Wembley. The hypnotic mantra continued to build with each repeat, until finally George signalled that the end had come, and finished with a long, drawn out 'Hey Jude', which was completely drowned out by a cheering and table-thumping audience.

The lads took off their guitars and placed them on their stands, waving, blowing kisses and pretending, just for one or two sweet moments, that they were the Beatles at the Shea Stadium. It was a night they would never forget, and for some it had hardly begun. David, drenched in sweat and hair like rat's-tails, descended the stage steps and went straight over to Suzanne and Katie, who both hugged him. Lazlo, never tardy when hugs are being offered around by girls in ball gowns, arrived soon afterwards.

Nicole had been absent from the proceedings for the last half of the encore, but now she cut a swathe through the crowd and walked up to David, virtually brushing his two women friends aside.

"Ah, so now you are ze pop star, David? I 'ave to warn you Suzanne, that he is not normal in 'is head. So far he 'as cavorted naked and frothing, not once but twice, showing 'is tiny little man to everyone. If mine were that small, I don't sink I would be showing it to ze world. He has blown 'is car to pieces, flooded expensive apartments and changed 'is sex in Italy. Tonight he is cavorting around in ze stupid shirt thinking he is George Harrison. What next for you, David? Try growing up, zat's a good idea I think!"

Suzanne began to say something, but David put his finger to his lips, gently advising her to hold her tongue.

"What exactly have I done to offend you, Nicole?" he asked. "I may be a fool, but I'm not malicious, I would have said. All you've done since we first met is be nasty to me. You've just belittled me in front of my friends, and all I was ever guilty of was thinking how beautiful you were. We men are often tongue-tied with girls, because it's us that are expected to bite the bullet and make the first move, and I can tell you that it's nerve-wracking. For once in your life, just think about it. You repay our interest in you by belittling us and laughing amongst yourselves if we aren't exactly the handsome hunk that you had on your shopping list. It's easy for you, you're beautiful, but I can tell you this. Your *mind* isn't beautiful. Inside your pretty head it's ugly, and anyone who goes out with you for more than a week would discover that for themselves. Just leave me alone, and I'll do the same for you. How's that?"

"Why should I?" sneered Nicole, taken aback. "You are a fool, and I like to remind you of it."

"Can *I* add something?" asked Suzanne.

"If you wish," replied Nicole aloofly.

"Well, firstly, all the things you hate about him are the very things I like about him. *Vive le différence* eh, Frog Face? Secondly, did you just pop out to the portaloo by any chance?"

Nicole considered this new line of questioning totally beneath her, and refused to answer. She began to walk away towards the bar, but Suzanne, who was in full flow now, shouted after her.

"The only reason I ask is that you have a long trail of soiled toilet paper tucked into the back of your dress, that's all. It rather spoils the effect, in my humble opinion."

Nicole spun round and realized, with a look of absolute horror, that her one-time friend was not wrong. She tore off the offending, malodorous article, and ran from the marquee into the night.

The circle of friends looked in blank amazement at Suzanne.

"What?" she asked, visibly shaking, like a pest-control officer who doesn't like doing his job but knows it has to be done.

"Remind me to stay on your side," said Lazlo. "What a girl!"

Katie gave her new acquaintance a comforting hug, adding that if Suzanne hadn't intervened, she'd have done the same, only maybe with a fist to the snout instead. David had his head in his hands, reliving the moment when Nicole had seen the toilet paper. He had long dreamt of revenge, but for some reason it now gave him no pleasure at all. His head was full of conflicting emotions, but the overriding one was that a lovely girl who looked more like Ingrid Bergman with every passing minute had stood up for him, and given his chief protagonist a piece of her mind. No, he felt nothing but sorrow for Nicole's plight now, but it *was* largely self-inflicted. Sad as he was to see her so distressed, she would think twice before coming on like the Ice Queen again.

David, meanwhile, suddenly caught a glimpse of his watch, which yanked him back to reality with a start.

"Jesus Christ!" he shouted, scaring Suzanne and Katie out of their wits.

"It's ten past nine!"

"Do you turn into a pumpkin?" asked Suzanne, intrigued.

"Worse, if I don't get out of here now!" he said. "Lazlo, get Mo. NOW!"

CHAPTER 33

Round up the usual suspects

David beckoned to Mo, Lazlo and the two girls to follow him to the car park as quickly as they could, adding breathlessly that all would be explained later. As he reached the marquee entrance he saw Jack, deep in conversation with Tony Catalano. David pointed to his watch, mouthed the words, "See you later," and then ran to catch up with the others.

"We'll go in my Mini," he said. "It'll be quicker than the transit van."

David got into the driver's seat with Mo in the passenger seat. Lazlo sat Katie on his lap with Suzanne next to them in the rear. It was what a car salesman would describe as 'cosy'. If David had hit any speed bumps on the journey, Lazlo would have risked producing a child out of wedlock.

"What on earth is going on?" asked Suzanne, clutching the door handle for support.

David repeated that all would be explained in the fullness of time, and asked everyone to bear with him. The car screeched through the black and winding country lanes, causing Katie's head to buffet continually against the low roof of the car. Lazlo just crossed himself theatrically at every new screech. After ten hair-raising minutes, the car pulled into the front gates of Twopenny Green Aerodrome, near Bobbington village, where once the mighty Dambuster Squadron had rehearsed their manoeuvres prior to their famous raids. He drove past the car park and onto the runway, heading for what looked like aeroplane lights at the far end of the dark, remote airfield.

"Have you gone completely bloody barmy?" yelled Lazlo, exasperated. It was not an unreasonable question given the circumstances. The car skidded to a halt on the wet tarmac, and David got out, asking Mo to follow him. The others were asked to remain in the car, and talk amongst themselves.

"If anything big with wings comes your way, and I don't mean a heron," David shouted to Lazlo, "make yourselves scarce."

Mo and David moved as stealthily as they could in the direction of the plane, a twin-engined affair that looked to David's untrained eye like a four or six-seater, rather than the smaller Cessna single-engines that often flew over his house *en-route* for the aerodrome. He could see the silhouettes of several figures inside, and could hear what sounded like a heated discussion. They approached the plane from behind, and David crept below the window line to listen in on the conversation.

"Do you think, you stupid French imbecile, that I was born yesterday?" asked Herr Grunstrasse angrily. "Zis painting is still wet. It is painted on a canvas that is patently modern in construction. I haf not flown all the way to England to be treated like a fool."

"But I don't understand it, Herr Grunstrasse!" whined Jean Jacques. "I know that the original was behind the old portrait. I placed it there myself, and it was definitely the real thing. I can't explain it!"

"You stole that picture from me, you little frog-faced shit!" snapped Lord Hickman, reaching out to grab the Frenchman's collar and being restrained by Pierre the Pilot. "What did you do with it?"

"Ah, so now we are getting all moral about stealing are we?" sneered Jean Jacques. "How do you suppose you came by the picture in the first place?"

"Ja, you shut your mouth," snarled Herr Grunstrasse. "You both try to sell me the same Monet and neither of you have it to sell in ze first place. I get very vindictive when my precious time is vasted. I must admit, Lord Hickman, that your fake is better than zis idiot's fake, but fakes zey both are. I suppose the Botticelli is also laughable?"

He opened Lord Hickman's portfolio and pulled out the drawing, removing its tissue paper covering. He added a pair of wire-rimmed spectacles to his fat sweaty face and studied the picture for a few moments.

"Ha! Pierre, it gets funnier. Now His Lordship is trying to sell me a forged Botticelli...."

David knocked loudly on the aeroplane door, in a style that suggested he was the next-door neighbour returning the garden shears. The door swung open, and David popped his head inside. He saw Lord Hickman, Jean Jacques and two people he didn't recognize. One was fat and wore a crumpled cream linen suit. The other was small and thin with bulging eyes that seemed to swivel independently, like a chameleon's.

"Ah, gents, good evening, guten Abend, bonsoir!" said David breezily. "Lord Hickman and J.J. I know. You'll be Mr Grunstrasse, and I guess you're his pilot."

"Who the hell are you?" asked Herr Grunstrasse. Pierre felt inside his flying jacket for a little reassurance.

"Oh me? I'm David," he said smiling, "and I bet I can guess what's going on. Our French friend here is trying to flog you a forged Monet, and Lord Hickman here is trying to do likewise, and throwing in a Botticelli for good measure, unless I'm very much mistaken. The trouble is, I have the real things in my possession, tucked away safely, and I intend to return them to their rightful owner. Now, I know I run the risk of spouting a real cliché here, but in about one minute, this aerodrome will be crawling with police, so if you wouldn't mind getting out of the plane and giving yourselves up, I'd be most grateful."

* * * * *

Meanwhile, at nine-fifteen pm, on the car park of the Whittington Inn, near Kinver, the observant drinker would have noticed a panda car containing three members of Her Majesty's constabulary eating smoky bacon crisps and drinking bottles of Vimto. The Whit, as it was known by the locals, was a fourteenth-century building that was built by William de Whittington, the grandfather of the rather more famous Dick Whittington, one time Lord Mayor of London and cat fancier. It was also the childhood home of the unfortunate Lady Jane Grey, whose head was parted from her body at an age when most young girls would be looking forward to their first disco.

Now, the Whit was the temporary base of constables Donald Woolley and Reg Bate, plus a 'wet behind the ears' rookie recruit in the back seat whom they had seen fit to rename Toxic. They had received a call on their radio asking them to attend an incident at the aerodrome at precisely nine-fifteen, where hopefully they would be able to catch a felon or two red-handed as they tried to fence stolen property. The caller had stressed that timing was of the essence, but our boys in blue had become becalmed and unable to proceed, due to the huge beer lorry that had broadsided across the notorious A449 and demolished a tractor coming in the opposite direction. Luckily for all concerned, no one was seriously injured, though the farmer did need new underpants.

The Wombourne police and the other emergency services were currently dealing with the accident, leaving the three musketeers marooned, frustrated and itching for action. In the meantime, they sought solace in snack foods and fizzy pop. Toxic, his gangly young frame squeezed into the back seat, had been drafted in at the last minute by Donald, who couldn't stand to see him at a loose end doing crosswords at the station. The lad was a raw recruit, as yet untested in an emergency situation, but he was also the West Midlands Police One Hundred Metres Sprint Champion, and could well come in handy should one of the criminals decide to leg it.

The responsibility of potentially having to chase and manhandle a vicious thug who could well be armed to the teeth weighed heavily, and manifested itself in what the more polite observer would call 'excess gas.' The fact that he'd consumed copious quantities of fizzy drink and three packets of crisps didn't help either. Ever since leaving the station, Toxic had let rip at alarmingly regular intervals, filling the panda with a pungent block of stale air, much to the chagrin of the other two officers.

"For Christ's sake man, can't you get out of the car to do that?" complained Reg, as he opened the window for the umpteenth time and fanned the vile gases away with his peaked cap. Toxic, who rather enjoyed the smell of his own creations, sat looking pleased with himself as he lifted his left leg to release another one into the wild.

"Don't be such a girl!" he grinned. "They won't 'urt yer! Take deep breaths – it'll soon be gone."

* * * * *

Back at the airfield, things were getting tetchy. Pierre, annoyed by this young upstart's intrusion, took out his pistol and pointed it at David's head. Had the lad been having trouble with constipation, this gesture would almost certainly have helped him greatly, just as the out-of-control beer truck had done for the farmer. Unfortunately, David's bowels were, as has been well documented, usually afflicted by the opposite problem, and it was only the timely clenching of his firm young buttock muscles that saved him from certain embarrassment in front of strangers. Kinver and its environs were certainly experiencing some scatological activity that night, what with one thing and another.

"Okay, I am now sick of playing around," Pierre snarled, his eyes swivelling from side to side at an alarming rate of knots. "Back slowly out of the plane, joker. Lord Hickman, Jean Jacques, you too."

The would-be art dealers stood in line outside the plane, hands aloft, followed by Pierre and Herr Grunstrasse. Mo, who was still crouching beneath the window, was caught cold by the suddenness of their exit, and stood transfixed like a muscle-bound rabbit in the headlamps.

"Ah, welcome to the party, big boy!" sneered Pierre, and waved his gun, gesturing for Mo to line up with the others.

"Nicely done," said Herr Grunstrasse to his colleague. "Now, gentlemen. I may be a fat man but my patience is wearing a bit thin. Correct me if I'm wrong, but the place is hardly swarming with police, as you suggested. Maybe they stopped off for fish and chips on the way. You will now hand over the real paintings, or Pierre here will begin to get nasty."

"This is your fault, you slimy French shit," snarled Lord Hickman. "I gave you a job and paid you well, and is this how you repay me?"

"I treated you the way you treated Signor Bonini, you hypocrite!" spat the Frenchman.

"Ladies, ladies!" pleaded Herr Grunstrasse.

"And did you know that Brigitte was my wife, you moron, or did you really think she fancied you?"

"What?" spluttered Lord Hickman incredulously. "You bastards - you were in it together?"

"Of course. We conned you, as you conned others. It was fair game, I think," said Jean Jacques.

"What on earth is going on?" asked Mo, puzzled.

"I am losing patience. The originals please," growled Herr Grunstrasse.

"She was running away with me to Australia. She was sick of you. You never paid her any attention. I gave her a good time, if you know what I mean," said Lord Hickman.

"Thirty love!" said David.

"She only did as much as she had to, to gain your confidence," yelled J.J., seriously wounded.

"That's what she told YOU!" shouted Lord Hickman, almost apoplectic now. "She told me you were useless in the sack. I thought you frogs were supposed to be good at it."

J.J. lunged at his adversary, swinging his fists. Pierre, who had had quite enough of this cat fight and was eager to get home, stepped forward and pointed his gun at them, promising to end their argument once and for all by putting neat round holes through their respective brows. This seemed to quell their aggression more than somewhat. He barked out an instruction for them all to turn round, so that his gun was now pointing at their backs. David, shaking uncontrollably by now and lips trembling, tried to reason with his captors, but his mouth was too dry to speak. He had seen this scene played out in cheap gangster movies many a time. It was the moment when someone traditionally got shot. Usually the one who wouldn't tell the hoodlum where the loot was. As they turned, Mo suddenly dropped one arm to the ground, and using it as a pivot, swung his left leg skywards like a scythe with breathtaking speed, catching the diminutive Pierre squarely on in the jaw. He was probably unconscious well before he hit the ground, which he did whilst giving his best impression of a sack of King Edwards.

"Oh, look at the little feller. He's fast asleep," said Mo, pushing himself up from the ground with an athletic spring. "It's probably all the travelling." He retrieved the gun and pointed it at the others, who duly raised their hands once more to show respect for their new master.

"Right," he said, breathing heavily and trying to compose himself. "Anyone else need a little nap?"

"Attaboy!" smiled David proudly. "Now where are the police when you need them?"

"Look!" said Herr Grunstrasse. "We're all business men."

"God! All the clichés tonight, eh Mo?" laughed David. "Actually, Herr Gobstopper, or whatever your name is, I'm an artist, not a business man."

"Now listen here," interjected Lord Hickman, a trifle too stroppily for David's liking, given his currently reduced circumstances. "I've been good to you, old son. I've given you a lot of well-paid work this last month."

"And I never saw a penny. Work's not much use without reward."

"Ah! Well I was coming to that. Besides, I thought we were friends," pleaded the upper-crust con artist.

"Well you know what thought did don't you? He thought he'd farted but he'd shit himself!"

"Charming!" said Herr Grunstrasse, disdainfully.

"Don't you *dare* talk to me that way," snapped Lord Hickman. "I'm a Belted Earl."

"You will be in a minute," growled Mo.

"We could *share* the money," suggested J.J., sweating profusely now. "He'll get his pictures, and there's enough there for all of us."

313

"The pictures go back to Mr Bonini. That's it. *Finito!* " said David firmly.

"Just out of interest, how much…" Mo began.

"Don't even *think* about thinking about it, Mo," said David. "It's a lot, but we have to do the right thing, okay? We may get a reward though. You never know."

Mo nodded. He felt a bit like a lion that had narrowly missed out on a Wildebeest and instead had to be content with an under-nourished gerbil. Their debate was interrupted by the distant sound of a police car siren, which seemed to be getting closer by the second. A pair of bright white headlamps burnt through the low fog which had now descended on the airfield, and the panda car skidded to a halt next to Pierre's plane. The doors swung dramatically open, and for a moment David thought he could detect the pungent aroma of boiled egg sandwiches, like when the lid is taken off a lunchbox. Then three uniformed officers burst from within, wielding their torches and truncheons, and walked over to join the throng.

"Thrice Hello!" said the first one to arrive. Here was a man who didn't like spending too much time on formalities. "So what's going on here then?"

"You'd better relieve me of this, for a start," suggested Mo, as he handed over the pistol, handle first. "The money is in that case over there. You'd better look after that too, before I get tempted again."

"I'm the one who called you, officer," piped up David. "These two gentlemen and the one fast asleep down there are trading in stolen works of art, and it's major stuff! The fat one here has a briefcase full of cash. The one resting on the grass had the gun, which my friend Mo kindly relieved him of, in his own inimitable fashion."

"David Day?" questioned the second copper, shining a torch into his face. "Is that you again?"

"Oh no! Heaven help us! It's you two - I don't believe it!" sighed David. "When you turned up half an hour late, I should have guessed."

"David Day?" shouted Toxic, the last to arrive on the scene. "Is that you, mate?"

Dennis Wills ran forward and hugged his old friend.

"Bloody hell! Dennis Wills. I thought you were going into the army," said David, stunned.

"I was, but I went along to the cop shop for an interview and just fancied it," replied Dennis, grinning from ear to ear.

"Have you been eating boiled eggs?" asked David, backing out of their bear hug.

Herr Grunstrasse, touched by this unexpected reunion, decided to quietly step back a few paces in order that old friends could mingle, uninterrupted by fat Germans. In fact, such was the carnival atmosphere that no one had noticed him quietly slip behind the plane and make for the wide open spaces. Then, suddenly, David awoke from his reverie and realized that the fat man had given them the slip. Dennis, clutching his torch, scanned the vicinity and could just about make out a ghostly blob-like apparition due west. In a flash he was off in hot pursuit like a Springer spaniel after an obese mallard. It was only a matter of time before the assembled cast heard a dull thud somewhere in the foggy night, which signalled the end of the fat man's freedom. A few moments later, Dennis and his handcuffed charge were back at the plane, the latter puffing and panting as if a coronary were imminent.

Herr Grunstrasse arrived back at base camp just in time to see his little stunned pilot return to the land of the living. Donald read him his rights and bundled him into the panda, making sure he cracked his head on the rear door frame as he did so. The two senior coppers returned to the plane and Donald informing David that he would have to follow them to the station, to help them file their report, and fill in a witness statement.

"Damn," he sighed, clasping his hand over his mouth. "I forgot that I'd have to do that. Oh bugger! I've made complex arrangements to get Mr Bonini's pictures back to him, and I need to get started right now."

"Sorry Dave," said Donald sympathetically, "but I can't allow that I'm afraid. It would be more than my job was worth, old son. You'll have to follow us back."

"Look, can you spare me ten minutes here at the airfield?" begged David. "I just need to sort out Plan B. Come on lads. I've handed you a big catch. These are international art thieves, and one of 'em's a real-life Lord. You don't nab one of *those* every week. It wouldn't surprise me if Dennis was made a sergeant and you two were made chief inspectors. Come on lads, just ten minutes and I promise I'll be down the station before midnight."

Donald looked at Reg, and they agreed.

"You're not in your exploding Mini tonight are you Dave?"

David assured them that his car could manage the short trip without incident. They walked towards the panda, but turned to shout back.

"Dave, can you give Toxic a lift back to the station? There's no room in the panda, what with this fat bugger and all."

David said that he could. The police car drove off at high speed, leaving David, Mo and Dennis to walk back to the Mini. As they approached, they could see another car's lights. Next to David's mini was a large Jaguar whose driver was chatting to Lazlo. David called out to his friends and walked up to them, smiling.

"Mission accomplished! Hello Jack. What kept you?"

"Sorry Dave. I couldn't resist having a listen to Tony Catalano's band before I set off. They invited me to sit in on one of their numbers, so I borrowed my Country Gent back from George. I figured you'd be a while sorting out your end of the deal, so I turned up just right, as it happens."

"*Your* Gretsch? I thought you'd tracked one down from another dealer for George."

"Well, I couldn't see the kid out of pocket, especially after we bloody sold his last one, so I gave him one of mine. I supported Sinatra on his British tour playing that particular weapon! I've got three more, and George looks like the kind of lad who'd appreciate it."

"Jack, you're a true gent, just like your guitar," said David, slapping him on the back.

"You're a hep cat, daddio!" added Lazlo, tongue firmly in cheek.

"Laz, we stopped talking that way twenty years ago," said Jack, a touch frostily.

Katie and Suzanne got out of the car, desperate to find out exactly what was happening. David had told everyone virtually nothing, and now it was time for a few overdue explanations. The only trouble was, he didn't know where to begin. He eventually began with Lazlo.

"Look old pal, I've got a job I need you to do. Someone I know, an Italian millionaire as it happens, has been swindled, big time. Lord Hickman and his Vineyard manager were both trying to sell pictures stolen from my Italian friend to an unscrupulous German art dealer. He flew in tonight with a sackful of cash to do the deal but I found out and scuppered their plans, hence the cop car you just saw taking the buggers away. So far so good, right?"

Lazlo and the girls nodded, with matching incredulous expressions.

"I arranged with Jack here to fly the real paintings, which I have in the boot of my car as it happens, back to Mr Bonini, who even now is probably waiting impatiently at a small aerodrome near Florence. The only trouble is, the police need me to give a statement, pronto, and I can't go."

"Hang on a bit," said Lazlo. "If I was going to choose someone to fly me to Florence, just hypothetically speaking, I probably wouldn't pick a jazz guitarist, good as he undoubtedly is. No offence Jack. I'd probably, and call me old fashioned if you like, be tempted to go for a pilot."

"Ah! Well you're right, but you're wrong, if you know what I mean," smiled David. "Jack *is* a pilot, and a very good one too, aren't you Jack?"

Jack was far too modest to join in. He waved a dismissive hand.

"Jack is a flying instructor here at Twopenny Green. He owns a big six-seater twin-engined thingy don't you Jack?"

Jack said that he did.

"In fact," David continued, "I didn't have an inkling, and I've been going to The Sound Hole for ages. He never mentioned it. I actually found out from Jethro, the gardener at the castle. Apparently, he used to give His Bloody Lordship flying lessons. Hickman's got a small Cessna parked here somewhere."

"Yes, but the sod never paid me," said Jack, "so I told him to sod off."

"Well bugger me!" said Lazlo, genuinely amazed. "You learn something new every day."

"Language!" said Katie. "You have a mouth like a sewer."

"Anyway," said David impatiently. "I can't go. So I need a big, big favour, Laz."

Lazlo could see where this was leading.

"Look, I wouldn't ask you unless it was life and death. I need you to go with Jack to keep him company, and deliver a Botticelli and a Monet to their rightful owner, now, tonight."

"Fuck off!" said Lazlo, after giving it a few second's thought.

"Laz, I'm begging you," pleaded David, clasping his hands together like an Italian footballer who's just been accused of diving in the penalty box.

"Let me get this straight," said Lazlo. "You want me to get on a small plane in the middle of the night, in a worsening fog, with someone who looks like Glenn Miller?"

"Do you think so?" asked Jack, flattered. "It's been mentioned before."

319

"He does look like Glenn Miller, I'll admit, but it's not him, you tosser," reasoned David. "Jack has been flying for…..how long is it Jack?"

"Over thirty years."

"Over thirty years, and he's an expert. Ex RAF instructor. Best in the business."

"Thirty years experience, man and dog, and I've only crashed three or four times," added Jack helpfully.

"Look, Mr Bonini is a bloody millionaire. He's agreed to charter our man here's plane at enormous expense. He'd arranged for Jack and me to stay at his luxury apartment in Florence overnight, and he was taking us all out to one of Italy's finest restaurants tomorrow, before Jack flew us home. Just think of it. Katie, you could go too. What an adventure eh? Romantic or what? Laz, you're my best mate. The one I trust with my life. I'd do it for you. What do you say?"

Laz stood, deep in thought. "You say Katie could come?"

"If you like."

"I'll go if she will."

"Attaboy!"

"And what if I don't want to go?" asked Katie.

It was a fair question. David made his excuses to the others and grabbed Katie's arm, taking her off behind his car for a private chat. If she refused to go, his plans could be in serious jeopardy. When they were safely out of earshot, David held her shoulders and looked into her eyes.

"Katie, you're my mate, and I need the biggest favour. Get on the plane kid, just for me."

Katie looked back at him in soft focus black and white. "You know when you asked me to come to the ball with you. I was longing to say yes, but something inside told me that it wasn't wise. You've always been my big friend, and I thought that if we - you know - got closer, and anything happened and we fell out, we wouldn't be friends any more. We'd dislike each other from then on. Its funny isn't it, how people who are intimate and fall out are less friendly to each other than two strangers on a train. We go from one extreme to another, and I didn't want that to happen to us. You're too nice to go out with. That's your problem!"

"Most girls say that. That's why I never end up with one."

"But this time you have. Suzanne thinks the world of you. It's obvious. And I'm jealous. I chose Lazlo because he's really good looking, and a bit wild too. He's exciting, but you're sort of comfortable."

"What, like an old shoe?"

"No, you know what I mean. You may not be as good looking…"

"Thanks."

"Or have such a big todger."

"Thanks again."

"Well, there's undoubtedly a physical attraction there. Who wouldn't find him attractive?" argued Katie.

"H" suggested David.

"What?"

"Oh nothing. Just the ramblings of a madman."

"But we get on great don't we? You and me."

321

"Until just now, yes. Until you made snide references to the size of my reproductive organ."

"Oh stop it. I'm trying to tell you that I made a mistake, and it's you I want really."

David didn't need a heart-to-heart at this precise moment. He had just found himself a beautiful new girlfriend that he was already falling madly in love with, and now here was another one flinging herself at him. It was all very flattering in one sense. Only the previous week his shares had been at rock bottom. Traders couldn't give him away. Now he was a sought-after commodity. He put it down to switching from classical clarinet to lead guitar in the sixth form, but right now he was seriously thinking of switching back in the hope that it would result in a quieter life. Sadly, he was going to have to tell Katie that their immediate future was as friends only. She had, after all, said the same thing to him only the week before, and she couldn't really expect to keep ducking in and out all the time. He felt like a man who had been staggering through the Gobi dessert living off dead locusts and the raindrops he'd managed to collect from parched old cacti, and then being offered *Pizza con Funghi* and *Spaghetti Bolognese* at precisely the same time.

He'd grown to love both, but they were very different.

"Look," said David. We'll have a long cosy chat about this back at college next week. My mind can't take this in right now." He shook her shoulders gently in an attempt to prepare her for his next sentence.

"Katie, listen. I'm about to be firm and masterful, which is not something I'm particularly noted for. You're getting on that plane. Go to Lazlo, he needs you. He looks all pitiful with that bandage on his wrist and that little scar on his brow, don't you think? Come on, you know you fancy him like mad. He won't go without you. As to us, we'll always have Wolverhampton. Our problems don't amount to a hill of baked beans at this precise moment. What's important is getting these pictures back. What do you say?"

Katie smiled a monochromatic soft focus tearful smile.

"Okay, just for you."

"Here's looking at you, kid."

"You'll have to fill me in when I get back," said Katie, wiping away a tear.

"That's the best offer I've ever had," smiled David. He could never resist a *double entendre*.

"No, I mean on who stole what from whom. I'm still totally confused. Did you say it was the vineyard man who double-crossed Lord Hickman?"

"Well, there's more to it than that, but that's about it in a nutshell, yes."

"So the bottler did it!"

"Very funny. Get your arse on that plane."

They joined the rest of the party, and announced that Katie was going with Lazlo. The two vehicles drove over to Jack's plane, a large silver affair with the legend, 'Country Gent' sign-written just under the cockpit, American Air-Force style. Jack told them to wait while he radioed the control tower and prepared for take off. Before long the mighty propellers roared into action. He opened the door, and Lazlo and Katie climbed onboard. David handed them the package from his boot, telling them to guard it with their lives.

"Say 'Ciao!' to Mr Bonini for me," shouted David, above the deafening noise. "I'll phone both sets of parents right

323

away to explain everything. We wouldn't want them worrying."

The plane circled in the damp mist that had settled on the runway. Jack waved to those who had to remain behind, revved up the engines and rocketed away across the tarmac. They watched, spellbound, as the engines droned and the wheels finally lifted from the ground, taking Lazlo and Katie into dark, romantic oblivion.

Eventually David, Suzanne, Dennis and Mo walked dreamily back to the car in the drizzly night air.

"Well, I'll go back to the marquee and hump all the equipment into the transit single handed then," said Mo stoically.

"Good man," said David, patting his back.

Suzanne, who had been as quiet as a mouse for the last fifteen or so minutes, suddenly began to shiver violently. She was dressed only in a satin ball gown, and was feeling the cold, now that the excitement was all over. David took off his coat and handed it to her. He put his arm around her and kissed her tenderly on the cheek. She flung her arms around him and kissed him as the rain began to fall heavily once more. He might have had better times in his nineteen years of life, but he was damned if he could remember when. Dennis coughed discreetly, and reminded the two new lovers that Stourbridge police station beckoned. David opened the car doors and let Mo and Suzanne get into the back seats. He looked over at the young, uniformed man waiting to get into his car and laughed.

"Dennis, I think this is the beginning of a beautiful friendship."

"What are you on about?" asked the young constable, puzzled. "I've known you since you were eleven."

"Oh, I don't know - it just seemed like a good line," replied David, as he started up the engine, "but knowing me, I've probably just borrowed it from an old film!"

THE END

Something to look forward to!

Coming soon, three more books in the David Day series.

VINCENT GOUGH'S VAN.

An art college murder mystery of Shakespearian proportions, littered with psychic sewing teachers, entrail-painting students and lesbian assassins.

THE CURSE OF TUTTON COMMON.

David sets about trying to improve Britain's worst museum, and ably assisted by a cat called Hitlerina, he discovers an ancient Egyptian tomb in Kinver.

PAINTING BY NUMBERS.

Thirty-year-old David is having a mid-life crisis, made worse by the fact that his art studio has exploded, and the ninety-year-old 'paint by numbers' enthusiast he has befriended is not what he seems.

...and a new novel featuring a new hero!
LOSING IT!

Writer, Adam Eve hires a pantomime horse costume, but forfeits his deposit when he loses one of the hooves. His obsessive efforts to locate it create mayhem!

For more information, email gt@geofftristram.co.uk

An extract from the opening chapter of
'Vincent Gough's Van', the sequel to 'Monet Trouble'.

CHAPTER 1

The Long Hair of the Law

David Day studied the policewoman from behind as she stood looking longingly at the window of the Tweedledum Coffee Shop.

A devilish grin spread across his face as he approached her. Treading carefully now, like a cat burglar, he was so close that he could smell her perfume. Had she been on guard, she would have noticed his ominous, looming shadow reflected in the window, but her mind was focused on other things.

The frosted apple turnover seemed to be calling to the depths of her soul. She had skipped breakfast that day because the alarm clock had failed to go off, making her late for work, and now, at eleven thirty a.m., she was ravenous.

He was inches away now, admiring that incredible hair. It was in a bun, of course, as she was in uniform, but still shiny and wonderful. It had fascinated him throughout his infant, junior and grammar school days, all four glorious feet of it.

When unfurled, it covered two thirds of her athletic six-foot frame. He had often imagined her naked, her modesty both above and below protected by this vast tidal wave of hair. She could have played the part of Lady Godiva, or featured in those sensual T.V. hair shampoo advertisements, but neither career options held any fascination for her. Ever since junior school, she had confided in David that she wished to join the force. He remained convinced that she had been brainwashed in those impressionable years by the pathetic careers advisors of the nineteen-sixties, and, for that matter, virtually every adult that clapped eyes on her.

"Ooh! You are a tall young girl," they observed, "You should join the Police Force!" As if her height eliminated her from any other role in life.

He held his breath now, so that she couldn't hear him. They had always got on well, in that brother and sister kind of way, had David and Maggie, or Teragram Snosrap, as he always called her. At grammar school they had all written their names backwards at the start of one new term, and hers was unanimously voted the funniest. He'd never forgotten it.

It was time to pounce.

He shoved his banana into the small of her back and clasped his left hand over her mouth.

"Don't move, Teragram Snosrap," he barked, "or I'll drill you with my banana!"

What happened next was something of a blur, but he was acutely aware of an unbearable pain and a cracking noise as his banana arm was twisted up his back. This was followed swiftly by the sickening thud of hard, cold pavement coming up to meet his ear, which began to throb horribly.

To add to his considerable discomfort, someone appeared to have dumped a two-hundred-weight sack of coal on his back.

"You are under arrest for assaulting a police officer," said the sack of coal, which, like Queen Victoria, was not amused.

"Gnah!" moaned David.

His rapidly swelling left eye was about half an inch from a rather unpleasant cigarette butt, which had pink lipstick all over the tip and was still glowing red at the business end. It was funny how he was still so observant, given the trying circumstances. Perhaps it was his artistic training coming into play.

A small crowd had now gathered to watch the arrest, and an old lady shouted, "Good on yer love. Throttle the bastard!"

David struggled to articulate his feelings. His face was flushed red with the shame and embarrassment of it all.

"Snosrap! It's me, David. David Day," he whimpered.

"My name is WPC Susan Hobbins. I would be very surprised if anyone was actually called Snosrap. Are you on any medication, sir?"

"Yes I am, but I can't see what that's got to do with anything!" he whined.

"What are you on, sir?"

David realised that she had the upper hand, and decided to help the police with their enquiries.

"It's called Benylin. I've had a bad cough. My mom says it's because I go to B.J's club to see rock bands, and everybody smokes there, apart from me of course."

"That's not what I meant," said the WPC, trying her hardest to be patient. "Why did you attack me with a banana, sir?"

"I thought you were Margaret," he replied feebly.

"If you thought I was Margaret, why did you call me Telegram Snogwop?"

"I didn't!"

"You bloody well did."

"No I didn't," insisted David. "I called you Teragram Snosrap; it's Margaret Parsons spelled backwards."

The officer stared at him critically. "Are you *sure* you're not on some form of medication?"

"No. I mean yes. I thought you were my friend Maggie, the policewoman. She's got hair four feet long. We went to school together. Not me and her hair you understand. Me and all of her, including her hair of course, if you….."

"Not Maggie Evans?"

"Parsons."

"She used to be Parsons I think. She got married to Barry Evans, another officer."

"Oh! I didn't know that she was married. I haven't seen her for ages. This cigarette butt is burning my brow. I may have to scream any time now."

The officer seemed to soften a little. "Okay. I'm going to let you stand up. If you misbehave, I have a truncheon, remember?"

"Understood," he groaned.

"Have I hurt you?" she asked, concerned by his pitiful voice.

"No" he replied, "I'm okay, apart from my ear, which has been grated off, my arm, which is snapped in sixteen places and my eye, which may never see to paint pictures again. I also have a third degree cigarette burn on my brow, so I'm scarred for life, WPC Nasus Snibboh."

"What?"

"Nasus Snibboh. That's your name spelt backwards."

"I see," she said, half smiling now. "Well, in future, make sure you know someone before you attack them with bananas in shopping precincts. You've got a fag end stuck to your cheek."

"Thank you. I may leave it there."

"That's your choice, sir."

"And now," said David, dusting himself off. "If it's okay with you, WPC Snibboh, I intend to enter this café and partake of a large greasy sausage roll and a pot of tea. Would you care to join me?"

The WPC began to laugh out loud, and turned to the now substantial crowd.

"It's all over folks. Big misunderstanding. Nothing to see. Move along please!"

She waited till they had dispersed and returned her gaze to David.

"A friend of Maggie's eh? She never mentioned any lunatic acquaintances, but then again, she wouldn't, would she? Buy me that apple turnover and we're quits. I'm starving!"

David grinned. "It's the least I can do after you've dislocated my arm and fractured my skull. I will buy you this cake, but I must warn you that I am liable to call in this favour at any time."

He flicked the dog end from his cheek, retrieved it from the floor and deposited it in a nearby litter bin. He was damned if she was going to re-arrest him for littering. With a nonchalant flick of his hair, he entered the café, and emerged seconds later with the apple turnover in a paper bag.

"Just out of interest, my dear Snibbs, how long *is* your hair?" he asked. WPC Hobbins appeared to blush, which David found very appealing. These hard-nut females always softened eventually. They seemed to respond favourably to his boyish charm, once the initial violence had concluded.

"Oh, not in the Maggie Parsons' class I'm afraid," she smiled. "It was about two-feet-six, last time I measured."

"Well, from the back you and Maggie are identical, and you don't disappoint from the front either, if you don't mind my saying so. The good news is, I can stick my banana into the backs of two lovely police officers with impunity now that we've been introduced."

"I wouldn't count on it buster," she warned. "You can't bribe me with an apple turnover and think that gives you the right to prod me with your banana. I'm not a cheap date. Now, if you'll excuse me, Divad Yad, I have a job to do, protecting the good folk of Wolverhampton from nutters." and with a cheeky wink, she was on her way.